VHR
PRESS
VINE HILL ROAD PRESS

The General's Ambition

A Master Sergeant Harper Mystery

By

M. L. Doyle

VHR
PRESS
VINE HILL ROAD PRESS

DEDICATION

To the men and women of
the 364th Mobile Public Affairs Detachment,
Fort Snelling, MN
and all others who have answered the call to serve

The Box: noun \baks\: The portion of a military installation designated for combat maneuver training. Usually hundreds of acres in size containing; firing ranges, MOUT (Military Operations in Urban Terrain) sites, and expansive spaces to facilitate all types of tactical exercises. Also known as The Sandbox.

CHAPTER 1

COLONEL NEIL MCCALLEN COMMUNICATED his displeasure in his narrow-eyed glare. He'd already told me once to stop fidgeting but I couldn't help looking at my watch yet again.

"Endlessly checking the time won't make it go any faster, Sergeant Harper," McCallen said, scanning the crowd. "He'll be waiting for you no matter how long this takes."

I couldn't help myself. My impatience felt skin deep, like tiny zaps of energy assaulting random parts of my body. I simply couldn't stand still and if one more thing delayed this press conference, I'd go mad. Despite my best efforts, I had to glance at my watch one more time and sighed when I'd confirmed the minute hand hadn't moved much since the last time I'd checked.

Yes, I knew Harry would still be waiting for me, waiting and probably feeling the same impatience I felt. We'd been trying for months to get away together. I'd learned over my many years in uniform that dating another soldier is always complicated. Dating a soldier that serves in a different Army is nearly impossible. Since I'd met Sergeant Major Harold Fogg of the British Army, getting together had felt like a mythological quest involving golden fleeces, elfin rings or slaying six-headed monsters. Quests I felt wholly unprepared for.

Finally, after countless attempts and delays, we'd managed to arrange a long getaway. This final press conference, which marked the end of a three-week field exercise, was the only thing between me and a Greek island vacation with Harry. Despite my spit-shined combat boots, I could almost feel the sand between my toes.

An entire month. We'd both managed to arrange to take leave for a full thirty days and we planned to spend every one of them together. Harry had started his leave this morning when he'd boarded a plane to make the short flight from Stansted Airport to Frankfurt. There he'd rented a car and driven four hours to a small village near Hohenfels, Germany where my unit had been conducting field maneuvers. The imposing British Special Air Service soldier had sent me a text when he'd arrived at the *Gastehaus der Koenig,* a small, family owned bed and breakfast only ten minutes from where I now stood impatiently wishing to be with him.

We'd never shared a hotel room before. We'd never seen each other wearing anything other than our uniforms. I'd fantasized about what it would be like to be in civilian clothes, a dress even, off duty, relaxed and in his arms. Fantasized about it until I couldn't stand it anymore. In about an hour, and I checked my watch again, I'd finally get to see him. The distraction of our imminent meeting had my heart racing, making me feel as anxious as a teenager waiting for her first prom date.

All I had to do was get through this last damn press conference and I could be with Harry. At last, really be with him.

"What's taking so long," I finally asked my boss. McCallen started to answer then paused, as if he needed to rethink his response, glancing around to see if anyone was listening. When he leaned in to speak to me I figured whatever he was about to say couldn't be good.

"General Blunt is on the phone with his wife. The whole family arrived last night and are staying at the hotel on post.

Evidently, they're going on a road trip to Poland for the weekend."

"Pottery shopping? General Blunt?" It was a favorite past time for many of the Army spouses in Germany, road trips to an area just across the Polish border where factories and warehouses offered up colorful pottery at bargain prices. I knew Pauline Blunt was a big fan of the stuff, having seen her collection displayed prominently in their home. That she was dragging the general with her on one of her shopping trips was more proof of who ruled their household.

McCallen shrugged. "Not sure he had much say in the matter."

"Then why can't we get this show on the road?" I said. "He must be looking forward to finishing as much as everyone else."

McCallen glanced around rechecking to ensure no one was paying attention. The room was full of people who had come to watch the press conference, but everyone seemed to be ignoring us.

"Evidently, Brianna went missing for a while. She went out last night and didn't get in until the wee hours of the morning. Mrs. Blunt is furious."

Brianna Blunt, the eighteen-year-old handful of hormones and attitude was a neverending source of frustration for the general. The young woman wielded her beauty, her buxom body and her father's position like a satchel of sharp knives, any one of which could cut you down in an instant. She looked like a model and acted like a diva. On a military base chock full of warfighters, she was like a jewel in a den of murderous thieves. Everyone eyed her with greed, but no one was stupid enough to reach for her first, knowing it was bound to end badly.

"The last thing he needs is a Brianna distraction," I said. "At least she came back."

"True, but you know how Pauline Blunt is. She must be quaking with righteous anger."

I smiled at the accurate description. Mrs. Blunt, the epitome of military spouse perfection, hated scandal of any kind. To her, appearances mattered, which is why she'd evidently eliminated the Mississippi accent from her speech and never left the house without being perfectly coifed. I imagined she would be so angry at Brianna's antics, even her solidly shellacked hair would be quivering.

'It's not funny, Harper," McCallen said while attempting not to smile.

"You're right, sir. Not funny at all," I smiled back.

McCallen looked a bit tired, his face more pale than usual, his freckles and the long scar that started at his eyebrow and slashed across his face in a wide, violent line, looked stark in the morning light that filtered through the multiple windows surrounding the large room. His ruddy-colored hair, usually worn very short and trim, could use a trip to a barber shop. Despite his obvious fatigue, he seemed relaxed as if he were looking forward to the end of the long, exhausting exercise as much as I was.

We both lost our smiles when the general's aide opened the office door, motioning for McCallen to go inside. He would spend a few minutes making sure the general's uniform—his battle dress uniform in this case—looked in order, do a quick run-through of the talking points and things to watch out for before the press conference finally began.

My public affairs team had set up shop in a tiny, old chapel building, converting the one-story structure into office space, our living quarters and a place to hold press conferences. On a small riser in the front of the room, near where the old chapel pulpit would have been, we'd arranged an American flag, the Ninth Army guidon flag and a two-star general officer flag. Centered in front of the three flags was a podium with the Ninth Army shield on the front. In the section of the floor where pews would have been, we'd set up rows and rows of metal folding chairs, most of which were now populated with civilian media role players. In the area formally used for child care for the chapel, our captain, my two soldiers, and I had set up our office. Our cots tucked in various corners had served just fine for our sleeping arrangements. Opposite us was a small storage room we'd converted into Colonel McCallen's office and quarters where he was now ensconced with General Blunt going over final notes for the press conference.

The building had worked out perfectly for us, but I was ready to be done with it. As soon as the press conference was over, all we had to do was turn in our weapons, pack up our gear and get the hell gone. I couldn't wait to take off the holster strapped to my thigh and turn in my nine millimeter.

Staff Sergeant Tracy Patrovski approached me with her camera, asking for help with the complicated settings. I noticed she'd put a bit of an extra shine on her boots and her raven hair was pulled back severely in a neat bun. She'd even applied a bit of makeup for the occasion which was unusual for the young woman.

"What's taking so long?" she asked. I chuckled at our similar frustrations, but kept McCallen's explanation to myself, instead felt grateful to have something to do while our wait continued.

In the middle of fixing the problems with camera settings, Captain Leon Jerreau sidled up next to me and whispered, "What's taking so long?"

Patrovski and I both laughed. "McCallen just went in to do the final brief," I said. "Hopefully they'll be coming out soon."

Jerreau had only been with us about a year and seemed to take well to the job. His Cajun ancestry gave him olive-colored skin that was almost as dark as mine. I'd always wondered if there wasn't a little African mixed in his blood somewhere. I noticed him fingering the small silver charm he wore on a chain in addition to his dog tags, his faced tinged with a redness that betrayed his agitation. He'd once told us his Cajun grandmother had given him the small disk as some kind of protection charm.

"What's wrong, sir?" I asked.

He turned his dark brown eyes to me, a wrinkle in his brow. "I don't know," he said, rubbing the disk. "Somethin' ain't right."

The captain's tightly curled brown hair looked a bit mussed, as if he'd been running his fingers through it. In the months since Jerreau had joined our team, I'd learned to take his superstitions and beliefs as seriously as I could out of respect. While I didn't believe all of his folksy ideas, he did, and more often than not his predictions of both good and bad events had been correct.

A burst of laughter drew our attention to the side of the room. A group of soldiers, most of them covered in dirt from the field, their helmets off, their faces streaked with worn-off camouflage paint and sweat, were all smiles and loose amusement. A handsome blond man seemed to be the entertainer. I noticed they all wore the same unit patch and Ranger tab and figured they must be here to see General Blunt who'd also worn the tan beret and tab during his career.

With his forehead pulled into a frown, Jerreau furiously rubbed his charm, staring at the group of Rangers. "What is bothering you, sir?" I asked him again.

He shook his head. "You go on and pooh pooh all you want, Sergeant Harper. I got the sniff of nasty swamp gas up in here."

Patrovski voiced her doubts. "Sooooo, there's something evil around?"

"Yeah, you laugh now," he said. "Go on and laugh, you."

Patrovski and I exchanged smiles for a second before someone called the room to attention. I turned to see McCallen stepping out of his office with General Blunt following close behind.

"*Endlich*," I mumbled the German word at the same time Patrovski said the same thing, only in English.

"Finally," she said.

We swapped smiles before she moved closer to the front of the room to take pictures.

McCallen adjusted his shoulder holster as he walked past the media role players with their notebooks, cameras and recorders and the bystanders who'd come just to watch the event. He tapped the microphone to ensure it was on, cleared his throat, arranged his notes on the podium and began. The people running video cameras and other recording devices, including one of my soldiers, Sergeant Dominic Owens, took it as their cue to start rolling.

"Ladies and gentlemen. Thank you for coming," McCallen said. "In a minute, Major General Preston Blunt, commander of Ninth Army Forces, Europe, will come to the microphone to answer your questions."

My boss ran through his opening remarks. I glanced at Blunt who stood next to McCallen looking serious, and for good reason. The group of mock reporters had been a tough bunch, asking pointed, biting questions that backed you into a corner if you weren't careful. Blunt had started the exercise with a few bad turns but had gained confidence and skill in high-pressure situations. Patrovski would take pictures and Owens would record the entire experience so that we could review the results with him later. If he followed the pattern he'd established so far, I expected Blunt to wade through the minefield of questions without tripping any dangerous wires.

As McCallen delivered the introduction, he looked relaxed and frankly, handsome. The kind of handsome that made women fix their hair and wet their lips. His ruddy complexion, freckles, red hair, and the jagged scar were all together sexy, like a hero in the flesh. He'd gained back the weight he'd lost after his newborn daughter died and his wife left him. He seemed better, now. Fit. Comfortable with the way his life had shaken out. And damn him, there were times when I still thought about him in improper ways. But I had blown out the torch I'd carried for him, once and for all. Still, the confidence and power he exuded were exceedingly attractive. The female role players all sat up straighter and fiddled with their hair whenever he was around.

I took a deep breath and clasped my hands behind my back, squeezing my fingers, trying to prevent myself from looking at my watch again.

"Ladies and gentlemen, Major General Blunt," McCallen stepped aside as Blunt made his way to the podium.

Blunt cleared his throat and glanced down at the notes McCallen had left for him on the podium. He would see his own opening statement, along with some bulleted talking points he could use for questions we anticipated.

He glanced up, scanned the crowd, pausing now and then to acknowledge people scattered about the room. He focused for a moment on the cluster of Rangers, then on the reporters in front of him and began to speak in a clear, confident voice. We'd provided him with a microphone, but he didn't need it. His voice was easily heard where I stood near the back of the room.

I tried to pay attention, but since I'd written the statement, I already knew what he would say. I glanced around the room, listening only to detect any stumbles or if he misread my carefully written remarks.

Aside from the people serving as the media, about fifty observers stood around the back of the room, some of them obviously just coming out of the box, the Rangers forming the largest group of viewers. I remembered the story Patrovski had written about the Ranger battalion. The group had traveled from the states to participate in the exercise at General Blunt's request. They would be sticking around for a few days after we left. It appeared Blunt had some admirers amongst the ranks who wanted to watch the general in action.

"Clearly, things are returning to normal in most of the townships," Blunt said, wrapping up his opening remarks. "Publican civilians are returning to work, shopping in markets and sending their children to school. All of these are signs they have confidence in the peace and safety of their communities. I will take your questions now."

Every reporter's hand went up.

I sighed. This was going to take forever.

"General Blunt, Tracy Simonson, TNT News. How can you say that things are returning to normal when there is still so much unrest? Just yesterday, in Mayberry, people seemed to be expressing their displeasure with your continued presence there."

"I'm glad you brought that up, Tracy..."

I tried to hide my smile. We'd purposely left the protests out of the opening statement, knowing it would be one of the first questions asked.

"We don't see the protests in Mayberry as unrest as you have characterized it," Blunt said, almost reciting the talking points we'd written verbatim. "We see this as an exercise in freedom of speech. In the past, those demonstrations would have resulted in violence, arrests and perhaps even deaths. The results are far different today."

He continued with more, hitting the responses out of the park, sounding calm and in charge. I couldn't help but feel a bit of pride in how masterful he'd become at this. McCallen and I had worked closely with him and it seemed the training had been worth the effort.

"General Blunt, just yesterday, the mayor of Pleasantville accused your forces of being heavy-handed. He complained that the constant patrols, the check points and searches are interfering with his town's ability to conduct simple commerce. Why is Pleasantville being singled out for this heavy-handed treatment?"

"Jason, your own paper reported the story about the bodies of three men found in the Pleasantville schoolyard. We have confirmed that those men had been shot execution-style. Bottom line is, the local Mayor of Pleasantville has asked for our help and we are giving it to him. Look, insurgents throughout most of Publican have laid down their arms. There's a stubborn group in Pleasantville and we're not going to abandon that town's efforts to return to peace and bring security to their citizens."

In my head, I imagined myself screaming, "Blah, blah, blah. Just get on with it already!" I squeezed my fingers again to stop myself from doing or saying something inappropriate. Blunt demonstrated that he'd been trained well. He stuck to his talking points, and since many of the questions were ones I had anticipated, it felt like watching a movie I'd seen a million times. My attention wandered. I watched Patrovski as she moved about the room taking pictures. Sergeant Owens had obviously locked down the video camera and just let it roll on the General. I knew most of the people in the room, all from various units I'd worked with.

I glanced to where Colonel McCallen stood and found him staring at me, his blue eyes softened, his expression intense. I averted my gaze, feeling the heat rush to my face. It had been a long time since I'd seen that look of desire from him directed at me. Why would he be looking at me like that now? Telling myself I'd misread him, I looked back again but I hadn't been wrong. "Crap," I mumbled, before I directed my gaze at the floor, willing myself not look at him again, my heart racing.

I focused on the Rangers, needing something to distract me. They were all new faces to me. The tall blond major looked like a pleasant enough fellow. Standing next to him was a striking-looking Captain, a tall and burly bodyguard type who looked Native American. He wore his hair in an extreme high and tight, cut to look like a Mohawk. Another man, shorter and rather slight, looked familiar somehow but I couldn't see his name from where I stood. And next to him, was a burly-looking guy with a crew cut and a weathered face. Looking at him reminded me of Harry.

I sighed. Harry. Soon, very soon.

All of the men standing in the cluster of Rangers seemed completely focused on everything going on, their heads shifting back and forth as they followed the questions and the answers like a tennis match.

I felt the pull to glance at McCallen again, but managed to overcome it.

"General, we all know the Publican police are notorious for corruption. How can you break them of the methods they've employed for so long?"

Blunt had been asked this question before, which told me the reporters were running out of material. That was a good thing. It meant they'd be done soon. I glanced at my watch, my stomach still in knots of anticipation. I was going crazy with eagerness. I considered ducking into the restroom but thought better of it. I didn't really need to go that bad. I'd just wanted something to do besides stand in the back of the room.

I took a deep breath and tried to focus my attention on the matter at hand. Blunt continued to command the room, looked at ease and in charge. He said something funny and the media corps erupted in laughter. I didn't know what he'd said that was so funny, but I noted how loose everyone seemed and realized we were coming close to being finished. My relief at the idea that it was finally almost over distracted me so much that I didn't notice the soldier approaching them until he was right in front of the podium. McCallen noticed him first. He glanced over Blunt's shoulder, his eyes suddenly wide in shock. At first, I didn't understand why he looked so alarmed. He'd instantly lunged forward, reaching over the podium, but there was little McCallen could have done when the soldier raised his nine millimeter pistol and shot the general in the head.

CHAPTER 2

THE ROOM ERUPTED IN noise and motion.

McCallen had reached over the podium, striking the shooter's arm just as the weapon went off. He then grabbed the man's wrist, shoving the podium out of the way and kicked the soldier's feet out from under him, forcing him to the ground. McCallen straddled the soldier as several of the Rangers rushed forward and joined the effort to restrain him, although he seemed to have gone limp and didn't resist. Once the others took over, McCallen stood. Great streaks of the general's blood covered his face and uniform as he kicked the weapon to send it skittering across the floor.

All the media role players had run away from the podium, knocking over chairs, screaming, shouting obscenities, clamoring over each other to get away. I moved to the side of the room to get out of the way, my attention riveted on McCallen, not sure if he'd been hurt. There was so much blood on him.

As soon as I found an opening in the mass of people, I moved toward him. My legs felt as if they weighed a hundred pounds each. McCallen turned and bent down, disappearing from my view. By the time I reached him, he was leaning over Blunt.

"Medic!" he shouted. "We need a medic in here now!"

I didn't want to see what that bullet had done to Blunt. I'd seen my share of bodies lately and wasn't looking forward to another. The instant, enormous spray of blood I'd witnessed had been enough to make me want to proceed cautiously, but as much as I wanted to turn away, I had to help.

"Patrovski!" I yelled. "Get the first aid kit from the office!"

"On it," she shouted.

"Hold on, sir," McCallen said.

Blunt lay on his back, his eyes open, staring at nothing. His chest rose and fell in rapid hitching gasps. Kneeling next to him, I saw that the shot had deeply grazed the side of his head, leaving a large bloody gash, his face a horror show of blood, with a larger pool growing on the floor beneath him. The last time I'd seen skin that pale had been on someone already dead.

Patrovski rushed over with the inadequate first aid kit, dropped it off, then went back to taking pictures of the scene. McCallen and I rummaged through the metal box, ripping open every gauze pad we could find, but nothing we did could staunch the flow from the gash in the side of Blunt's head. McCallen continued to offer words of encouragement, but Blunt didn't appear to be cognizant of anything. Several other people came to help, one soldier handing me the black and white Keffiyeh he'd worn around his neck. I wadded it up and pressed it to the wound and it quickly turned just as red as everything else.

I glanced over to where the shooter lay, but couldn't see him buried under all of the men who had rushed to restrain him. Every soldier's face I saw displayed shock and anger. The screaming and the shouting continued around the room. There was such an uproar it was hard to distinguish any words.

"Medic, damn it!" McCallen called again. "Someone get a medic in here."

I heard radios squawking as people reached out for help. Others ran out of the building, presumably to spread the word of what happened or to just get away from the horror.

The Rangers had flipped the shooter onto his stomach, pulled his arms behind his back and used flex ties to bind him. They were handy, those flex ties. Everyone who worked a check point or walked patrol kept a supply in their pockets. They were uncomfortable but effective. I knew that from personal experience.One of the Rangers screamed directions in fury. "Hold him down now," he said, pacing and red faced. "What have you done, Major! What have you done?"

Finally, two soldiers arrived with combat medical kits, pushing McCallen and I out of the way. They quickly took over, replacing our inadequate attempts to staunch the flow with bleed stop bandages, their hands flying through the process of stabilizing the general. In seconds, they'd inserted an IV line.

McCallen, now that he didn't have anything to do, seemed frozen in place, his body limp, his eyes out of focus. I wrapped a hand around his arm, pulling him to his feet and away from the activity.

"Sir, are you okay?"

He stood staring down at Blunt, his face, hands and the front of his uniform drenched in blood. When he didn't react to my words, I repeated myself. His eyes, when they met mine, appeared unfocused. He opened his mouth to speak but nothing came out. He glanced around, then down at his blood-drenched hands.

I pulled him further away from the commotion, keeping my eye on him. He followed me docilely, glancing back to the general and the activity around him. I settled him into a chair.

"Neil. Neil, are you okay?" The blood on his face was thick and horrifying. I took out my packet of wet wipes, and used them on my own hands first before trying to clean him up. I sat on a chair next to him, held his chin in my hand and attacked the gore. When he finally spoke, his words were slurred.

"Jesus, Lauren. Did you see that?" he asked, his skin pasty, his lips colorless.

"Yes, sir. Everyone saw it."

"That guy. He just walked up and shot him. He was smiling when he did it. Did you see that? Jesus."

McCallen had worked closely with Blunt. I didn't know what his personal feelings for the general were, but it didn't matter. Something this horrifying, McCallen would be seeing the event in his head for years to come. I grew alarmed at the glassy look in McCallen's eyes. I'd never seen him so out of it. I kept working on cleaning his face, tossing the used wipes on the floor. They formed a bloody pile.

"I can't believe he survived that," McCallen said.

"You saved him," I said. With a head wound like that, Blunt could still die, but I wasn't going to say that.

He closed his eyes as I tried to clear them of the thick, sticky substance. The sight of all that blood turned my stomach, but I didn't want to alert McCallen to the amount of gore on his face He sat passively, his hands palm up and limp in his lap. He trembled a bit, as if he were cold.

"I saw him coming. He was right there. I just couldn't move fast enough."

"You did everything you could."

"It felt like I was in slow motion, like in a dream," he said, the words mumbled and slurred.

"But you stopped him, sir. He'd surely be dead if it wasn't for you."

"Is he going to be okay?" Jerreau asked as he handed me a bottle of water. I didn't bother to answer him. He could see for himself that McCallen wasn't responding. His lassitude was alarming.

"I told you," Jerreau said, his hand on my shoulder to get my attention, while fingering his charm with his other hand. "Something evil was in this room."

"Captain Jerreau, you are not being helpful right now," I said.

He mumbled something under his breath, then quickly walked away.

The sound of sirens grew in the distance until they stopped right outside the door. Paramedics rushed in rolling a gurney.

As they rolled past the shooter, I realized the men who'd captured him had been replaced by several MPs. I wondered how they'd gotten here so fast. They pulled the man to his feet and backed him up into a chair, their hands on his shoulders pressing him into the seat.

It didn't take the paramedics long to get the general on the gurney and on the way to a hospital. I wondered where they would take him. There was a medical clinic on post, but I didn't think it was staffed to handle anything this serious. They'd probably take him to the landing zone, load him in a helicopter to medevac him to the nearest trauma center, mostly likely a German hospital.

I turned my attention back to McCallen and realized he still hadn't moved. The plastic water bottle hung limply from his fingers. I took it from him. "Come on now, Neil. Drink the water. Drink it."

He opened his mouth and let me feed him a couple of sips. The more he drank, the more he seemed to want. His gaze wandered to me and he stared as I fed him more water, taking bigger and bigger gulps. He took the bottle from me, his fingers lingering over mine, before he took over, taking a long sip.

"Is that better?" I asked.

"I need to talk to you," he said. He had that look in his eye again as his gaze roamed my face. His eyes were glassy, his breathing heavy.

"Colonel ... "

"Don't colonel me, Lauren. We need to talk," he said in a soft voice. He reached up to touch my face, but then noticed the blood on his hands and thought better of it. "Lauren. You know we need to talk. You have to hear me out."

I glanced over my shoulder to see if anyone was near. I didn't know what he was about to say, but I had a feeling it wouldn't be appropriate.

"Sir, this isn't the time or the place."

"You're about to go off with that guy. I've waited too long already."

"You've been through a terrible shock. You don't really mean..."

"Bullshit." He grabbed my wrist and squeezed, leaning in until he was inches from my face. "I love you. You know that. Don't pretend you don't."

"Neil, you're hurting me."

He let go of my wrist like I'd burned him. "I'm sorry. I'm ... I'm not crazy, Lauren. I mean every word." He licked his lips and tilted his head back, taking in great gulps of water. The color began to return to his face. He stopped drinking, panted a moment and fixed his blue eyes on me. When he spoke again, he sounded calm, but a pleading note remained in his voice. "We could be together now. Now that my marriage is over. Don't think I haven't thought about it, Lauren. I have. A lot."

I had to look away from the intensity of McCallen's gaze. When I glanced at the shooter, he was staring back at me. Despite his rumpled uniform, the redness of his face, there was something familiar about him. The MPs kept their hands on his shoulders as if he might get up and make a run for it. To me, he looked completely compliant. He turned his gaze to the floor, a strange smile on his face.

"Don't ignore me, Lauren," McCallen said.

"Ignore you? Sir, you're not making sense…"

"Stop sir-ing me. That won't change anything. And I'm making perfect sense. I had to say something before you run off with him."

He leaned into me now, the force of his stare more frightening then the vacant look I'd seen before. Traces of blood still streaked his face. It made him look a bit off the rails.

"My feelings haven't changed, Lauren. I can't stop thinking about us. About us, together."

"Damn it, Neil. Stop it. Just stop." Nine months ago, I would have reacted very differently to his words. I'd spent so many years wanting him, craving time with him even though he was completely unattainable. Now, his words were an intrusion, like a destructive jab at the tender web of feeling I'd built around my new relationship with Harry.

Harry. I hardly knew him. I had no idea if our relationship would work. In total, we'd only spent hours together, but it had been enough time to know that he was brave, confident, and charming with a rare intellect that kept me delightfully on my toes and utterly fascinated. Not to mention, when he trained his green-eyed gaze at me, the chemistry brewed a combustible heat so intense, I felt scorched. He'd seen me at my very worst and still wanted me. Nothing, not this exercise, not anything Neil could say, absolutely nothing would get in the way of my plans with Harry.

Except maybe an assassination attempt on my commanding general.

"Un-fricking believable," I said, finally realizing what the horrible event meant. Investigators would soon swarm over the place. Everyone would have to be questioned. It would be hours before I could get away now. Not to mention we could expect a media mob in no time.

"Damn it," I said, shooting up out of my chair. I'd spoken louder than I'd intended and my outburst had attracted the attention of one of the medics who had worked on the general. She glanced over, her eyes growing large in alarm when she saw McCallen with the streaks of blood on his face and uniform. She rushed over.

"Are you hurt?"

McCallen simply looked at her, unaware that his appearance might cause someone distress.

"That's not his blood," I said. "He's fine, but he might need to be treated for shock."

McCallen narrowed his eyes at me. "I'm not in shock and you know it."

"Well, you're not making sense."

"I'm fine, sergeant," he said to the medic. "You may go."

She hesitated, then picked up her bag and left. McCallen turned his gaze back to me. "I know you still have feelings for me."

"Oh for Pete's sake!" I said, fed up with his distraction. "Go wash your face. You look like a crazy man."

I stomped away, my boot heels vibrating across the floor as I walked toward the door. I could never get a decent signal in the place we'd been using as an office and I had to make a call. When I got outside, I hit the speed dial button for Harry's phone. It rang once.

"About bloody time," he said.

My entire body flushed with warmth at the sound of his voice.

"Harry..." I didn't know where to begin.

"Something's happened hasn't it?"
"We might have a slight delay."

CHAPTER 3

I GRIPPED THE PHONE TIGHTER, wishing I could jump through it to tell him in person. "Harry, I'm so sorry."

"You've nothing to be sorry for, love. It's not your fault. The most important thing is that you're alright. You are, aren't you?"

"Going a bit crazy here, but yes. I'm fine."

"It's just a delay. It doesn't do to get cheesed off about it." The disappointment in his voice belied his words.

"I don't know how long I'll be."

"However long is too long, darling."

"You know I feel the same. I can't tell you how frustrating this is."

"It's bleedin' rotten, what's happened to your general and that, but the timing couldn't be worse, yeah?"

"I know, Harry."

"It's not like we've been trying to muck up the plans on purpose. It just seems it somehow always happens."

It had happened over and over again. Weekend plans, holidays, multiple chances to see each other had been carefully plotted and missed. He'd have a last minute mission or I'd have some sort of emergency, the demands of our careers throwing up one obstacle after another. But now, with him waiting only ten minutes away in a cozy, romantic hotel, my level of frustration oozed thick and viscid as if I were wading through a sea of quicksand. The more I fought against it, the more helpless I felt.

"I'll get there as soon as I possibly can." I tried to sound hopeful but failed, as I walked away from the building, heading toward the spot where I knew I could get a good signal and away from the hubbub behind me. Police sirens, squawking radios, people shouting; I could barely hear Harry through the bad connection, but the further I walked, the more his voice came through clearly and the more I wanted to just keep walking to divorce myself from the awful truth.

Yet again, our plans had been thwarted. How can this keep happening?

"You'd tell me if you weren't okay, wouldn't you? It must've been horrible to see that."

"I'm fine. Shook up of course, and right now, feeling very much like I could strangle someone, but I'm fine. I promise."

I made it to my chosen spot, a pocket of quiet at the edge of the parking lot. Standing under a large shade tree, I looked down the sloping terrain out to the area we called the box, a vast training area we'd occupied for almost a month. Set foot in the box on any training post during an exercise, and you needed to make the mental shift from your real-world location to whatever country the exercise scenario had set for you. From where I stood, I saw long convoys of vehicles kicking up billows of dust as they snaked out of the box, headed for the main post on their way home. A mock town, used for Military Operations in Urban Terrain or MOUT site, sat in the near distance. The small cluster of buildings appeared like a quiet rural village populated with structures that represented schools, churches, shops and homes, set in a five-acre area. During our exercise, the little village had been called Pleasantville. It was just one of several MOUT site towns used in the exercise scenario which had put us on a post-invasion, nation-building mission in the made up country called Publican. Scores of role players had been stationed in the fake towns scattered throughout the box. Our soldiers had patrolled the streets where role player civilians had protested, rioted and falsely accused us of countless wrongdoings. The Publican newspapers had misquoted us, printed inaccurate information and published stories for the sole purpose of whipping up angry sentiment. And to enhance the training experience, it all happened at a pace that was so constant it made you breathless.

While the MOUT sites had very American sounding names like Pleasantville, Mayberry and Fairtown, the most current events of rising tensions between ethnic Albanians and Serbs in Kosovo led many of us to believe more appropriate names for the towns would be Pristina, Mitrovica or Glodjane. No matter the town names, as preparation for potential real-world missions, it had been excellent training. Now I just needed it to be over. "I'll probably have to give a witness statement. And I'm sure they'll want to hold a press conference."

He was silent for a long moment.

"Harry?"

"Just don't dally, love. Get it done and come to me, on the quick, yeah?"

I leaned on the tree, my knees suddenly weak with desire to be with him. "Roger, that. On the quick," I said, a smile threatening. He understood the lack of choice I sometimes faced because of the uniform I wore. His service to the crown. My service to my country. The career choices we had made were bigger than our own wishes and felt most burdensome when what our duty required conflicted with what we most desired. I didn't have to explain things to him. He knew, just as I did, that the freedoms our professions worked to secure for others didn't necessarily extend to us.

Still, hearing Harry's voice had lightened my mood, despite how dark things felt. I glanced at my watch. "It's almost noon. If I have my way, I'll be there by dinner time. Don't give up on me, Fogg."

"Never that."

From behind me, I heard someone calling my name. I turned and saw that my day wasn't getting any better. "Holy hell," I said.

"What is it, pet?"

"Harry, I've got to go," I turned my back on the person shouting at me, wishing he would go away but knowing he wouldn't. "I swear. I will get there as soon as I possibly can. Pick out a nice place for us to have our first meal together." I checked my watch. That would give me five or six hours to be done with my statement, get on the road, and start my leave.

"Harper! I know that's you."

"Alright, love. Sounds like you're needed. Just get the job done. I'll see you sooner than you think."

I disconnected the call, took a deep breath and walked toward the man who had been calling me. "Chief Ramsey," I said, shaking his hand. "And here I hoped to live the rest of my life without ever seeing you again."

He regarded me with his icy blue eyes, now crinkled into slits, his large dimples on display. "Oh, you wound me, Sergeant Harper. I'm one of your biggest fans."

"Now perhaps. At one time, that wasn't the case."

Chief Warrant Officer Four Paul Ramsey was the CID investigator who had accused me of murder. He'd been a doggedly persistent and stubborn adversary. Somehow, after a great deal of trauma, I'd won him over. The last time I saw him, he had apologized for his treatment of me. Since then, I'd managed to forgive him for his mistakes, but some things are too hard to forget. His smile made him seem almost human, although I knew from experience he only pretended to be Homo sapien. In reality he was some sort of organism whose main characteristics were suspicion, narrow-mindedness and inflexibility.

He wore a dark blue suit, a starkly-white shirt and a blue striped tie since civilian clothes were the proper uniform for a CID investigator. The dark color of the suit with his blonde hair and tan complexion looked good on him even though I would never tell him that.

"I admit to drawing the wrong conclusions about you, Master Sergeant Harper," he said, as he turned to walk toward the building and the wild scene I'd just left. "You look wonderful, by the way."

I stopped and focused my attention on him. "You sound like someone who wants something."

"Me? No." He started toward the building again, but my mistrust of the investigator made me linger in place. "Are you coming?" he said.

I followed him, but my danger gauge felt twitchy. Ramsey smiling? Dishing out compliments? It was too out of character to take lightly.

When I walked into our building, I hardly recognized the place where I'd lived for three weeks. Chairs, once arranged in neat rows, now formed a mad jumble of obstacles covering the floor. A multicolored pile of flags, even Old Glory, covered the floor in a disturbing clump of disregard. I found myself staring at the pile of satin and fringe, the stars and stripes mixed in with the blood-red general officer flag and the Ninth Army guidon heavy with battle ribbons. Every instinct directed me to rush to the United States flag, pick it up off the floor, to right it, to clean it off and return it to its stand. I struggled to ignore the discord the image caused.

I noticed the edge of the fancy Ninth Army shield we'd hung on the front of the podium lay partially in a large puddle of blood, and there were bloody footprints everywhere, as if someone were using them to teach a complicated dance step.

The murder attempt had taken place in my home and seeing the scene again, felt like a new violation.

"I take it you saw the attack?" Ramsey said.

"Yes, along with a room full of people, not to mention a video camera was rolling the whole time and there were several people taking pictures. The entire thing has been recorded start to finish."

"That should make my job easier," he said, an eyebrow raised.

The noise had died down but chaos still prevailed. Ramsey's partner, Chief Warrant Officer Three Hector Santos, stood with a clipboard, assessing the room, taking notes. Santos, also wearing a dark suit and tie, glanced our way, saw me and nodded a greeting, then went back to work.

Military Police had replaced the flex ties with handcuffs. The man in custody now sat with his head down, his shoulders hunched as if he wanted to curl into a ball.

"Ah, I see Colonel McCallen is here. So, you two are still working together." Ramsey smiled at me an eyebrow raised. When I narrowed my eyes at him he laughed and smacked me on the shoulder. "Relax Harper. You're not under suspicion anymore."

"Colonel McCallen is my boss. There wasn't anything going on between us when you accused me of murder. There isn't anything going on between us now, so don't even go there."

He put his hands up and laughed, "Okay, okay. Don't bite my head off. I'm just giving you a hard time."

"And you should know," I added without joining in on his laughter, "that McCallen was standing right next to the general when it happened. I think he went into shock or something. He's not acting like himself."

As if he knew we were talking about him, McCallen came over. He'd washed much of the blood off his face and had shed his uniform jacket since it had been covered in gore. He held a damp rag and scrubbed the tiny creases in his hands, trying to get them clean. Evidently, he'd heard everything I said.

"I am not in shock," he said, directing an accusatory gaze at me. "I'm perfectly lucid and rational and I meant everything I said."

"Oh? Something you want to share," Ramsey asked.

McCallen and I answered together. "No."

"I see. Well, then," he said, his calculating gaze bouncing back and forth between us. "You two might as well get comfortable. I'll come back to take your statements as soon as I've walked through the scene."

"Don't you need everyone to clear out?" I asked. "Are we compromising your crime scene?"

"We know what happened here," Ramsey said. "We just need to collect evidence for documentation but we'll be at it for a few hours."

"Chief, I don't want to be pushy," I said. "But, I really need to be somewhere. Would it be okay if I were the first in line to provide my statement?"

"Master Sergeant Harper has a date," McCallen said, his words ringing with a sarcastic bite.

"Actually, Chief, I had plans to go on thirty days of leave. I've had the plans for a long time and I'd like to keep them." I said the last part looking at my boss. Ramsey had busied himself scanning the room and didn't hear the tension between McCallen and me.

"I'll put you on the list first, but this interview probably won't be the last. Eye witnesses will be important to this investigation."

"You don't expect me to stay here until the investigation is over." When he didn't respond I started to panic. "How long are you talking about?"

Ramsey snapped on latex gloves, his gaze busy scanning the crime scene. "Hard to say. I understand your desire to leave. I just can't make any promises about when that might be."

Ramsey's mild assurance sounded hollow. I had never trusted the investigator and I wasn't about to start now.

"Even he agrees this situation makes everyone's plans a bit fluid, Sergeant Harper. This is a crisis situation."

My focus snapped to McCallen and I froze for a moment, thinking, surely he wouldn't use this as an excuse to keep me here. When I was finally able to speak, I hated how meek my words sounded. "Sir, you know how long I've been waiting for this. You can't…"

"I think you know that I can." He uttered the simple fact gently, as if he regretted the power he had over me. He took a wide stance and crossed his arms. It was his I've-made-a-decision-and-I'm-not-budging posture. I felt as if my head was about to explode. He checked his watch. "Any minute now, a Stars and Stripes reporter is going to show up here and we'll have international media at the gate in no time. I'm going to need all hands on deck."

The period of my speechlessness stretched for a long moment, so frozen in shock I feared any sound I allowed out of my mouth would come out in a scream despite my best efforts. When I did finally speak, my voice shook in a humiliating display of my lack of control. "Sir, Captain Jerreau is more than capable of assisting you..."

"You're my senior NCO, Harper. You know this incident will cause a shit storm of media attention to rain down on this place. You can't possibly think I can allow you to go on leave now."

From the corner of my eye, I saw that Patrovski and Owens watched us. Owens, his dark skin glistening in sweat, looked concerned as he moved around shooting video, carefully stepping over chairs that had been tossed about in the melee. Jerreau stood talking to one of the MPs but his attention stayed focused on McCallen and me. They could see my distress. I'd spent days preparing them for my departure. I considered us a disciplined and skilled team of Public Affairs Officers, each one of us perfectly capable of handling the situation. And being the lead NCO in an event like this would be good experience for Patrovski. Captain Jerreau, a newly trained PAO, had never been quoted in the media, had never served as a spokesperson yet, but he was ready. They didn't need me. The most disturbing thing was, even with Ramsey's need for a statement, McCallen knew their capabilities. He was looking for excuses to keep me here, and, I thought, to keep me away from Harry.

I stared down at my boots, clenched my hands into fists and attempted to dampen down my temper but there were too many heated words I wanted to throw at my boss. I could almost hear my sister, Loretta, whispering in my ear to take deep breaths and not say anything I would regret later. "Don't start acting like the angry black woman, shaking your head and pointing your finger. It will just be used as an excuse not to take you seriously," she'd say.

With my hands on my hips, I met McCallen's gaze. It had been awhile since I'd really looked at him and made a frank assessment. There were a few more lines around his eyes and mouth from recent trauma; the death of a child, the ending of his marriage. His freckles had always fascinated me. At one time, the scattering of color across his pale skin led me to fantasize about playing connect the dots with gentle strokes on his face, to run my finger along his scar, so large and impossible to ignore, the thing that should have marred his face but instead, gave him a look of mystery and sex appeal. I'd never had a chance to live out those fantasies. He stared back, his gaze softening. What I said next came out calm and quiet so that only he could hear. My tone was meant to assure him I wasn't joking.

"Colonel McCallen, if you attempt to prevent me from taking this leave, I'll have no option but to go over your head."

He cocked his head at me. "I thought you'd say that." He let his gaze roam my face for a long moment. "You won't believe this, Lauren, but I am sorry."

I was about to argue my point when he glanced over my shoulder. "General Roderick, sir," he said.

Brigadier General Stanley J. Roderick was the Ninth Army Deputy Commander. I turned to see him stride into the room and head directly for us. The imposing African American officer had recently told me he wanted to recommend me for the Sergeant Major's Academy. I'd always felt he respected my work and my opinion and it was to him that I had intended to report McCallen's behavior, knowing he would back me up. In seconds, he dashed those hopes.

"Colonel," he said shaking my boss's hand. "I've heard you saved his life."

"I did what anyone else would have," McCallen said.

Roderick smiled. "Yeah, all heroes say that." He turned to me. "Harper, I'm sorry I had to delay your leave," he said. "But this is a crisis situation. Lots of people had family plans for after the exercise. I've had to delay them all. The colonel argued on your behalf but I need you here, at least until we can assess this state of affairs."

I could almost feel my face drain of color. McCallen had used the same words – a crisis situation. I'd directed my anger at the wrong place.

Roderick was still talking. "Neil, we need to get the news about this out to the lowest levels. I don't want the ranks to hear about General Blunt's injuries from a national news report."

Roderick started walking to the front of the room. Neil naturally fell in by his side but sent a glance to me over his shoulder, apology evident in his look.

It was a good thing there was something to sit on nearby or I would have ended up on the floor. Plopping down on the metal chair, I put my face in my hands and doubled over, tears of frustration threatening.

"Oh my god," I said into my hands. "Not again." How would I explain this to Harry? He'd come all this way. What could I say to him?

CHAPTER 4

I SAT THAT WAY, MY face in my hands, trying to catch my breath and come to terms with my reality when someone spoke to me.

"Are you hurt?"

I didn't realize the question was directed at me until I felt a hand on my shoulder. I jumped in response.

"I apologize," he said. I recognized the blond Ranger who'd been watching the press conference. He'd squatted down next to me, a hand on the back of my chair. I pulled away from him, surprised to have his unfamiliar face so close to mine. His squint-eyed gaze seemed full of concern.

"I didn't mean to startle you, Sergeant. I merely wanted to ensure that you were unhurt."

"I'm fine, sir. Just a bit in shock I guess."

"It was a rather shocking incident." His southern accent sounded almost fake it was so textbook, as if he'd imitated it from studying movies of the Civil War era. He rose to his full height and looked down at me. "May I get you something? Water or…"

I was surprised by his question. It was unusual for an officer to offer service to an NCO. I stood to demonstrate that I really was fine. He stood average height, with wide shoulders on a slender build; hard looking, as if a great deal of muscle lie in wait beneath his uniform.

"No, thank you, sir. I'm fine. Really."

"Good," he said, studying me. "I shall take your assurances to be fact."

Something in his expression made me think he didn't altogether believe me.

"I'm Master Sergeant Harper," I said extending my hand.

"Major Mathias Albert Beechwood." His calloused and large hand gave a firm but not overdone handshake. "Most people call me Math."

I smiled. Despite the almost humorous and a bit pretentious introduction, there was something charming and open about his regard. His gaze felt penetrating and honest, his concern genuine. His chiseled cheeks, narrow-eyed squint, deep dimples and yes, that southern accent, made you want to know more about him, hear what he had to say. For some reason, he'd decided to direct his attention to me and that made me feel privileged somehow.

"And this fine fellow is Captain Joshua Pratt, my right hand." He indicated the Native American soldier standing next to him. Pratt looked down at me while shaking my hand before he crossed his arms, his expression without emotion but focused. My attention was drawn to the massive signet ring he wore, one that looked very similar to the one that rarely left McCallen's finger. He observed me looking at it, and raised an eyebrow. His intense gaze felt a bit disconcerting, as if, simply by noticing it, I'd somehow challenged his right to be an alumnus of West Point.

"And this is our Command Sergeant Major, David Eldnik."

I shook hands with the large NCO who had reminded me of Harry. "Nice to meet you Sergeant Major," I said.

"Considering the circumstances, I would have rather met anywhere but here," he said, his dark eyed gaze looked genuinely sorrowful. "We all know Blunt," he said. "I just...I just can't believe this." He pinched his nose between his eyes, scrunching them shut. Then he glanced at me briefly before mumbling an apology and walking out of the building.

I shifted my attention back to Beechwood.

"Our Sergeant Major has always been an emotional man, but he's right," he said. "We all know the general and his family. Terrible." Unlike Eldnik, neither he nor Pratt seemed to have been as emotive about the attack. "Course, we know that one too," he said, looking at the shooter. "Unbelievable."

"Do you have any idea why he would do such a thing?"

Beechwood kind of chuckled and wagged a finger at me. "I've heard about you," he said. "We participated in an exercise with that unit of Sappers you were with in Honduras, didn't we Pratt?" he said, soliciting agreement from his companion. "Some of the boys we know told us about what happened down there. You were lucky to have come out of that jungle unscathed. They said you were impressive."

Unscathed is not how I would have described my condition after what happened in Honduras, but I didn't bother to correct his assessment. I smiled. "Is that a compliment, Major? Or should I regard it as an attempt to avoid answering the question?"

His smile widened and he glanced at Pratt. "See Pratt? What they said about her was true." He crossed his arms and the mirth left his face. He looked down as if ashamed of his association with Newberg. "No, I don't know why he did it, but I do feel a bit responsible for what has happened here."

"Why?"

"Major Newberg is a member of my unit. A fellow Ranger," he said. "I feel as if I should have known that he was not in control of his faculties."

Pratt grunted. "He seemed perfectly in control to me."

Beechwood shot him an annoyed look. "We both know he has been under a great deal of stress lately." He directed his next comment to me. "He'd recently been given some disappointing news. I had no idea he would react to it in such an extreme manner."

"What kind of disappointing news?"

"Some change in his next assignment. Evidently, it wasn't the position he'd hoped for. Our Major Newberg has quite the career progression mapped out for himself. Not getting the assignment was a source of great frustration."

Pratt grunted again. "Doubt this was because he didn't get the job he wanted."

"We may never know what was in his head when he committed this horrible crime." The rebuff from Beechwood drew another grunt from Pratt.

"Surely General Blunt didn't have anything to do with a change of assignment," I said. Even if he had, what job could Newberg have wanted so badly that he'd kill over not getting it? Considering the flash he wore on his uniform, he'd already completed most of the skills-related courses available and seemed about the right age to be a major.

"I was not privy to the reasons why his assignment was changed. I simply know that Newberg was disappointed. I...that is, many of us know the major very well. It is out of character for him to do something so rash."

Something about this exchange began to feel like an act they were performing for my benefit. Pratt and Beechwood exchanged looks during the brief speech, then directed their gaze back at me as if waiting for my reaction. I had several questions I wanted to ask but didn't get a chance to when Melody Spencer, Mrs. Blunt's sister, stormed through the door.

She rushed in, her eyes sweeping the room. When her gaze landed on me and the Rangers, her eyes widened and she paused as if about to say something. A moment later, she turned away from us and moved quickly to where General Roderick and Colonel McCallen stood.

"It was nice to meet you both," I said. "Please excuse me."

Beechwood flashed a perfect set of white teeth in a charming and flirtatious smile. It felt as if, in a different time, he would have bowed and kissed my hand as a form of farewell. "Of course, Sergeant. I'm sure you have plenty to keep you occupied."

As I made my way toward McCallen, I had the feeling they were still watching me. I glanced back at them and found both Beechwood and Pratt staring. I smiled nervously and turned away wondering if the major always laid on the charm so thickly or if he had been flirting with me.

When I joined McCallen, Melody was in the middle of speaking to General Roderick.

"She and Brianna are on their way to the hospital. They called from the car to tell me the news. This is just ..." She paused as her gaze took in the disarray of the scene around her. When the dark pool of blood on the floor as well as the blood and gore on the podium finally registered, she sucked in a breath and covered her face with her hands, peeking at the carnage thorugh her fingers as if they could minimize the shocking image. McCallen and I both reached out to steady her but she evidently felt more comfortable with me and nearly collapsed in my arms.

"There's a chair right over here, ma'am."

She glanced at me vacantly and allowed me to get her seated, McCallen and Roderick reaching out to assist.

"Oh my god," she mumbled. "It's just so horrible. Why would anyone want to do this to Preston?"

There'd been much speculation about Melody Spencer over the years the Blunts had been in Germany. Speculation about why a seemingly capable and attractive woman chose to live with her older sister's family. Rumors were that she'd joined them after she'd suffered some kind of life changing event, but no one knew exactly what that was.

She wore her strawberry-blonde hair in her usual style of a half ponytail pulled back tightly in a colorful scrunchy with the rest of her thin, wavy and fizzy hair hanging down her back. She favored almost floor-length bohemian-style skirts with loose-fitting tops. Her thick cat eye glasses came in multiple colors that always matched her wardrobe.

I'd always thought her the much more approachable Spencer sister and could imagine having talks with her about books or theatre over a glass of wine. I liked her style which seemed complimentary to her profession as a grade school teacher, a profession that had allowed her to move with the Blunts from duty station to duty station, and easily find work wherever they went. In her mid-thirties, she was attractive in a quiet, bookish way but I knew she had her secrets. I often saw her in the gym in Heidelberg and figured her sister, the general's wife, would never have approved of the many, discreet tattoos she wore, like the Celtic cross on the back of her shoulder, the serpent that wrapped around the top of her thigh, or the bloody, cracked heart with the initials C and S on her breast. There were stories behind those tattoos I'd never have the courage to ask her about. All evidence of the fact that there was very little I knew about Melody Spencer aside from what I'd learned by using the same gym, undressing in the same locker room and hanging out in a sauna. Superficial, surface deep things.

I may not have known much about her, but I could see that she felt the attack on her brother-in-law deeply.

"We will get to the bottom of this, I assure you," General Roderick said. "In the meantime, I think it best that you keep Mrs. Blunt at the hospital. I'll call my wife and ask her to come to assist."

"Good. I'm sure Julia will be a comfort. But I came to remind you about Trent," she said. "Someone has to tell Trent at the academy before this is all over the news. Melody asked me to do it, but I can't. I simply can't tell him his father…"

"The Red Cross has already been notified so his travel orders can be arranged," Roderick said. "I know the commandant at the Point personally, so I reached out to him. I'm sure he will deliver the news to Trent within the hour."

Even at the military academy, no one ever wanted to get a Red Cross message. It meant someone close to you had died or was gravely ill. Trent, in his third year at his father's alma mater, would be called out of class, given the grave news and issued orders to join his family as soon as possible.

"I feel bad that I can't tell him myself. I just can't bring myself to do it, but lord knows, it's beyond Pauline's abilities. She is never good at delivering bad news. Especially in this case."

"Understood, ma'am." McCallen said. "It's taken care of. One less thing for you to worry about."

"Good," she said, her gaze roaming the room again. She turned to General Roderick. "Stanley, please keep us informed."

"Of course. Now, I'll have my driver take you to the hospital."

"Please, no. I don't want to be a bother. I drove myself…"

"Nonsense. You shouldn't be driving," he said, while waving a young Sergeant over and giving him instructions.

"I don't want to be a bother," Melody repeated, but her protest went ignored. She moved slowly as she stood and, taking the arm offered her, walked toward the door escorted by the soldier.

"It pains me to see that family in such crisis," Roderick said, his hands clenched at his sides, his forehead pulled into a deep frown. He almost vibrated with the intensity of his emotions. He stepped away from McCallen and me and addressed the room. "Who is in charge of this investigation?

Ramsey stood from where he'd been squatting, examining something on the floor. He walked toward us, a wary expression on his face.

"May I help you, sir?"

"I want to know why Major Newberg would do such a thing. If he's simply a disturbed man, why didn't we see that? We must also consider that this was a part of a larger plot. What if other senior leaders are in danger?"

Roderick's hands were on his hips as he leaned into Ramsey's personal space. I'd seen him do that many times and I'd never envied the person who'd attracted such attention. "I want hourly updates. You find out what the motivation was behind this. I refuse to believe Major Newberg suddenly became deranged."

"Sir, we may never know..."

"You *will* find out," Roderick demanded. "This is your only mission." His gaze swept the room. "This is the priority for all of us. Anyone who doesn't cooperate with this investigation will face the most grave of consequences." He turned to my boss. "McCallen, with me. We need to hold a press conference as soon as possible."

They strode toward McCallen's office. When they closed the door, it was like someone had unclogged a drain, the sudden release of tension leaving a sucking sound in its wake.

I turned to Ramsey and tried to hide my smile at his red face and troubled look, recognizing an unpleasant satisfaction in seeing the investigator looking so uncomfortable. I tried to keep the laughter out of my voice when I said, "Looks like you've got your work cut out for you."

He glanced at Santos, then crossed his arms and gave me a pointed stare. Santos joined him, both men directing intense gazes toward me.

"What?" I said.

"You just keep your nose out of this one, Harper," Ramsey said. "Every time you get involved, things get complicated."

"Every time I... Are you out of your mind? You act as if I had a choice before."

Santos and Ramsey swapped looks. "It may be true that circumstances complelled your involvement before," Santos said. "You have a choice this time."

"And this time, we want you to stay out of it," Ramsey said.

"Fine by me." I threw my hands up as if being robbed at gunpoint. "I've got plenty of other things to do."

For a brief moment, I felt as if I'd been granted a reprieve but it felt temporary and that left me feeling uneasy. I scanned the room and saw Beechwood and Pratt watching me. Beechwood stretched his mouth in a fake smile.

Ramsey must have seen a change in my expression. "What is it?"

"If I tell you not to look, I know you're going to look."

He rolled his eyes at me. "Don't look where?"

"There's a group of Rangers that were here to watch the press conference. There's a tall, Native American guy and the blond major...I told you not to look!" I said to the back of his head. He turned back to me, smiling.

"Trust me, they know we're talking about them," Ramsey said. "What about them?"

"Well, they're in Newberg's unit and they came here with him. You might want to talk to them. They said something about Newberg being upset about his next duty assignment."

Ramsey smiled. "You see, Harper. You're already getting involved when I just finished telling you..."

"Believe me, I want nothing to do with this. I'm just telling you what I know. Would you rather I kept it to myself?"

He pointed a finger at me. "Stay out of it, Harper. I mean it."

I threw my hands up again in protest. "Hey, I've got my own job to do. I wouldn't dream of doing yours. Again."

Ramsey narrowed his eyes at me, before showing me his back.

Like most things that come out of my mouth, at the time I said it, I'd meant every word.

CHAPTER 5

JOE GAVIN LOOKED AGITATED, on edge, like he wanted to see and hear everything at once. The Stars and Stripes reporter had been invited to attend the press conference but had decided not to. He'd already seen several of Blunt's practice media events and knew the last one of the exercise wouldn't be much of a news story. He'd decided instead to hit the road early for the five-hour drive back to Frankfurt. A call from his editor had turned him around and sent him speeding back.

"I cannot believe I wasn't here," he said, running his fingers through his beard. "My editor is going to kill me for missing this." The active duty soldier was allowed to wear his hair longer than regulation and have facial hair since he worked in civilian clothes most of the time. Unlike some, Gavin was a reasonable and professional reporter. Early on in the exercise, I'd purposely offered a one-on-one interview to him with Blunt, knowing the reporter would be fair and not take advantage as some liked to do. The story that resulted had been front page, above the fold and had contributed to the confidence Blunt needed in himself, improved his trust in the media and more importantly, his trust in his PAO.

Gavin had arrived just as the military police were leading the shooter out of the building.

"Is that the guy?" He asked.

"Yes, but he hasn't been charged with anything yet. I'd appreciate it if you wouldn't publish his name until they do."

'Okay, okay, I know the rules. But that doesn't mean I can't give a good description."

Everyone in the room stopped to watch as they left, as if we were all going to write our own description of the man who had tried to kill Major General Blunt.

He was average height with black hair shorn in military style, a true high and tight. A bit brawny-looking with a large chest and muscular arms, his camouflage uniform was covered in subdued flash -- jump wings, air assault badge, the pathfinder badge, the Combat Infantry Badge, and just below the shoulder on his left sleeve he wore the Ranger skill tab above his unit patch. He wore the gold clover leaf of a Major and the embroidered name on his uniform read Newberg.

I wondered how long he'd been planning the attack. He'd shown up with the rest of the Rangers as if he simply wanted to watch the press conference. How could he have hid his intentions so thoroughly? The more I looked at him, the more he seemed familiar, but I couldn't place him. No longer wearing the strange smile, he stared straight ahead, not acknowledging that he was the center of attention. The MPs on either side of him kept firm grips on his arms as they walked him out.

What could have motivated Newberg to do such a thing? The flash on his uniform meant he was an exceptional soldier. You didn't earn that many specialty badges without discipline. You couldn't even get into most of those schools unless you were recommended. Perhaps he'd suffered some kind of psychotic break.

I glanced at my watch, the minutes and hours still marching toward the time when I'd promised Harry I would be with him. A wave of melancholy washed over me, but I didn't have time for it. I called Patrovski over and put Gavin in her care while he furiously took notes of everything going on around him.

Then I approached my captain, skirting the splatters of blood and papers scattered on the floor. "Can I speak to you for a moment, sir?"

He immediately started fingering his charm, again. "I knew something bad was 'bout to happen, me," he said.

I'd only known the young Captain a few months, but he always surprised me with the way he jumped into his dialect at will. He could stand in front of a room full of people and give a lecture or class with a barely detectible Louisiana accent. But let him get comfortable or upset, and the Cajun came out. I learned that he only used it around those he trusted, so when I heard it, I felt somehow privileged.

"Sir, we need to start pulling some products together."

He regarded me with his large brown eyes and noticed me looking at his charm.

"My grandmother's charm works, Sergeant Harper. It's still warm, like the evil lurking up in here."

Or from the friction he built on it with his furious rubbing. "You put a lot of trust in voodoo things."

"You go head and laugh, you," he said, dropping the disk, his hands going to his hips.

"I'm not laughing, sir," I said. "If it's a protection charm, I could use one myself."

He locked gazes with me for a moment to gauge my seriousness. "I don't need to have precognition to know that what you say is probably true." He smiled, in that way he would, when people questioned his beliefs, as if anyone who didn't believe in voodoo didn't understand the true way of the world. "If protection is what you want, what you think you need, than perhaps I can help you with that," he said.

"In what way?"

"Nev'ah you mind," he said with a sly smile, which he erased before saying, "What do you need, Sergeant Harper?"

He'd dropped the Cajun dialect and focused his attention on me. While his transition seemed instantaneous, I needed a second to order my thoughts. He waited patiently.

"We'll need to get started on some products," I said.

Jerreau nodded his head. "A press release, some talking points, a media kit and a plan for a press conference. A large one."

"We'll have the whole international media corps wanting in on this one," I said.

The phones in both offices were already ringing. Owens looked up from where he sat at my desk, his forehead wrinkled into a frown, a phone cradled between his head and shoulder, then returned to furiously taking notes and messages. As soon as he hung up from one call, another one came in.

"I already have the release written in my head," Jerreau said, pointing to his temple. "It'll take me about five minutes to knock it out."

"I think you should be the spokesperson for this, sir. The colonel can take the first press conference but after that..."

He remained expressionless, save for a small quirk at the corner of his mouth. His nod this time was almost imperceptible. "I'll be ready."

"Just so I know for sure, if you were to hold a press conference about this right now, what would be the first thing you'd say?"

He grinned, widened his stance and crossed his arms as if to signal he was ready to be challenged. "A condolence message for the Blunt family and a promise for a thorough investigation."

"Good man. See the guy over there with Patrovski? That's Joe Gavin from Stars and Stripes. He's your first reporter. I'm sure he'll ask to speak to witnesses."

"Not until they've given their statement to the investigators," Jerreau replied. "And it will be up to them if they want to speak to him."

"Good. He'll want to know more about the shooter," I said.

"We can't release his name until he's been charged. We'll release the information as soon as it's available."

I smiled. "Almost sounds like you've been trained for this."

"Don't worry, Sergeant Harper. I'm ready for true."

"I'm sure you'll be great."

"I'll take over for Patrovski and have her help Owens on the phones," he said as he took a couple of steps toward Gavin, then stopped. "I heard they delayed your leave."

"Whatcha gonna do?" I said, with a shrug.

"Only thing you can do. Pretend it's Mardi Gras and *laissez les bons temps roulent,*" he said, with a smile. "Let the good times roll."

With Jerreau on a mission, my next goal was to get a holding statement together for Patrovski and Owens to give to any media who called and determine when we wanted to hold the press conference. The media would be clamoring for a presser tonight. I hoped a release would hold them until tomorrow. I figured we'd have a better picture of Blunt's medical condition by then and wondered how he was doing.

As hard as I attempted to focus on the job at hand, my attention bounced around between my official duties and Harry. By this time, I should have already been with him, staring into those deep green eyes, smelling his scent that reminded me of woods and fresh water. I'd been yearning for him for so long, imagining our reunion so vividly, I could almost hear his voice.

"Wait a minute…" I said to myself. When I turned around, I realized it hadn't been my imagination.

CHAPTER 6

HARRY WALKED TOWARD ME, excusing himself and shouldering his way past anyone who wanted to question why a British Army soldier had come strolling into our area. He'd tucked his beige beret under the epaulet on the shoulder of his camouflage uniform, the pants of which were tightly tucked into the tops of his spit shined boots. He held a thick folder under one arm and made his way toward me, dwarfing most of the men in the room and refusing to be deterred. He stopped inches from me, and chuckled at my shocked expression. He took one of my hands and kissed it. His eyes literally twinkled.

"Feeling rather proud of yourself, are you Sergeant Major Fogg?" My smile couldn't have been wider. I never knew what Harry would do from one minute to the next. If I'd had a tail, it would be wagging wildly.

"A bit chuffed, yeah," he said. "You look so lovely."

The softness of his gaze made me feel woozy. "What are you doing here?"

He glanced over my shoulder, his forehead pulled into a frown. "I had a feeling you'd have trouble getting away. I realize a major catastrophe has occurred here," he said, as his gaze swept the room, taking in the chaos, the blood and gore. "Despite that, I hoped I could help free you up. At least for a time."

McCallen approached, his negativity radiating off him in the set of his mouth and the tenseness of his posture. In contrast, General Roderick seemed openly curious. Harry snapped out a proper British salute which Roderick returned smartly.

"Sergeant Major Harold Fogg at your service, sir."

As Harry and the general shook hands, Roderick asked the same question I had asked.

"Not that you're unwelcome, but what does the British Army have to do with this incident?"

"With this incident, nothing, sir. We do however have an interest in Master Sergeant Harper here." Harry said. "I realize this is an improper time, but if I could just have a moment."

Harry held out his arm, tentatively touching Roderick on the shoulder to lead him away from McCallen and me. He'd performed the separation so smoothly, I was sure Roderick was unaware of the masterful way in which Harry had taken charge.

"What's that about?" McCallen said, his jaw clenched. When I didn't respond, he focused angry eyes at me. "Well?"

I shrugged. "I have no idea. I'm as shocked as you are.'

Harry was showing Roderick something in the folder he held. Roderick looked at the document then glanced at me. The two men continued to confer.

"You knew he was coming," McCallen's face was about as red as it ever got.

"No, sir, I did not."

"What did he mean? That the British Army had an interest in you?"

I crossed my arms and cocked my head at my boss. "Do you have any idea how you're acting?"

He pressed his lips together as if attempting to stop himself from saying anymore, but he couldn't keep his mouth shut. He leaned toward me, the intensity of his gaze froze me in place. His words came out sharp and angry.

"Lauren, I can't lose you now. Not after everything...not after waiting so long." He raised a hand as if he were going to touch me, but stopped himself, curling his fingers in a frustrated fist. "I know that if I let you run off with this guy, I'll lose you forever."

For years. That's how long I'd wanted to be with him. I'd worked by his side, fantasized about him, wrote about him in my journal, and knew the entire time that we'd never be together. His wife, his two kids and the threat of the end of both of our careers were hurdles I could never leap. We'd kissed one time, in a moment of weakness. It had been an earth-shattering moment that I still remembered when I stole looks at him, when I allowed myself to wonder what might have been. The kiss had also been more destructive than any kiss should ever be.

"Lose me? Neil, you never had me. There isn't an- us."

"There could be."

Harry had Roderick laughing. Neil and I watched them walk toward us. I took a step away from him, seeking to lower his intensity and catch my breath.

"Well, Sergeant Harper," Roderick said. "Evidently I'm not the only one who thinks you deserve recognition."

I stood, with my mouth hanging open, not understanding a thing. Harry merely grinned and let the moment stretch on. Finally, he pulled an over-sized envelope from the folder he held, a large red wax seal on the back, and handed it to me.

"Open it, lu ... ah, Sergeant."

I tried to keep myself from grinning at Harry's stumble. I so looked forward to hearing him call me love again.

The huge wax seal on the back of the envelope bore the image of a crown stamped into it. Sticking my finger into the fold, I opened the seal and pulled out a card.

At the top, in fancy cursive writing, I read, *The Lord Chamberlin is commanded by Her Majesty to invite Master Sergeant Lauren Harper to Buckingham Palace.*

"Buckingham Palace?"

There were a lot more words, but I was too confused to take it in. I kept staring at the card, my forehead wrinkled, my mouth open. When I glanced up, all three men were staring at me. "Harry, I don't understand. What is this about?"

"Master Sergeant Harper, you are a hero of the crown. You saved the life of two British citizens despite grave danger to yourself. Her Majesty, Queen Elizabeth the second, will present you with The George Cross which is awarded to military or civilians for acts of great bravery exclusive of war. The ceremony will take place in Buckingham Palace where the Queen shall present the cross herself, six weeks hence."

"Holy crap," I mumbled to myself, embarrassed by the way my hand shook, holding the invitation.

Roderick crossed his arms and laughed. "Not exactly an appropriate response to an invitation from the queen, but I can understand your shock. I can honestly say I've never seen anyone with the GC. I imagine it'll be a medal you'll have to explain every time you wear it."

My mouth went suddenly very dry and I avoided wiping the sweat from my face. "It's ... it's worn on ... any formal occasion." I felt mortified at the shaking of my voice. Every time I wore my dress uniform, for every ceremony, every special event, I'd have to explain.

Roderick exchanged looks with McCallen. "Of course. Sergeant Harper. From what Sergeant Major Fogg tells me, it's well-deserved."

"Thank you, sir."

Most days, I went out of my way to avoid remembering what happened to me in Bosnia. Nothing about the experience had made me feel like a hero. I'd been petrified, not to mention unable to defend myself against almost constant assaults. In the end, I'd managed to get myself and the two kidnapped British reporters out of our predicament, but I'd never be healed. I would never forget. The idea of getting a medal for it, of having everyone know what I'd been through, to hear the details of my torture read out to an audience while I stood in front of them, and the thought of having to explain to people every time I wore the damn thing....

My stomach cramped. I almost doubled over and put my hand to my mouth in a panic. I managed to mumble an apology before I ran for the latrine.

CHAPTER 7

SERGEANT HARPER ARE YOU alright?" Patrovski said in the most timid voice I'd ever heard from her. It was the third or fourth time she'd asked the same question. I'd lost track.

I retched again, my stomach knotted into a fist. I hadn't had much for breakfast, but my body kept trying to empty itself and there simply wasn't anything there. Panting, I stood up slowly, thinking surely I had to be done. Wiping my face with a wad of toilet paper, I hit the flush handle to call an end to it and stumbled out of the stall, past Patrovski and leaned on the sink. I sucked up handfuls of water, rinsed my mouth out and spit.

"Sergeant Harper ... "

"Yes, Patrovski. I'm fine. Just ... just give me a minute."

I made the mistake of glancing in the mirror. Curly wisps of my dark hair stood on end, my brown skin sweaty and pale, dark circles under my bloodshot eyes. "Careful, you'll make yourself sick again," I said to my image, then scooped up handfuls of water to splash my face.

"Sergeant Harper?"

"It's okay Patrovski," I said, my face drenched. She seemed more uncomfortable than me. "Really, Tracy. I'm alright."

As my heart slowed, I stared at myself in the mirror. The experience had changed me. The memories still hadn't faded and the talk of what had happened hadn't died. I'd forever be known as *that* Master Sergeant Harper, as helpless to expunge the reputation that followed me as I had been in that barn.

"Fucking Bosnia," I mumbled, turning my back to the mirror. I leaned against the sink and sank my face in my hands. Everyone knew what had happened to me. I'd tried to keep it quiet when I came back, but the rumors had already made their rounds and Ramsey had written a very thorough report, a report that had only been partially classified. He'd not left anything out about my abduction, the torture, the rescue, the killing and capture of the people responsible. Just about everything had been available for reading except for names which had been redacted. If anyone wanted to know, they could find out that the man at the center of the events was alive in a prison somewhere. Exactly where, even the country that held him, were classified, which was a good thing since there were days when I still fantasized about killing him.

For weeks, I'd received calls from reporters requesting interviews, a publishing company had offered a fat sum for a book deal and someone from the United Nations Council on Human Trafficking asked me to speak before their committee. I'd survived my experience, but there was no way I could narrate the details to a worldwide audience. Some of the information passed about was inaccurate and speculative. I'd been given scores of opportunities to correct the record, but I'd refused, deciding it better to let them get it wrong than to have to tell it myself.

I took a deep breath and looked at my young soldier. She stood with her arms crossed, avoiding my gaze. "Seriously. I'm fine. I suppose they're all freaking out."

She shrugged. "You know how men are. A woman gets upset and they start acting like little boys."

We shared a smile for a moment, then that expression crept onto her face. The raised eyebrows, the sorrowful eyes, the I'm-so-sorry-that-happened-to-you look. I'd seen it so many times it made me want to puke again.

I stared at my boots, thinking about how covered in mud they'd always been in Bosnia. I'd tried some talk therapy, tried writing about it, tried simply to avoid all things that reminded me of it. Eventually, I came to the conclusion that I would never forget it and I would never accept it, and I definitely didn't want those three days to define me. Somehow, the idea of getting a medal for the experience had been too much.

I took a deep breath and turned back to the mirror. "Did you hear?" I said to my soldier's reflection in the mirror. "I'm going to meet the Queen of England."

Patrovski grinned. "That's pretty cool. Do you think William and Harry might be there?" She waggled her eyebrows at me.

I had no idea, but her comment made me think about my Harry. He would be going crazy, blaming himself for upsetting me. I took a deep breath and accepted that it was time to face the music.

When I opened the door, I found him pacing. He froze and stared at me, his mouth open. The look of anguish on his face could have been funny if it didn't send a stab through my heart.

He took a couple of slow, tentative steps toward me. I'd seen him cool and confident in the most difficult of circumstances. Now he stood, literally wringing his hands, his lips pale.

"I'm okay, Harry," I said. "Please don't freak out."

"I thought, well I thought it would… I only meant to…"

"Really, Harry, I'm fine. I'm sorry I lost it. It's an unbelievable honor. You just took me by surprise."

"Oh, I've cocked it up is what happened." He ran a hand through his short-cropped hair, his face flushed.

I glanced behind him where McCallen stood with his arms crossed watching us. General Roderick seemed to be holding his breath, as if waiting to see what I'd do. I directed a smile at him that I didn't feel and he grinned and exhaled with relief.

"Well," he said loud enough for us to hear. He clamped a hand on McCallen's shoulder. "In light of the great news Sergeant Major Fogg just gave us, I think you can release Harper for the evening, don't you think Colonel? Give her and her friend a chance to celebrate her impending recognition."

I bit my lip. Letting me off for the rest of the evening, especially after all the drama that had just occurred, was the last thing Neil wanted to do. He stiffened at the suggestion then relaxed. There was plenty to do. The team had their hands full, but they would get along without me here and he knew it. "Yes, sir," McCallen said. "She deserves some time to celebrate."

"Exactly. So, congratulations, Sergeant Harper," The general said, as he gathered up his entourage, and left the building.

I grabbed Harry's arm and squeezed, staring into his eyes. "Harry, wait for me outside." I said. "If you stay here, he might change his mind. Just give me ten minutes, okay?" My heart thudded in my chest. It was possible, after so many weeks and months of wishing for it, that Harry and I could spend an evening together. The prospect almost brought tears to my eyes.

He looked down at me, his lips parted, the possibilities dancing in his gaze. The electric charge I felt when he was near made the hairs on my arms stand up.

A slow grin spread across his face. "I can't wait to kiss you, love," he whispered. He paused for a long moment, staring at me then tucked the folder he held under his arm and walked toward the door.

Just as Harry was about to leave, Command Sergeant Major Eldnik, one of the Rangers Beechwood had introduced me to, walked in the door. The two men froze for a second then with shouts of surprise, they shared a boisterous hug with lots of back slapping and exclamations of shock and joy. The reunion, one I was sure to hear more about later, made me smile.

When I glanced at Neil, my smile felt inappropriate. He directed his gaze at the floor, walked to his office and sat down behind his desk, his attention riveted to his computer. His dejected look sent a sharp pang to my gut, but I shrugged it off. He'd get over it.

I walked into the office across the hall. My team had heard the exchange with the general so they knew what was up. As soon as I shut the door, Patrovski and Owens put their calls on hold. Captain Jerreau looked up from his computer where I was sure he was working on the press release. I explained to them that I'd be gone for the evening. My news resulted in three smiling faces. They knew how much this night meant to me and I could tell from their eagerness, that they wanted to do what they could to help me.

"Don't worry, Sergeant Harper. We've got this," Captain Jerreau said.

We ran through the game plan. We'd been holding press conferences for weeks, over and over again. We'd been answering reporter questions and issuing press releases. This team was ready.

"Sir, you'll need to be prepared for someone to ask for a copy of the video," I said.

"Roger. I'll run it by the colonel, but I'm sure he'll just say it's been turned over as evidence and they'll have to file a FOIA request."

A Freedom of Information Act request was the usual way criminal evidence ended up in the hands of the media. Aside from the video, I couldn't think of anything that could cause them any trouble. I stood looking at them, trying to think if there was anything I'd forgotten.

"It's okay, Sergeant Harper," Owens said. "If I were you, I'd get out of here before something else happens."

Something about the way they all looked at me, their smiles, their obvious feelings of support, made me get a bit choked up. I looked away and blinked a bunch of times, then blew out a long breath.

"Okay," I said, nodding. "I'll see you guys in the morning."

I grabbed one of the bags I'd already packed for my leave and made my way toward the door, pausing a moment to glance at McCallen where he sat in his office, his eyes glued to his computer screen. I ignored the urge to say goodbye and just kept walking, hoping neither of the investigators would notice my absence until I was long gone.

I found Harry and his new-found friend standing outside. Harry stood with a comforting hand on Eldnik's shoulder. It was clear the man had been emotional about what he'd witnessed. "Nick here tells me you two already met," Harry said. "He's an old friend, love. We've been in the dirt together a time or two, yeah mate?" His attempt at drawing the man out of his funk worked only partially.

Eldnik managed a slight smile as he greeted me. "Harry was just telling me about your impending visit with the Queen and ... well, of course I read some of the stories about you in the paper and ..."

"Steady on, Nick," Harry said. "I'm already in the crapper over it."

"It's alright, Harry." I said. "I'm sorry about what happened to the general, Sergeant Major. Did you know him well?"

He gave me first a confused look, then understanding. "Oh, you thought...No, it's not the general I was upset about. I mean, I know him and all and it's terrible. It's Newberg that's really got me baffled. I can't believe what he did. I mean, I was standing right next to him."

"You had no idea..."

"Of course not," he said, his frustration evident. "But I should have. I should have seen something. Shouldn't I have?"

"Don't blame yourself, Sergeant Major," I said. "He must have planned this for a long time."

"Evidently," he said. "Which makes it worse that I missed it. What the hell set him off like that? You know he..."

He was interrupted when he heard his name called. Captain Pratt stood in the doorway, motioning him over.

"Looks like I've gotta go," he said. "Hey, we're going on a jump tomorrow morning," Eldnik said. "You want to join us?"

Harry looked at me with a question on his face. "I'll be busy holding a press conference," I said. "Go ahead and do it if you like."

"Brilliant, I'd love to have a go."

They exchanged numbers and information about where to meet and Eldnik jogged away, leaving Harry and me smiling at each other.

CHAPTER 8

WHEN WE ARRIVED AT the *Gastehaus der Koenig*, which basically translated to, the King's Inn, my lack of knowledge about Harry smacked me in the face. He strolled up to the front desk, leaned an elbow on the counter and proceeded to flirt shamelessly.

"*Gutten Tage, Frau Wexler. Wie gehts?*" How are you, Harry asked her.

"*Sher gut, Hern Fogg.*" she replied, a smile brightening her weathered face. "*Und ist das die junge Dame von dem ihr spracht?*" She asked him if I was the young woman he'd told her about. I blushed at the idea that they'd been talking about me.

He chuckled and turned his gaze to me. "*Ganz shone ist sie nicht?*" Isn't she beautiful? Harry replied, the smile he gave me melted my heart.

"*Alls was sie sagte.*" Just as you described, she replied, her checks turning ruddy.

As if all the compliments weren't enough, I stared at him open-mouthed. The first shock being that Harry could speak perfectly accented German. It wasn't a big surprise. He seemed to be able to do just about anything. He'd evidently told her I was beautiful, which she had confirmed. The bigger surprise followed.

"*Alles in Ordung,*" Mrs. Wexler said, brightly. "*Ich habe einen Tisch für zwei Personen reserviert für sieben heute abend fur sie. Und hier sind die Schlussel fur Zimmeren, sechs und zwanzig und neun und swanzig.*"

She was proud to have accomplished everything he'd requested, including a reservation at seven o'clock for a table for two, which I'd expected. What I hadn't expected was what she'd said next, as she handed him keys for two rooms, numbered twenty-six and twenty-nine. He'd planned for us to stay separately. I tried to hide my surprise, but he noticed and smiled as if to reassure me.

I'd chosen the little bed and breakfast because it was typical of the unique mom and pop places all over Germany and it was private. It offered simple, spacious, yet comfortable rooms, home-brewed and bottled beer, and the restaurant served all locally-raised meat and produce. Another factor in my selection had been that I knew I wouldn't run into anyone from my unit or the exercise. The original plan was to only stay one night, but for that night, I hadn't wanted any distractions.

We both signed our registration forms. He picked up our keys and my overnight bag, and taking my hand, led me up the stairs and down the hall. I was surprised that I felt some relief that he'd reserved the two rooms. Relief that I wouldn't, suddenly, have to change in front of this man I barely knew, and further surprise that he would understand my hesitance even before I did.

When we reached my door he turned to me and smiled, then held my cheek in his hand. He glanced at my door as if he wanted to go in. "I'm not one to go diving into the water head first. I like to walk in slowly, feel the water rise around me, take my time getting comfortable, yeah?"

I smiled and shook my head. "I swear. You always manage to keep me guessing."

He stepped closer and traced my lower lip with his thumb. "In an hour, I'll come and knock on your door and we'll have our first proper date. Perhaps we'll take a walk before dinner, a little stroll to that old palace down the road. How would that be?"

"Perfect," I said.

"In an hour then," he said, and hesitated. I thought he might kiss me but he didn't. He took the key from me, unlocked my door, and with a hand to my back, pushed me gently inside. We stood on either side of the threshold smiling at each other.

"In an hour," I said and couldn't take my eyes off him as I slowly closed the door.

✑❦

EXACTLY AN HOUR LATER, after shampooing, shaving, exfoliating and carefully applying just the right amount of makeup, I was ready. I'd changed into a yellow tank dress with a little flare to the skirt and strappy low-heeled sandals. I had a yellow cardigan handy just in case. The dress had a scooped neck which was perfect for a simple gold chain and matching small hoop earrings. Yellow and gold looked good against my brown skin. I had dabbed a bit of perfume behind my ears and diffused my hair dry. It now hung halfway down my back in its usual, unfettered thick, curly mass.

When the knock on the door came, I suddenly realized why I was so nervous. Since I'd never seen him out of uniform, I had no idea what I would see when I opened the door. Would he be standing there in a wife-beater t-shirt, plaid shorts, black socks and sandals? It seemed unlikely, but he could be wearing Wrangler jeans, cowboy boots, a western shirt and a string tie. He could even be wearing a shirt unbuttoned to display his hairy chest, gold chains and polyester pants that were too tight. I didn't think any of those possibilities would change the way I felt about the big British soldier, but they would solidify the certainty that I didn't know much about him at all.

I moved to the door, took a deep breath and opened it.

"Oh, bloody hell," Harry said, the words rushed out in a whisper.

"Hi," was all I could manage, looking up at him. I'd anticipated all of the worst scenarios. That anticipation hadn't prepared me for the reality.

Freshly shaved, his face looked soft and touchable, despite his crooked nose that always made me think he'd earned it doing something violent. I smiled at the touch of gel in his hair, just enough to add a spike to the short crop of it. He wore a black crew neck that hung loosely past his waist from broad shoulders and his wide chest. The loose-fitting shirt somehow emphasized just how much brawn Harry had been hiding under his uniform. Dark gray cargo-pocket slacks and comfortable-looking loafers completed his outfit.

When I realized again that breathing was essential, I took in a deep breath, exhaled, and grinned so widely I thought my face would break. He looked perfect. Standing before me was exactly what Harry Fogg with two Gs should have looked like if I'd taken the time to truly imagine him. Instead I'd been unable to form a picture and had let my anxiety get the better of me.

"Well, say something." His worried expression almost made me laugh.

I grabbed his arm, tugged him into my room and surveyed him from head to toe. "Look at you," I said, kicking the door closed. "Just look at you."

Almost against my will, I drifted closer, my hands rising to touch his face as if I needed to reassure myself that he actually stood in front of me. I used both hands and simply enjoyed the feel of him. Since my eyes weren't enough proof, my fingers had to bear witness over his forehead and brow, down his crooked nose, his high cheeks and square jaw. I stopping to rub the cleft of his chin with my thumb, smiling at the knowledge that he was real— this was real and not a scene I'd made up in my head. I could get my fill of looking at him, although it seemed impossible that I'd ever feel fulfilled. He took possession of my hands and kissed my palms, one at a time, his eyes closed. Then he spread my hand to his chest and looked at me, looked through me. I felt his breath catch and his heartbeat gradually slow to a steady rhythm.

"I take it you won't be throwing me back then," he said, wrapping a thick curl of my hair around his finger, his green eyes crinkled into slits. He pressed his lips to my forehead, then gazed down at me again.

"Nah uh," I said, unable to form coherent words.

"I'd kiss you, but ..."

"Oh," I said, almost jumping away from him. "Maybe we should … It would be like that diving head first thing."

He flashed his teeth at me. "Spot on."

We should have felt a bit silly, standing there, just gazing at each other, but it didn't feel silly at all. It felt like a necessary pause, an acknowledgment that this was us, the people we were out of uniform. Lauren and Harry. A woman. A man. Not soldiers. No weapons, no body armor, no pressing mission to divert our attention. Just us. He took a deep breath. "I think you'll need a wrap. There's a bit of a nip in the air."

I stepped away from him, unable to stop staring. I managed to pick up my cardigan and my bag. He took the sweater from me and held it so I could slip my arms through.

"It's a rococo palace I'm told," he said, as if he'd memorized the tour brochure, his warm fingers brushing up the length of my bare arms. "The gardens are maintained by an historic trust." He spoke as if he had to struggle to concentrate. Before he covered it with my sweater, he bent down and gently kissed my shoulder where it met my neck, his warm breath brushing across my skin.

"Sounds perfect," I mumbled, the lingering feel of his lips on my flesh a beguiling distraction.

He moved toward the door, his hand out to me. I allowed my fingers to interlace with his. Our hands felt as if they'd been made to fit together.

He tugged me toward the door. "The dinner special tonight is schnitzel, and Gerta has made her famous strudel."

"Gerta? You and Mrs. Wexler are on first name terms now?"

"Gerta is her daughter. She runs the kitchen."

"I see," I said. "Is there anything you don't know?"

"Plenty," he said. "But I'm a quick on the uptake and I've got hours to learn much more."

The way he looked at me, the powerful current that seemed to sing across our connected hands, I wondered if we could make it through another couple of hours without taking that splashing dive into the water.

෨෬

I WAS TAKING MY final bite of the strudel we'd shared when the muted vibration of my phone disturbed our peace. We both stared at my bag where it lay on the corner of the table.

"Shit," I whispered.

I let it continue to vibrate. Harry wiped his mouth with his napkin and leaned back, crossing his legs. "You'd better get that."

The display said it was McCallen. I didn't want the intrusion, didn't want to talk to him, but it was my duty.

"Harper," I said.

"Hold on," McCallen said. I heard some fabric rustling, conversation in the background. The next voice wasn't McCallen's.

"You ran out without talking to me," Ramsey said.

"I had more important things to do," I said, smiling at Harry.

"So I've heard." He lowered his voice. "Which could explain why your colonel has been walking around here all evening looking as if someone killed his puppy."

"I wouldn't know about that."

"Hmm. Well, that's not why I called."

"I didn't think so. What is it?"

"The shooter is Major Winston Newberg, an intelligence officer from special operations command."

"Excellent investigative work. Took you this long to come up with the name he had printed on his chest?"

His strong exhale demonstrated his frustration with me. "Finished with your joke now? Are you ready to take this seriously?"

"Yes," I said with a sigh. "Go ahead, Chief." Harry looked comfortable, one arm draped over the back of his chair. He appeared relaxed but present, his focus riveted on me, listening intently. I loved looking at him and loved the way he watched me. His presence was an almost impossible disturbance.

"Does the name sound at all familiar to you Sergeant Harper?"

"Newberg? No. Why would it?"

"Think, Sergeant Harper. Doesn't the name ring any bells?"

"Major Winton Newberg? No, I...," *Oh crap*, I thought. I looked across at Harry, his focus still with me. One other couple sat on the opposite side of the restaurant from us. They had stared at us openly when we first sat down. Now they held hands and seemed totally into each other. Harry glanced at them, then turned back to me, an eyebrow raised.

"Win-the-lottery Newberg," I said, with a heavy sigh. "That's why he looked familiar. I met him on a Cobra Gold exercise in Thailand. Jeeze, that was ten years ago. He was a Lieutenant then, an operations officer I'd sometimes run into in the TOC. But I've not seen him since then. He's just another soldier I met on an exercise."

I'd been in charge of assignments for the three long weeks of the exercise plus a week of working as the advance party. Instead of going out each day to cover stories, I'd been back at headquarters much of the time, working sixteen hour days. Everyone in the TOC became friendly, having most of our meals together, entertaining each other since we had been stuck inside a command post while everyone else was spread out over the countryside doing what we'd all thought of as the fun stuff. It had been drudgery, sitting in the TOC, answering media calls, arranging logistics for everyone else. The handful of us who'd stayed back had made the most of it but it had been hard to set schedules for chopper rides to Chiang Mai, to send journalists down to Phuket, all while I sat chained to a desk spending what little off time I had playing cribbage in a command post surrounded by exotic scenery.

"Win the lottery?" Ramsey asked.

"He was always buying local gambling tickets, getting everyone to contribute to the pool. It became one of the few high points of the day."

"I see. And that's all you remember? Because, I have to tell you, there are references to you in recent emails he wrote, in journal entries..."

"Emails with who?"

"We don't know. To whoever hooah boy six is. We're trying to trace the IP address."

"Hooah boy. That's original." Hooah. A word used often in the Army but something difficult to define. It meant yes, no, thank you, hello, good bye, good job and just about anything in between. On long exercises, I got tired of hearing it because it was mostly shouted as a motivator, entire rooms full of people blasting it at the top of their lungs. Everyone used the word. With an email address like that, it could belong to anyone.

"It doesn't matter who he wrote to," I said. "I've not seen him in ten years. I barely remember him."

"He remembers you. He has newspaper clippings in his battle book about your assignment to Ninth Army, about what happened in Bosnia and about you in Honduras. He's been following you."

I shook my head. It didn't make sense. "Okay, so he's some kind of stalker. What does that have to do with anything?"

"It's a connection. Investigations are built on connections."

"Isn't the fact that Newberg was in a unit with Blunt a connection?"

"Of course," he said, sounding impatient. "But it's an obvious one."

"And weren't all those men from the Ranger unit connected to Blunt? Did you talk to Beechwood and Pratt?"

"Of course, we interviewed each of them and several others. There's only one other person with a connection to both Newberg and General Blunt that we haven't interviewed yet and that's you."

I allowed my frustration to come over loud and clear. "I'll be more than happy to answer your questions in the morning."

"We need you to come in tonight."

I stared at the phone then looked at Harry, my lips pressed together. It was only 8:30, but that didn't change the way I planned to respond to the investigator.

"Now, love," Harry said. "Don't let him get under your skin." He laid his hand over my clenched fist. It helped to calm me. Still, it took great willpower not to throw the phone to the floor. I took a deep breath and steeled myself. When I spoke again, I had decided to edit the expletives and just about everything else I could have said out of my response and answered simply. "No."

"This isn't a request, Sergeant Harper."

"No," I repeated.

"The stuff he wrote about you is significant. It's some kind of connection and we need to find out what that is." Ramsey's words become more heated. I didn't care.

"And I'd be happy to talk about that with you. In the morning."

I could almost picture the apple-red color of his face as his voice rose in volume. "General Roderick ordered everyone to cooperate. Right now, you're being uncooperative."

"General Roderick also released me for the evening. If I recall, he specifically told me to go celebrate and that's what I'm doing."

"You are impeding this investigation."

"If I'm an impediment to your investigation then you have far more problems than I'm sure you're willing to admit." He started to sputter a response but I was losing patience. "I was on an exercise with your suspect for the better part of a month over ten years ago. That's it. Aside from what I've just told you, I don't know anything else of value about the guy."

"What is or isn't of value is up to me to decide."

"And you can do that in the morning. In the meantime, why don't you just ask him why he's been writing about me?"

Ramsey paused. His next words were mumbled. "We did. He's not talking."

"And neither am I."

He responded with a bunch of talk about my obligations and following orders. I took a final bite of the strudel, smiling at Harry. He raised an eyebrow at me. Staring at him, I knew there was nothing Ramsey could say that would make me leave. I smiled. "I will be in at zero nine hundred tomorrow and not one minute before. Any questions you might have about my brief exposure to your suspect will just have to wait until the morning."

"General Roderick will hear about this."

"Go ahead and tell him. In fact, in the morning, I'll tell him myself."

"Master Sergeant Harper..."

"Good night, chief."

As I disconnected the call, I could hear him demanding that I obey orders, words I cut off as I closed the phone, powered it off, and dropped it back into my clutch. I glanced up to see Harry grinning at me.

"What are you smiling about? I just disobeyed a direct order."

He picked up my hand and brought it to his lips. "If you hadn't said no, do you really think I ever would have let you leave?"

CHAPTER 9

WE STROLLED DOWN THE hall, my arm threaded through Harry's. I felt content, warm, like I would purr if it were possible. I worried a bit about the consequences of disobeying Ramsey's order to report back to base, but I wasn't going to let it ruin my evening. It had been too perfect so far.

When we got to my door, I fished the key out of my bag and Harry gently plucked it from my fingers. He unlocked the door, let it swing open then with a hand to my back, pushed me inside.

For a moment, I thought he planned to deposit me there and go to his own room. I opened my mouth to protest, but he followed me in, closed and locked the door behind him.

After an exhale of relief, I went to the table, dropped my bag there and hung my sweater on the back of a chair. When I turned around, he still stood at the door watching me. He ran a hand through his hair and chuckled. "I've never been so bleedin' nervous in my life."

"Yeah, me too."

"It's just that I've been waiting for this for so long. Sitting down to a meal, having all the time we need for a chat. Just the chance to see you..." he let his gaze wander up and down, drinking me in. "To see you like this."

I took a step toward him. He stayed rooted in place.

"Just you," he said. "Without the uniform and the muddy boots and your hair all tucked up and orderly."

"I hope you think it was worth the wait."

He smiled. "Oh love. If I'd known you'd be this gorgeous, I'd never have had the nerve to chat you up in the first place."

"Harry, I haven't been … well, there hasn't been anyone since Bosnia, and …"

"I know, Lauren. We don't have to do anything you aren't ready for. No pressure."

I'd already decided that I wasn't going to allow the animals who'd attacked me in Bosnia to ruin my happiness. I'd spent hours wondering what it would be like to make love to someone for the first time after what I'd been through. While I was nervous, just looking at Harry, the way he looked at me and the desire it conjured inside me, made me think I was ready for this.

And I trusted him. Trusted that he would take me through any issues, any fears I might have.

I reached out to touch him, my palm to his chest, then ran my hand up and over his shoulder. I'd always marveled at the size of him. Any adversary would be afraid when they saw Harry, and for good reason. He looked lethal. Like a war fighter. Someone willing to do whatever might be necessary, which made it all the more intense to see the emotional warmth in his gaze.

"You've been too far away from me all evening," he said, his voice quiet as he wrapped his arm around my waist and dragged me to him. I lay my hand against his cheek. He smiled, grabbed a handful of my hair, gently pulled my head back, and bent to kiss me, but stopped. "Is this okay?" he asked.

"Yes, Harry. Yes."

He slanted his lips over mine and kissed me, tentatively at first. It felt as if we both held our breath, as if we feared what might happen, the emotions too intense. I peeked at him through half-closed eyes. He looked back at me, then parted my lips with his tongue and began a slow but thorough exploration of my mouth. My breath came in jagged huffs, my head spun with the scent of him and the force of his stare. I finally had to close my eyes and just give into him. His moan sounded like a deep growl as we allowed ourselves to melt into the kiss.

Eventually, he pulled away and stared down at me, his eyes glassy and intense.

"Bloody hell."

I smiled up at him, enjoying his distress, the way he trembled under my touch. "Do you remember Honduras?" I ask him, as I slipped the shoulder of my dress down to reveal my lacy bra, white this time. I'd done the same thing in Honduras while we lay on the jungle floor. There, we couldn't relax, couldn't fully give ourselves over to the physical yearning we felt. We'd been in uniform, filthy and tired and under the extreme pressure of all that had gone on there.

Here, now, we could take our time.

His breath caught for a moment as his gaze roamed over me like a caress. He met my eyes as if to ask permission.

"Please, Harry."

His brow furrowed as he hooked his finger into the lace of my bra and pulled down, exposing my breast. He cupped me in his hand, ran his thumb over my hardening nipple and bent down to trace it with his tongue. When he gently clamped his lips down, I let my head fall back, gasping, pressing myself further into him. His responding moan vibrated across my skin.

When he returned his attention to my lips, I barely noticed his insistent pull on the zipper of my dress. He pushed the straps off my shoulders until the outfit I'd so carefully selected sat in a yellow mound at my feet. He stopped kissing me long enough to reach both of his arms behind his head to pull off his shirt. In an instant he stood before me bare-chested. What I saw there made me gasp and take a couple of steps away from him.

He stood slumped against the door, his arms hanging loosely at his sides.

"Sorry," he mumbled. "I should have...sorry."

After a moment of gaping at him, I righted my bra. Harry avoided looking me in the eye as I stared at him.

In all of my imaginings of seeing Harry this way, I'd never thought that his flesh would be so marred. His scars left me shocked, speechless. There were just so many of them. I took a tentative step forward and traced my fingers over two, deep, star-like indents in his chest, just below the rise of his shoulder.

"These are gunshot wounds," I said.

"Wasn't bad though. Only hit the fleshy bits."

"Harry, you were shot in the chest. Twice." I stared at him, incredulous.

He gently rubbed my bicep where a bullet had gone straight through. The scar was new. I hadn't grown accustomed to it yet. "You've got one too, love," he said.

"Yes, but one. Just…just look at you." He still wouldn't meet my gaze while my fingers skipped over several small ridges and patches of skin that simply looked damaged, to trace a long slash that went from below his arm, down and across the ridges of his stomach. The scar was at least two inches wide. The marks where the stitches had held his skin together were still visible. "What the hell did this?"

"A very dirty machete." He shifted from foot to foot. "It just looks bad, really. It was mostly a flesh wound but it became infected and it just…well, it wouldn't have been as bad in a proper hospital."

A machete. That meant he'd earned it hand to hand, in a deadly fight with someone. Someone who'd looked him in the eye and tried to kill him. Since Harry was standing here, I could only assume the someone who'd wielded that machete was dead.

He met my gaze for a moment, then looked away again, his face reddening. I traced another dark, wide scar, one of several that formed large, welted hash marks down his arm. All of them appeared equally painful. "Are these burns?"

"A hot iron. They were meant as a … a bit of a motivator."

"To talk you mean?"

He didn't respond, which left too much to my imagination. He'd been held against his will. Interrogated. "Jesus, Harry."

Some of the scars were minor; short ridges, bumps, darkened patches, but there was very little of his flesh that didn't have some kind of mark on it. I put my hand to the side of his face so that he would look at me. "Are there more?"

He looked down again, then took a deep breath and turned around. I almost gasped, but didn't. He watched me over his shoulder.

"It wasn't as bad as it looks."

"Wasn't as bad? Harry, this looks like you were dragged. It's like your skin was scraped off."

From just below one shoulder blade and down his entire side, a dark patch of scar tissue half a foot wide, looked deeply welted and hard. I traced my fingers along the welt. He laughed.

"Harry!"

"Well, it tickles."

"Oh, you're impossible," I said, walking away from him. I wrapped my arms around myself and turned back to stare at him. Almost every injury could have killed him. His body read like a road map to the dangerous life he'd led. He'd escaped death more than once, had obviously escaped capture at least once and many tight scrapes in between. I'd seen him in action with my own eyes, guns drawn, bullets flying. What I'd seen left little doubt that he was skilled and professional.

I squeezed myself tighter, one hand to my face. I'd known all along he was a special operations soldier, had known that he did dangerous things. I liked his lethal look—that swagger he had that said nothing could touch him. Well, plenty had touched him and done significant damage. My Harry was indeed skilled and professional but also, mortal.

Now, every time I was away from him, I'd worry that he might not come back.

He bent to pick up his shirt. 'I'll put it back on..."

"Don't you dare."

"But you think I'm hideous."

"Oh, Harry. Hideous is the absolute last thing I think you are and you know it."

"Do I?" He tossed his shirt onto the chair and stood with his hands on his hips. "If I'm not hideous, then what?"

When I couldn't answer, he walked toward me, kicking off his shoes one foot at a time, and kept making progress across the room to me.

"There are more," he said, unfastening his belt, a smile creeping onto his face. "Want to see?" He dropped his pants and kicked them to the side, stepping over them. He wore black, tight-fitting boxer briefs.

"Oh, mercy," I whispered.

He pointed to a long, thick scar that traced down from below his boxers to just above his knee. "A misstep as I went over a fence. Almost impaled myself."

He sat on the edge of the bed and pointed to a puncture wound in the top of his foot and showed me the matching scar at the bottom of his foot. "Jump accident. Didn't see the bloody thing sticking up from the ground in the pitch black. Could've been worse. Could've sat on it. Imagine explaining that."

"How can you joke about it?"

"Near death experiences are always funny later," he said. "Didn't you know?" He grinned and reached out his hand to me. "Come here. Come here to me, love."

I put my hand in his and let him drag me to him. He wrapped his arms around my waist, turned his face to the side and laid his head against my belly, snuggling in. I pressed him to me and gently ran my hand over his head, taking a deep breath and sighing with the perfection of the moment. I had to blink rapidly to keep a tear from escaping.

"I should have warned you. I am sorry."

"I've always known you had a dangerous profession."

"Yes, you have."

"There's a difference between knowing something, and really understanding it."

He looked up at me, then sighed and scooted back onto the bed, pulling me with him. He lay on his side and propped his head in his hand. I mirrored his position.

"It's not like you've had the most peaceful life, Lauren." He traced the scars on my wrists that I'd earned when I'd been hung from them for hours on end, the small scar on my thigh where a knife had embedded itself. Then traced the surgical scar at my hairline behind my ear, the scar I'd earned when they repaired the damage to my shattered cheek, a reminder of my Bosnian ordeal.

"Those are different. I didn't intentionally walk into dangerous situations."

"Oh, so stumbling into them by accident is better?"

He had a point. At least he'd been trained for the danger he faced. Still, the idea that he could put himself in harm's way so often made me shudder. Goose bumps erupted along my arms. He tsked and reached out to run a warm hand over them.

"It's like silk, your skin. How can it be so soft?"

He pulled me to him and held me, rubbing warmth back into my body. After a while, he pushed me back and leaned over me, stroking my face, his green eyes like pools of jade. Rich and expressive.

"We can compare our battle scars, love. The ones we can see anyway. What about the ones you can't see?"

"You mean Bosnia."

He kissed me on the forehead. "A woman goes through something like that, it's bound to leave scars much worse than anything on my flesh."

"At the time, the thought of anyone ever touching me again seemed impossible. But now that we're here, now that I'm with you, I'm not sure I've ever wanted anything more in my life."

He closed his eyes as if in relief. When he opened them again, they were shining. He ran his fingers down my cheek. "I'm going to kiss you now. Then I intended to make love to you. If at any time, you want me to stop ..."

"I don't want you to stop, Harry."

At first his kisses were tentative, taking his time, but soon they became possessive, demanding.

"Is this okay?" he asked, his breath hot against my neck.

"Yes, Harry. Please yes."

There was something natural, organic in the way we came together, no thought or hesitation in what came next. At some point we both slipped out of the rest of our clothing until we were finally, gloriously naked, the delicious friction of our skin touching, all of our skin, making us both gasp in delight. Despite his scars he was beautiful. His large, calloused hands were gentle but firm in their instruction as he captured me completely. I couldn't get enough of touching him, the reality of him, of us finally being together.

We'd left the light from the small bedside lamp on, but it was soft and yellow, giving what we did a dreamlike quality. He teased me to desperation then let me rest, sometimes coaxing laughter from me, as if he needed the pause to acknowledge the joy of what we'd waited for so long. Then, he'd start over from the beginning, controlling every movement, every sensation. I realized there was more I knew about Harry than I'd thought. I'd known he would be a passionate and attentive lover. I'd known he would take control and enjoy watching me as much as I enjoyed watching him and I'd known making love to him would be well worth waiting for. I'd been right on all counts. I marveled at the spectacle of him, at the grace of his touch and the easy pace he kept, a question in his gaze at each turn, checking to see that I was okay with all that we did. I was more than okay.

He rolled onto his back and smiled up at me above him, whispering words of reassurance, our gazes locked, joined so completely I felt enveloped in the pulsation of us. He guided me until I felt beyond restraint. Then he wrapped his arm around my waist, pulling me tight and allowed me to use him as I wished.

"Yes, love. Yes," He whispered, until he couldn't talk anymore and we were both left sated, exhausted and pleasantly stunned.

৯৩৵ড়৲

SOMETIME LATER, I UNCURLED myself from Harry to go to the bathroom, rolling off the small edge of the bed without disturbing him.

When I came back, he still lay peacefully. I crept closer to the bed and stared down at him, appreciating the view. He'd claimed the center, leaving me with little room, but I hadn't cared. He lay with one arm up and bent over his head, his face turned and resting on his bicep. His other hand was pressed against his chest as if he were swearing an oath of allegiance. I felt overwhelmed at the sight of him.

"You going to stand there all night gawking?" he asked in a sleepy mumble, his eyes still closed.

I smiled and crawled in next to him, resting my head on his chest. "Just appreciating the scenery."

He wrapped his arm around me and pulled me closer, my body coiling around his, our legs and feet entangling as if our limbs had been fabricated with curves and grooves designed to slot together perfectly into one warm and living entity.

"You'd better get some sleep," he said. "You have to be up in a few hours."

"I don't want to sleep. It feels like a waste of time when you're finally here."

He stretched, long and slow until his entire body was taut and vibrating. He relaxed with a heavy sigh and leaned over me with a crooked smile. "You wanna have another go then?"

CHAPTER 10

W E WENT DOWN TO breakfast as soon as it opened at six. We were starving. I tried to be in a bad mood over the meal, but Harry wouldn't allow it. I didn't want to go back to base, didn't want to deal with the media, or McCallen or any of it.

Our original plans for leave had been to return to Heidelberg, show Harry around my home, introduce him to some of my friends, tour the city and the like. After that, we were to fly to Athens for a couple of days followed by some island hopping. We planned to ride the Greek ferries from island to island as the mood suited us.

Harry tried to stay positive. "As long as we can keep our flight plans, the delay won't ruin our trip. Chin up. It won't be so bad, pet."

"That gives us three days before our flight leaves. What if they don't let me go in three days?"

"We'll deal with that when and if it happens."

"You'll go on the jump today, but what are you going to do with yourself after that?"

"Well, I'll extend our reservations here," he said, picking up a large roll. He tore it in half, slathered it in butter, stuck a piece of ham and a slice of cheese on it and took a massive bite, chewing noisily.

"And aside from that?"

Around his food he mumbled an answer I couldn't understand. I narrowed my eyes at him and waited. He was trying to avoid telling me because he didn't think I'd like it, whatever it was. When he tried to take another bite, I grabbed his hand.

"Answer me, Harry. What do you plan to do while I go off to work?"

"I said I'm going to hang about with you."

"Wha..? Oh, no you're not," I said, vigorously shaking my head. McCallen would be impossible with Harry around. But Harry just popped more food into his mouth and shrugged as if it were all decided.

"You're going to ignore my wishes, aren't you?" I said.

"See? You already know me so well."

"Harold Fogg…"

"Firstly," he said, while spreading orange jam on another roll, "I figure, the more I hang about, the more I'd be throwin' a spanner in the works and the more people will realize that you aren't supposed to be there in the first place. I'd like to be a reminder of the holiday you are supposed to be on with me."

"But, Harry…

"Secondly," he said interrupting me. "Twice in the past, when someone has committed a violent act near you, somehow or other, you've managed to get yourself into something dodgy. I plan to be there to ensure you remain safe."

"Harry, the bad guy is already in jail. Besides, it doesn't have anything to do with me."

"Neither did that fellow in Honduras, and look what happened there." He stood and walked to the buffet table. He wore sweatpants and a loose t-shirt. The more I looked at him, the more I wanted to touch him.

"You would be too much of a distraction," I said, as he sat back down.

He smiled at me wickedly. "That's the whole point, darling. Besides, I'll go on the jump with Nick and the boys so you'll be on your own today. You can have your press conference and get the major work done. After that, I want you to myself and I want them to know it."

"You've got it all figured out, haven't you?"

"Absolutely."

We were the only ones in the morning room. It was still too early on a Saturday for most guests to be up. He gingerly put hot, soft-boiled eggs onto egg cups, blowing on his fingers. He sat one in front of me then began work on his own. Tapping the pointy end of the egg with the edge of his butter knife, he cracked it evenly around, then neatly sliced off the top and sprinkled a bit of salt on it. He picked up his spoon and took a scoop of the soft-boiled goodness.

"Perfection," he said. "Want me to open yours?"

"Yes, please." I said, with the intense desire to watch again how his large, scarred and calloused hands performed the delicate work.

"Besides, I heard what Ramsey said to you last night on the phone," Harry said, as he reached across the table. "Something about a stalker?"

"Oh, it's nonsense. If Newberg was such a stalker, how could it have been more than ten years since I met him? It's got to be just a coincidence."

"Or not," he said. "In any case, I intend to be by your side."

"But Harry ..."

"Hush, now," he said, depositing the perfectly opened egg before me. "I'm going to be by your side as much as possible. Full stop."

"Bossy, aren't we?" I took a bite of my egg and hummed with the delicate taste, then shook my head. "I'm not looking forward to seeing McCallen's face when he realizes you're going to be hanging around." I took a sip of coffee, knowing there would be some kind of confrontation between the two men.

"Why would he object?"

I shrugged, sipped my coffee again, trying to look casual. I didn't want to explain the crazy things McCallen had said to me. Hopefully, he would have recovered himself by the time I saw him next, and realized how foolish he'd been. Again, Harry proved that he wasn't easily distracted. He put his hand over mine, staring at me intently. "Why would he object, Lauren?"

"Ugh!" I groaned and rolled my eyes. "It's too embarrassing."

"Once more, why would he object?"

"It's nothing. He just... yesterday he was talking crazy." Harry kept staring at me but I couldn't meet his gaze. I blew out a rush of air and came clean. "He said, now that his wife has left him..."

"I KNEW it," Harry exclaimed, smacking the table. "I bloody well knew he fancied ya. He's been trying to chat you up from the start. The bloody wanker. Well that settles it then, doesn't it? I'm not letting you out of my bleedin' sight."

I couldn't stop the smile from revealing itself on my face.

"Think it's funny do ya?"

"As crazy as McCallen was acting yesterday, he was right about one thing."

"And what was that exactly?" he asked, still brooding.

I brushed his cheek with the back of my fingers. "He said that if I left with you, he'd never have a chance."

Harry let a slow smile spread across his face. "Well, that's brilliant isn't it?" He covered my hand with his and leaned toward me. "I hope you know ... I don't want to assume that you do, so I'm going to tell you. This isn't a one off. I'm all in. I know we're just starting to get to know each other and all, and we'll have a whole month together—I just wanted to say it straight. I fancy you, Lauren. Something fierce."

His declaration ignited an uncontrolled blaze in my chest. I glanced at my watch. "Do you think we have time ... "

He softened his gaze at me and flashed me a toothy grin. "Come on, love," he said. "No time to dawdle."

⁂

I DROPPED HARRY OFF near where the Rangers were billeted. Eldnik would meet him, get him suited up with the necessary equipment, after which they'd attended an hour-long safety briefing before boarding the plane for the jump.

"Have fun, Harry," I said, before he stepped out of the car.

He kissed my hand. "You be careful. If you need anything, you call me, understand?"

"Of course."

He moved to get out of the car, then stopped and turned back to me. "Have I told you, you look smashing today?"

He didn't wait for a response before he stepped out of the car and I watched as Eldnik greeted him with enthusiasm.

By the time I arrived, the rest of the team had been up and working for some time. They'd already stowed their cots, converting the sleeping area back to an office and were eating breakfast on the run, consuming handfuls of granola while balancing mugs of coffee and yogurt cups. Patrovski and Owens were busy rearranging the main room, lining up chairs in neat rows in preparation for the press conference. The lectern and flags we'd been using over the last three weeks had been splattered with blood when I'd left the night before. They'd simply removed the podium and put a standing microphone in its place. And while they'd managed to come up with clean U.S. and general officer flags, the Ninth Army guidon was one-of-a-kind. Someone had unsuccessfully attempted to clean it but removing the large, brown splatters that now covered most of the silk would be impossible. Many of the irreplaceable battle ribbons would remain forever marred with dried blood.

Jerreau stood behind a desk working the phones that rang steadily. They'd announced the press conference in a news release and on the website, but questions were still coming in. Most of them requests to come to the scene and shoot video for b-roll. To avoid having to accommodate so many requests, Owens had put together a reel of generic video shots around post, of General Blunt with soldiers in the field, a variety of images broadcasters could use in their reporting. He'd uploaded it all along with some still images to our official website available for download. Still, the phones kept ringing.

Patrovski took over phone duties so Jerreau and I could review the press kits the team had put together. The initial press release, biographies, contact information, were all ready and waiting. "You guys have done a great job. I'm not sure why I'm here," I said.

"Frankly, Sergeant Harper, neither do I," Jerreau said, leaning in to whisper his doubts about decisions senior officers had made. "There's no reason...well. Hopefully, once this initial press conference is over, they'll let you go, don't you think?"

There was always hope.

"Where's your boyfriend?" were the first words out of McCallen's mouth. He'd stepped out of the men's restroom near the front door, a towel around his neck and his hair still damp from a shower. A small bit of toilet paper covered a bloody shaving nick on his neck.

"Good morning, sir."

"Did you send him back to England?"

I shook my head in disbelief. "He's traveled all the way here and we're going to make the best of things. Right now, he's going on a jump with the Rangers. After that, he'll probably come here, sir."

"He'll be a distraction."

Jerreau guffawed rudely. McCallen shot him an angry look while I tried not to smile. I wasn't very successful in hiding my amusement. "I'm well aware of how distracting he can be," I said, my loaded meaning not lost on the colonel.

McCallen opened his mouth to object further, but I changed the subject. "Looks like we'll have a full house."

"The attempt to kill an American general has been at the top of every major newscast. The president called Mrs. Blunt last night and General Roderick. Then the SecDef and the President spoke from the Rose Garden this morning about it. That pretty much guarantees we will be mobbed."

I exchanged looks with Jerreau. "We'll be ready, sir," I said.

McCallen leafed through the media packet, but I could tell he wasn't really looking at it. He seemed fidgety. Finally, he said what was on his mind. "Captain, give us a moment."

"Of course, sir," Jerreau said.

McCallen watched him walk away then checked over his shoulders to see if anyone else was close.

"Did you give any thought to what I said to you yesterday?" He hadn't slept well. That was evident in the folds of fatigue under his eyes and the sea of red in them. It made him look vulnerable, in need of comforting.

"Do you mean the stuff you said to me when you were still in shock, sir?"

He stared at me for a long moment, as if to be sure he'd heard me correctly. "Lauren, …" he began.

"Sir, you know better than anyone that your wife wasn't our only obstacle." He began to say something more, but I simply couldn't listen to it. "Harry is very important to me, sir, and grows more important by the day. That is not going to change. He's a good man. At this point, I wouldn't do anything to jeopardize whatever future I might have with him."

He digested my words silently. The moment stretched on while he stared at me, glimpses of competing emotions flashing in his eyes. Finally, he took a deep breath, straightened and pulled the towel down from his neck and used it to wipe his hands. "If anyone needs me, I'll be working on my opening statement," he said, his back ramrod straight as he strode purposefully toward his office.

I'd hurt him. The knowledge made my chest feel hollow. After all the years of our silent flirting, all the time we'd played this game of pretending we didn't have a secret desire for each other, I wondered why it was so easy for me to say no to him. Had it been his unavailability that made him so attractive to me in the first place? I suspected part of the new feelings linked back to Bosnia. Our attraction had led to deep trouble for me, and when I needed him most, he'd abandoned me. It was that abandonment that I couldn't let go of or easily forget. And while his marriage might be rocky at the moment, he was still my commanding officer. Army regulations still precluded any possibility of a relationship between us.

I thought about Harry and felt my face flush at the memory of the night before. He'd been a glorious lover. I knew, at some point, time with Harry would be enough to erase the years I'd spent pining over McCallen.

"What are you grinning about?" Ramsey asked, a salacious note in his voice.

"Nothing I care to share with you," I said, feeling defensive. I'd been so preoccupied with thinking about relationship drama I hadn't heard him come in.

"I bet I can guess."

"Don't bother," I said, hoping to change the subject. "I still don't understand what was so urgent last night. I know you want my statement but I can't give it to you until after this press conference."

As if to demonstrate how busy I was, I started putting the press kits together. Fact sheets, the press release, Blunt's bio and other bits and pieces had to be collated and shoved into pocket folders. In minutes, reporters would start arriving. I didn't have time for Ramsey and his questions.

"Harper, you don't seem to understand the seriousness of this investigation. We have to move with as much haste as possible."

"So much haste, that you can't even stop to change clothes?"

He looked as if he'd slept in his suit. He needed a shave and his eyes were red-rimmed. "This is how one looks after you've been in an interrogation room all night, Harper."

"You say that as if I'm not already familiar with such things," I said, unable to keep the resentment from my voice. "As much as you may want to, you won't be able to interrogate me until after the press leave."

"That's fine. Before I take your statement, I want you to have a little chat with Newberg, see if you can get him to talk."

I stopped and stared at him. "You want me to talk to him? Why?"

"He's refusing to talk to me until he is allowed to see the visitors he wants. He's asked to see a couple of people from his unit but I don't want to grant him that. I figured he knows you. He obviously has some kind of interest in you. Maybe you can get him to open up."

"You must be desperate. I barely remember the guy."

Ramsey scrubbed his face with his hands, then ran his fingers through his hair and ended with an elaborate shrug. "You're right. I am a bit desperate. I've questioned him most of the night. He sits there, not saying anything. Now, given that I've reached the end of my persuasive abilities with the suspect, I thought I would try them, as inadequate as they seem to be, on you."

"Chief, I want to help, but I'm not comfortable with the idea of talking to him." I returned to working on the press kits, my hands flying fast through the repetitive motions until it became almost soothing, mindless work. "Besides, like I said. I barely know him. I don't see how I can help."

"I'm not asking for a favor. I have the authority to officially request your assistance, which I have done." He'd delivered the message in a cold voice, one that froze me.

"What does that mean?" I asked.

"It means, if I want to, I can officially make you a part of this investigation."

I sputtered in shock. "But you're not going to, right? You're not going to make this official. Right?" My heart thudded in panic. Taking care of the media aspect could take days. Getting sucked into the investigation could take much longer. I didn't want any part of it, not when my vacation with Harry was on the line.

"If you come and talk to him, I'll leave you out of it."

"I want your assurances that you won't change your mind."

He crossed his arms, his lips pressed together. "What, you don't trust me?"

I guffawed my disbelief. "Really, Chief. In what universe would I have a reason to trust you?"

He narrowed his eyes at me and shook his head. "You have my assurance, Sergeant Harper. Just come speak to him after this press conference thing."

"Okay. I can do that. Just don't make this official or anything. Who else has he asked to see? Has he seen a lawyer?"

"He doesn't seem to think he needs a lawyer as crazy as that may sound. He has asked to see Major Beechwood and some command sergeant major in his unit." He took out a notebook and flipped through the pages. "Eldnik. He closed the notebook and shoved it in a cargo pocket. "Newberg doesn't know it yet, but I'm only going to allow him one visitor and that's you."

"Lucky me," I said

"You already promised you'd talk to me today. I have a feeling a conversation between you two could be fruitful. Sitting down with Newberg shouldn't be any big deal."

"I wish you hadn't said that." Saying something wasn't going to be a big deal, usually meant it would. "Do you have a clean suit? You're going to be on television you know."

"Just be happy I'm here. I hate these things."

I turned away from him thinking that if his presence was the only thing I had to be happy about, I'd be having a miserable time of it.

CHAPTER 11

THE STREAM OF MEDIA had been steady for ten minutes. We would have standing room only.

"McCallen was looking for you," Jerreau said. "And we're already out of press kits."

"We're not gonna kill any more trees. Just tell anyone else who arrives that everything's posted on our website."

I glanced to the front of the room where Owens stood in the middle of an altercation between photographers. There were too many video cameras and still photographers, all attempting to elbow their way to the best vantage point for their shot. I knew he'd be able to sort it out.

I rapped on McCallen's door and stepped in.

Ramsey stood with him, the two men talking over the order of things. They both looked wired with nervous energy. Ramsey had shaved, but his suit still looked ridiculously wrinkled.

"You have a full house, gentlemen."

Ramsey's face flushed red. "God, I hate these things," he said. "I'd better hit the john once more." He ducked out the door leaving me alone with McCallen.

"You wanted to see me, sir?"

He looked up from the paper he'd been studying. I knew he liked to memorize his talking points and statements so he wouldn't have to refer to his notes during a media event. He claimed he didn't have a photographic memory, but he always seemed to be able to conjure the exact words necessary only moments after reading them. "Jerreau tell you that?"

"Yes, sir."

He stepped over to the mirror and fidgeted with his uniform. "It wasn't anything specific. I just wondered where you were." He looked at me over his shoulder. "I've never done a press conference without you." He turned back to the mirror. "It'd be too weird not to have you around."

"Oh." The awkward moment stretched on for several beats. He tugged on his collar, attempting to get it to lie flat, but it wasn't cooperating.

"Can I help you with that?" I asked.

In answer, he turned to me, dropping his hands. I walked behind him, reached up and fixed the lay of his collar, pulling and tugging, then walked around in front of him. He smelled good, like something citrusy. In times past, getting this close to him would have made my heart race. This time, the feather light feel of his breath on my cheek made me take a step back. I picked a piece of lint off one sleeve then found a long blond hair over one shoulder. "Hmm," I said. "Wonder where that came from."

He chuckled.

"I see you were able to make it to the barber. The haircut looks good."

He met my gaze and the awkwardness returned full force. I could feel my face heating up.

"We're a good team," he said.

"Yes, sir. We are. And there's no reason we can't continue to be. Now, can we go do this thing?"

"I don't know. Has Ramsey stopped pissing himself yet?"

We chuckled but the momentary easiness lasted only seconds before I had to step back from him. Thankfully, Ramsey returned even more flustered then he'd been when he left. "I got water on my tie. Damn it."

McCallen and I exchanged smiles. "Let's do this," he said.

"Okay then." I stepped out the door and raised my voice. "Ladies and gentlemen please take your seats."

☙◗◖❧

THE TEAM LOOKED EXHAUSTED. Jerreau, after having asked nicely a number of times, finally lost his temper and threatened to call the MPs if the last reporters continued their refusal to leave. Patrovski and Owens, when faced with the roomful of chairs that needed to be put away, argued it would be better to leave them up in case we needed to have another press conference. I agreed and smiled when they both exchanged looks of relief and began moving around the room straightening chairs and cleaning up, their movements slow, as if they could barely endure the heaviness of their feet.

Considering the circumstances, the press conference had gone almost exactly as anticipated. McCallen had given them a rundown of the current situation including the fact that General Blunt was in an induced coma with an unknown prognosis. The questions that followed were about Newberg, his motives, his mental state and questions about our security measures. Why did it happen and how could we stop if from ever happening again. And finally, who was running things now that the senior commander in Europe is out of the picture. The mood hadn't been hostile, just intense. I felt relieved it was over.

McCallen had performed like the consummate professional, barely consulting his notes, striking the right amount of authority and sympathy. He oozed a warm and friendly confidence that made you want to trust every word that came out of his mouth. The scar that slashed across his face seemed to disappear when he stood in front of the press, and his blue eyes drew you in until they captured all of your attention. The squared shoulders, broad chest and loose delivery reminded me why I'd slowly but surely fallen in love with him.

As soon as it ended, Ramsey had left and McCallen had disappeared into his office. I didn't blame him. He'd stood in front of the firing squad for more than an hour answering question after question with Ramsey chiming in now and then with what little information he was willing to provide, which wasn't much. All that time at the microphone saps your energy. McCallen would need the peace of his office after that long ordeal.

Despite our exhaustion, the phones kept ringing and we knew none of the reporters would go very far. We would have to feed them hourly updates, give them bits and pieces of information even if minor, just to keep them happy.

I knew Ramsey expected me to go talk to Newberg but I'd spent some time answering a few calls, taking notes and realizing the demands wouldn't stop anytime soon. I'd finally taken the phone off the hook, promising myself it would only be for a few minutes and then I'd get up and go see Newberg. I reclined into my chair, resting my head on the back, closed my eyes and immediately thought about Harry, wondering what he was up to.

In the distance, a wail of sirens started up, but I shut out the ever-increasing noise and reveled in not moving. The relaxation didn't last long before my cell phone vibrated in my pocket.

I sleepily reached for it. "Harper, here."

"It's Santos," he said, his voice loud and jumpy like he was getting tossed around inside a vehicle. The sound of the sirens I'd heard earlier now came loudly through the phone as he tried to speak over the undulating noise. He said something else that came through jumbled. I sat up, put a finger in my other ear, intensely trying to decipher what he'd said.

"I can't hear you. Say again."

His words faded in and out over static. "... accident ... drop zone," he repeated. "...dead...injuries..."

I stood so fast I knocked my chair over but barely heard the sound of it dropping. A wash of icy realization hit me. I ran outside and across the parking lot to look down the hill and watched the progress of a large plume of road dust moving deeper into the box. *Harry. What if it's Harry?*

CHAPTER 12

THE CALL HAD DISCONNECTED. My fingers shook as I punched in numbers, trying to call Santos back. He picked up but I still couldn't hear him. "Chief Santos, do you know who is involved? Who's been injured? Chief?" I clutched the phone then stared at it, wishing it back to life.

The mental worry gymnastics began immediately. It could have been any number of units making a jump today. It didn't necessarily have to be the Rangers. But if it wasn't Harry's group, if it wasn't the Rangers, why would Santos call me?

I hit the speeddial for Harry, but the call went directly to voicemail. That didn't surprise me. He would have turned the phone off while in the plane and probably hadn't turned it back on yet. As least, that's what I told myself as I jogged back to the building and found my whole team standing in the doorway, their faces tight with worry.

"An accident at a drop zone," I said, as I pushed my way past them.

"Is it Sergeant Major Fogg?" Patrovski asked.

"I don't know." What if it was Harry? But I didn't want to allow that idea to take hold. It couldn't be him. It simply couldn't. I'd only just found him. I'd only just realized how much he meant to me, how much I wanted him in my life. It couldn't be Harry. It simply couldn't. There'd have to be something totally jacked up about life and karma and rotten luck for it to be Harry.

"Holy, fucking, bloody hell, please don't let it be, Harry." I said it in a rush of words as I picked up a phone, not knowing who to call. Harry had probably done hundreds of jumps. He could do anything, handle anything. He was a professional soldier. The best of the best.

But he wasn't immune to injury. I'd seen the evidence of his past in the violent designs on his body. Evidence that starkly displayed the reality that bad things happen all the time, sometimes on purpose. Sometimes by accident—unexpected, unplanned, horrible, terrible, accidents.

I took a few deep breaths, in and out, forcing my breathing to return to normal, unclenching my brain from the almost crazed place I'd been headed. My knuckles were white and my hand unsteady as I clutched the phone handset, but I had no idea who to call.

"The EOC," Jerreau said. "They'd know."

"Right!" I said. The sergeant in charge of the emergency operations center answered on the first ring. I used the excuse of possible media interest to get the information I needed. Patrovski, Owens and Jerreau formed a concerned ring around me. McCallen joined them.

"One of the Ranger platoons," the sergeant said. "Preliminary reports are that one is dead and at least two others injured."

My next words came out shaky and weak. "The Rangers," I said, to let everyone in the room know what I'd learned. "Any names yet?"

"Should have the names soon. The EMTs are on the radio now. You want to hold or..."

"I'll hold," I blurted as I paced, the length of the telephone cord restricting my movements. I ignored the others and knew how crazy I looked. The sergeant hadn't put me on hold, only laid the phone down while he waited for the additional information. The squawk of the radio and the sound of several people talking were distant noises to the clatter of my own rapid and shaky breathing coming back to me through the handset. I needed to calm down, but every second of waiting only increased the horrible mental pictures already ricocheting around inside my skull. Harry's broken and lifeless body on the ground. Harry's face disappearing behind the zipper of a body bag. I shuddered at the vividness of the images, as if imagining it would make it true.

Jerreau stood, rubbing his charm. "It's not him, Sergeant Harper. I know dis."

I gave him a weak smile. "I hope you're right, sir."

When the sergeant picked up the phone on his end again, I held my breath.

"You ready to copy," he asked? He sounded so calm, as if the people he was about to name meant nothing to him. They were just names after all. They weren't people he knew, not people he'd just held and kissed, or with whom he'd imagined the possibility of a future.

My hand shook as I clutched the pen. "Ready to copy," I said.

"Injured are Sergeant First Class Stephens, Nicholas R. and Staff Sergeant Havlik, Brent T."

I asked him to spell the names and he did using the military alphabet.

"Stephens—sierra, tango, echo, pappa..."

I dutifully wrote them out, and I repeated them, trying to be professional, trying to do my job, but my voice sounded foreign to my ears and the tremble in my hands made it difficult to scratch out the letters in a coherent fashion on the pad that seemed to blur before me.

He hadn't said, Fogg, Harold...and I realized I didn't know Harry's middle name or even if he had a middle name.

The sergeant kept talking. I shook my head to try to focus.

"I'm sorry, can you repeat that last part?"

"Both have severe compound fractures, head, neck and back injuries. Both in serious but stable condition according to the EMTs."

"Okay," I said. I cleared my throat and tried to steady my voice but it was no use. "And the deceased?"

"Ah, hold one."

I wanted to curse at him. How much longer would I have to wait?

"The deceased is Captain Garron, Sylvester..."

I had to grab the edge of the desk, my knees suddenly weak. "I'm sorry, can you hold for just a moment?" I said.

I didn't wait for him to respond before I hit the hold button. "Oh thank God," I said as I collapsed into a chair and bent over with my head between my knees. Jerreau put a comforting hand on my back. "You just relax, you. Let me take this."

He picked up the phone and took down the rest of the information. "Can you spell that name for me please?"

I sat bent over, wondering who the Captain left behind — parents, siblings, maybe a wife and kids. His family would have sent him off knowing he had a dangerous job. Knowing never makes the earth shattering news any easier to take. I knew exactly how his people would feel when they received the terrible news. Loss. Terrible, gut wrenching loss. There'd been too much of it in my life recently.

By the time Jerreau hung up the phone, I felt limp with relief. I relaxed into the chair, reclining back into the tilt, my hands over my face. My relief was so intense it almost reduced me to tears, but I refused to let it overwhelm me. I took a moment, behind my hands, to take a deep breath then opened my eyes to see the team, Patrovski, Owens and Jerreau all smiling and expressing their relief that Harry hadn't been involved. McCallen stood stony-faced, but also flushed a vivid red.

After a long pause, McCallen asked Patrovski to write a preliminary press release about the accident. He sent Owens out to pick up lunch for everyone, handing him some money and instructions for the purchase of several pizzas. He asked Captain Jerreau to go to the EOC to get as much information about the accident as possible.

Once everyone had been given a mission, he stood over me, gazing down, a look of concern on his face. "I'm glad he's okay, Sergeant Harper."

"Me too, sir. Thank you."

He stared at me for a long moment, then turned and walked out. On his way out he said, "I'm going to see General Roderick. You can reach me at headquarters."

I tried to call Harry several times but it kept going straight to voicemail. "Please call me, Harry. Please."

Exhausted from worry, I crossed my arms on my desk and put my head down on them, listening to Patrovski's nimble fingers typing away at her keyboard as I attempted to force the morbid mental images of Harry, broken and dead, out of my head. I called up the vision of him giving me a cocky grin before he'd hefted his ruck over one shoulder and walked away from me with his long stride and rolling gait. Watching him execute such simple movements conjured up embarrassingly aroused feelings. I smiled at the positive thoughts but my peace didn't last long.

"Oh my god. Are you sleeping?"

The question, dripping in disbelief and accusation, made me scrunch up my eyes and wish I could keep them closed. Brianna Blunt, General Blunt's daughter, was the last person I wanted to speak to.

"No," I said, having not moved at all. "I'm quite alert actually."

"Well, you look like you're asleep. Where is everybody?"

I sighed. She obviously wasn't going away. I sat up, and looked at her. While her voice had held her usual taunting and insulting tone, she looked a bit of a wreck. Her pale face and darting gaze broadcast her agitation as she nervously tucked hair behind her ear. She stood in the doorway, shifting from foot to foot as if she wanted to come in, but didn't know if she should. She carried a large hobo bag, slung across her shoulder and riding low on her hip. The pretty little peasant top she wore fit loosely everywhere, except for across her chest where her push up bra created the illusion of a great deal of cleavage. Her short, shorts displayed long and lean legs. If she'd been my eighteen-year-old daughter, I would have told her to go to her room and put more clothes on.

I glanced a Patrovski who met my gaze for a second before returning her attention to her computer, divorcing herself from the conversation. I sighed, knowing I wouldn't get any help from her.

Obligation forced me to speak. "Is there something I can do for you?"

She took a few tentative steps toward me. The closer she came, the more visible her tension. I sat up and gave her my full attention.

"What is it, Brianna? What's wrong?"

She looked behind herself nervously as she worked up the courage to speak. "I was getting a hamburger in the bar at the bowling alley…"

"I thought you'd be at the hospital."

"I was. All night. I came home to shower and change and I just wanted a little time to myself. Between my mom and Mrs. Roderick and…ugh." She shoved her hands in her hair as if she planned to pull it out. "Anyway, I just wanted to sit down and have a burger, you know?"

"No one could fault you for doing that," I said.

She smiled at me and seemed to relax a bit more now that she knew I wasn't judging her badly.

"So, there were some MPs in there." She stopped in front of the desk. Her fingers shook as she gazed about the room, working herself around to the subject. "Their radios…they jumped up and left, but I heard…"

"You heard the radio chatter about the accident at the drop zone."

She opened her mouth to speak, but then simply nodded her head, her chest, neck and face suddenly flushed.

"Do you know someone jumping today?"

"I mean, I know it's like, ridiculous to think it's someone I know, but…"

"No it's not," I said. "I know exactly how you feel."

"You do?" Her eyes, now huge, appeared ready to well over in tears.

I went to her, put a gentle hand at her back and guided her to a chair on the other side of my desk. "You have no idea, Brianna."

"Can you…I came here because I thought maybe you guys could find out?"

And then it was as if I'd uncorked a champagne bottle as her thoughts came gushing out. "It's just that I heard about an accident on the radio and then they just rushed out and I thought, oh my god, it could be him but then I thought, that's crazy, it couldn't be him and then I thought, but what if it was, and like, how would I find out and even if it was him no one would tell me and..."

"Brianna, wait," I said. "Who is it you're worried about?"

The question put the brakes on her words. She opened and closed her mouth a couple of times, then popped out of the chair and gazed around as if she were surprised to find herself there. "I...oh, never mind. I shouldn't have come here," she said, on her way to the door.

"I have the names of the men."

She stopped and turned around, a hopeful look on her face. A look that slowly turned hard and appeared more like the Brianna I'd encountered before.

"Then give them to me," she demanded.

I glanced at Patrovski who stared back at me, her mouth open. She returned her attention to her work. Why did I think it wouldn't hurt to have a witness to this scene? You simply never knew what Brianna was capable of.

"Who is it you're worried about?" I repeated my question, wondering why she didn't want me to know. Someone had her wound up in worry. I wanted to know who.

"Just give me the names."

"I can't do that. The names of accident victims are always close hold until the families can be notified. You know that."

"But that could be hours."

I leaned against the front of the desk and crossed my arms. I knew I was being cruel. I'd just been her, felt exactly like her, sick with worry. Going crazy wondering if the person I loved was one of the injured or killed, but she didn't want me to know who she cared about and that sparked my curiosity in a way that couldn't be ignored.

"I'll find out some other way." Despite her threat, she stayed frozen in place.

I turned and picked up the notepad where I had written the names and read them again to myself, then glanced up at her. She licked her lips as if I were holding something she wanted to eat and she was famished.

"What name do you hope is not on this list, Brianna?"

She hesitated for another moment before blurting it out. "Beechwood. Major Mathias Beechwood."

I looked at the list again, even though I knew the answer to her question. "No, Brianna. He's not one of them."

She put a hand to her chest, and threw her head back in a dramatic swoon, a rare smile lighting up her face. "Oh thank god! Oh my god I was so worried. Oh my god!" She laughed lightly, reaching a hand out to include me in her relief before she realized who she was talking to.

"How well do you know Major Beechwood?" I asked. I knew he was a friend of the family, but her concern seemed far stronger than the kind of casual concern an eighteen-year-old girl might have for a Major in the Army who was probably at least thirty, if not older. And Beechwood had been one of the men who'd accompanied Newberg to the press conference—a press conference in which her father had almost been killed. My curiosity meter pinged into the red and Brianna's obvious agitation only added to the sensation.

Her eyes snapped to where Patrovski sat. She licked her lips and lowered her voice. "He's just a friend, okay?"

I nodded, not believing her for a second. I lowered my voice to match hers, the conspiratorial whisper meant to draw her in without promising that I'd keep any secrets. "Must be a pretty good friend for you to have been so concerned about him."

The look on her face turned calculating, broadcasting, at least to me anyway, that she was about to ask me for another favor. She moved toward me, slow, as if she were afraid to startle me.

"I heard my Dad talking about you once. He said you had gone through some kind of terrible experience but that you were really brave. Like, stronger than most of the male soldiers he knew."

"Your Dad said that, huh?"

She nodded and smiled. For someone so young, she seemed to be very aware of her puppet master skills. She'd tossed me a compliment. Next would be a request for something. She stepped closer, put a sweet smile on her face, conjuring up some innocent looking eyes and a soft girlish voice as if we were suddenly friends.

"If I gave you another name, could you tell me if it's on the list?"

"Let me guess. Would it be…Captain Pratt?"

The look of shock on her face was priceless. She wanted to ask me how I knew but didn't. I wouldn't have told her anyway.

"Brianna, how do you know these men?"

"What? I just know them, okay? I know a lot of the men who serve with my Dad. They…they come to the house and stuff. It's not like it's against the law."

Maybe not against the law. She was 18, the age of consent, but if Brianna didn't know it, the men surely knew their association with her was inappropriate. "Does your father know you've been friends with them?" Your mother?"

"Oh, my mother is impossible. You must know that. She sticks her nose into everything I do. I can't wait until I graduate so I can be on my own." She paused while her gaze darted around the room and halted on one of our press kits. The folder happened to be opened to her father's biography. His official photo in his dress uniform, the American flag hanging behind him, stared back at her.

"God. Everything is so messed up now," her voice shook and she suddenly looked like a frightened little girl. "Mom's a wreck. And Daddy's like, well I'll just say it. He's like a vegetable, right? They put him in a coma and they don't know if he's ever going to wake up. And now we'll have to leave Germany and leave all of my friends and everything is just horrible."

Her face had grown redder as she recited the litany of all the ways her life had gone wrong, and once the tears started to spill there was no stopping them. I pulled a few pieces of Kleenex from the box on my desk and handed them to her. She'd gone from a shrewd manipulator to a confused and scared kid, just graduating high school, her whole life in front of her and yet her world crumbling beneath her feet.

I pulled her into a hug and was surprised when she didn't resist and gave into hiccupping sobs. She tucked her arms in and buried her face in my chest as I held her, shushed her, rocking back and forth. She reminded me of my kid sister, Loretta at that moment, a teenage girl facing grown up issues. When our mother had died and I'd become Loretta's guardian, she'd often come to me with one catastrophe or another. At eighteen, everything, every problem, every challenge seemed like life and death weighted in the balance.

Brianna displayed that same vulnerability, but I wasn't fooled. She was still the spoiled, manipulative kid I'd known for years, but her sorrow for her father was genuine.

She cried herself out after a while, so I loosened my hold and moved her gently to a chair. She blew her nose and sniffled. I gave her a bottle of water from my supply and sat down at my desk again, giving her time to collect herself.

"Thank you," she said. "I've never been very nice to you."

"It's okay. You've been through a lot."

She sniffled some more and I couldn't help myself. I had to find out what she knew, if anything.

"Brianna, please be honest with me. How do you know Pratt and Beechwood?"

The sudden blush that washed up her neck to her face felt like a warning light, cautioning that I might not want to know the answer to my question.

CHAPTER 13

"OH, WHY DO YOU care?" Brianna sounded weak and exhausted as she clenched the used up tissue in her fist, her face still flushed in embarrassment. "Guys my Dad knows come and go all the time. They were like my brothers. Some of them were my babysitters when I was a kid. They'd pick me up from school sometimes. I mean, there was always someone around." She shook her head, staring at the floor.

"Beechwood was your babysitter?"

"No, not him. Jeeze. Just... some of them."

Her voice faded as if she didn't want to go into detail. Her father had probably changed units a number of times in her young years. While the Blunts had spent most of that time at Fort Bragg, there still would have been constant change in her life with each new assignment, new schools, new friends, new homes and new men under her father's command. Even if she weren't moving, the people around her were in the Army's constant shuffle of soldiers from job to job and place to place.

"Brianna, do you know Major Newberg too?"

She looked at me for a moment before her gaze flicked away. In answer, she gave me a petulant shrug of her shoulder.

"Brianna?"

"What of it?" She said, hopping out of the chair. "It's not like I knew he was going to do what he did. Seriously."

I glanced behind me and saw that Patrovski still acted as if she were ignoring us, but I knew she was listening and I was glad for it. The more Brianna talked, the more interesting information flowed. Having a second set of ears never hurt.

"Brianna, please explain to me how you know Major Newberg? Did you guys hang out? And how do Beechwood and Pratt fit in? Was it just casual? What do all three of these men have in common with you?"

"God. You ask a lot of question." She stared at the wadded up tissue in her hand.

"I need a lot of answers."

She wouldn't look at me but she wasn't leaving either. I wasn't doing anything to make her stay. It felt as if she didn't understand her own desire to talk to me.

"I'm not a little kid you know."

"I know you're not," I said, not meaning a word of it and trying to hide my exasperation.

"Well, it's nothing bad if that's what you're thinking."

"At this point, I don't know what I'm thinking."

She stood and paced a bit, working herself into it, her fingers touching things—the stack of press kits, giving a squeeze to a stress ball I had on my desk. She picked up the mini-slinky I'd tossed in my office supplies at the last minute and smiled for a second as she let it run back and forth over her palms. She put it down as if ashamed that something so small had given her a moment of pleasure. "They were just...around, you know? Nothing special. They're like my brothers, most of them." She picked at her nails then looked up as if she'd just thought of something. "Like last year when Trent was getting ready to do the SLE course at the Point."

"SLE?"

"Some kind of summer training program they have for kids graduating high school who want to go to The Point...Senior Leader Experience or something. Anyway, I guess it was a big deal. Whatever. Dad tried to make me do the program this year but I said, no way. I applied for The Point because he made me, but I never intended to go there. I told him so many times that I'm just not into the Army stuff but he ... he wouldn't ever listen to me." She slowed down for the last bit, as if just realizing she wouldn't be having that conflict with her father anymore. She mumbled the rest under her breath. "I suppose I won't have to go now. Maybe Trent can go somewhere else now too." The vacant look in her eyes appeared more sad than hopeful.

"Trent didn't want to go to West Point?"

She shrugged. I wasn't sure what that meant. "If he didn't want to go," I asked, "why would he do the SLE course?"

Her gaze snapped back to me. "Like he had a choice. God." She tsked her disappointment that I'd ask such a stupid question, as if I'd never understand her world. Perhaps she wasn't that far off.

"Dad had gone to so much trouble. It's all he talked about for weeks. He practically forced the parents of all the other kids from the base to get involved, everyone who was applying the same year as Trent. Made this mega deal over it…stories in the base paper and stuff. God. Every weekend in the spring for like two months, Trent had to do all this Army stuff. It was insanity."

"And Pratt and Beechwood were involved in this training?"

"And Major Newberg, yeah. But I had no idea he was such a nut job. I mean, neither did Dad. He liked those guys. They used to come over a lot."

"Can you think of any reason why Major Newberg would have done what he did?"

"NO!" Her shout startled me. Patrovski cursed under her breath, the outburst probably startling her as well. "I mean, how could I know that? My mom keeps asking the same thing. Why, why, why? It's gonna drive me crazy. And Aunt Melody…" She suddenly stopped, then looked at me, her mouth open. "I've gotta go."

"Brianna, wait." But she was already leaving. She dug in her bag and came up with her cell phone, her thumbs quickly typing out a text message as she walked to the door.

"Brianna, just be honest with me. Do you have a crush on Beechwood?"

She threw an angry look over her shoulder at me. "As if," she said. She turned to walk out the door but stopped when her phone rang. She answered it, then froze, her face turning red. "What? Oh my god!"

I assumed it was something to do with the general. I went to her as she directed her wide, shock-filled eyes to me. "But he doesn't do drugs," she said. I realized she couldn't be talking about the general. "I'll be right there," she said. "Oh my f'ing GOD, can anything else go wrong?" she said, staring at her phone, shaking her head.

"Brianna, what happened?"

"It's my brother. Trent's been arrested." She delivered that news with a look of disbelief before running out of the door.

CHAPTER 14

PATROVSKI STOOD WITH HER mouth open in shock. "Did I just hear her say General Blunt's son has been arrested?"

"Can anything else happen to this family?" I picked up the phone on my desk and called Santos.

The investigator answered on the first ring. When he learned it was me, it sounded as if he cupped his hand around the phone, delivering the news with a strange echo and a very soft whisper.

"Are you calling about the arrest?" he asked.

"How did you know?"

"Trent Blunt's flight arrived on time at Frankfurt International." Santos spoke as if afraid he'd be caught delivering the juicy gossip. "The general's driver couldn't find him at the airport. He searched everywhere for him, finally discovering Trent had been arrested for possession."

It took a moment for the news to sink in. "Possession of what?" I finally asked, not hiding the shock in my voice.

"Heroin. Not a lot, but enough. He was taken into custody at passport control."

"Jesus," I said, taking a minute to digest the implications of the news. "Why are you whispering?"

He chuckled. "My partner is rather averse to giving out information unless absolutely necessary."

"I bet he is. Does Trent have a lawyer?"

"Yes, yes," he said in a normal voice, the muffled echo gone. "We will have that file to you as soon as we've completed our review. Yes. Yes of course."

I chuckled as he made up crap to say. "So Ramsey is standing next to you now?"

"Yes. Yes, thank you. I'll give you another update as soon as I can. "

He hung up. I turned to look at Patrovski. "Have you noticed how everything has suddenly gone completely bonkers?"

"Ah, yeah," she said.

"Why do I get the feeling this confluence of events is not a coincidence?"

స్ళ

I IMMEDIATELY CALLED COLONEL McCallen. He answered on the first ring. The news about Trent Blunt, the general's son, would only further complicate things.

"Does Mrs. Blunt know?" he asked. I could tell he was standing in the tactical operations center. The TOC was always loud and buzzing with activity.

"It was either her or Melody Spencer that called Brianna and told her. Either way, I figure she knows."

"Christ," he said, his voice strained. "Who travels overseas to be by his father's deathbed with a bag of heroin? Wait, does heroin even come in a bag?"

I chuckled. The comment wasn't that funny but I seized on his attempt at humor. Several uncomfortable seconds ticked by.

"You may as well get Patrovski working on another release about the arrest," he said, a strange detachment in his voice as if he was beyond caring about the series of bizarre events that had occurred in the last twenty-four hours. "The media probably already know about it so we've got to get some kind of statement out there."

"Yes, sir."

"And call the Pentagon. Army public affairs needs to know."

"Yes, sir."

"I'll inform General Roderick now. After that I'll be back in the office to settle last minute arrangements. We may as well schedule a second presser for tomorrow. We can confront the Trent situation then."

"Okay, sir."

"Jesus, Lauren," he said, his voice harsh. "Hold on, a minute."

I listened to the hubbub of the TOC diminish in the background then suddenly disappear as he moved behind closed doors. "Stop sir-ing me, damn it. It's like you use it as a shield or something. Just stop. Please." He'd lowered his voice to a harsh whisper but his anger came through five by five. "It doesn't matter how many times you say it, it won't change anything."

"Neil...,"

"Damn it; just listen to me for a minute. We still need to talk. There are things I have to tell you."

"But I..."

"You've got to give me five minutes. That's all I ask. You owe me that much."

The desperation in his words made my gut ache. This was Neil. The last person in the world I ever wanted to hurt, but there was nothing he could say, nothing he could do that would knock me off the course I'd set. I had every intention of giving a relationship with Harry a chance, but we'd been through too much to just turn my back on him.

"Alright, alright. Jeeze. I'll listen to what you have to say, but you have to hear what I say in response. You have to listen and hear it. Promise me."

"I just...I just need a couple of minutes," he said. "After that, I'll not say another word."

I agreed to listen to him, just to get him to shut up about it. I hung up the phone feeling angry that I'd been forced into a corner. My anger didn't last long. Almost as soon as I hung up, it rang again.

"Hello love."

"Oh, thank god," I said. "I've...I've been beside myself."

"I'm all aces, love. I'm alive and breathing and all my bits are in working order. They took all of our phones so no one could call home and muck things up. I wish I could have called sooner."

He tried to make light of it, but something in his delivery made me think the accident had had some kind of impact on him. One minute he'd been on a lark with an old buddy, strapping on a parachute and jumping out of a plane for the hell of it. The next minute, life seemed much more precious.

"Poor devils," he said. I could almost feel him shudder his revulsion at the thought of plummeting from the sky without breaks. "There will be hours of questions now," he said. "They're not wasting any time going after the gen, but I suspect I'll be here a while."

"I'm so sorry you have to go through this, Harry."

"Well, nothing to be done about it. Best just settle in for a long wait. I'm sorry for the blokes taken to casualty. Nasty breaks they had. Bloody awful."

"Let me know if there's anything I can do. Ramsey still wants me to try to talk to Newberg and there have been some other developments." I told him about Trent Blunt and the plans for a follow up press conference. "Between the accident, Trent and the assassination attempt, tomorrow's press conference is going to be a bit more complicated. Hopefully, we can still plan on a late dinner together tonight."

"That would be lovely, and a perfect thing for me to think upon as I sit here with nothing to do but play mindless games on my phone."

"Harry?"

"Yes, darling?"

I swallowed, feeling as if I wanted to babble all kinds of nonsense that would embarrass the both of us. "I'm so glad you're okay."

"I'm right as rain, Lauren. Don't you worry."

☙❧

OWENS CAME BACK WITH far more pizza than we could possibly eat. That was okay. Leftovers never went to waste when we were going full tilt. He sat down at his video editor, shoving pizza in his mouth, put his headphones on and got to work.

Jerreau returned with nasty details about the accident he'd learned from the EOC. He shared them with Patrovski for her press release then sat down and started writing some talking points.

I let them all know we'd be calling another press conference for the morning.

"That'll be a tough one," Jerreau said, his fingers working furiously on his charm. "It's gonna get hot up in here."

"Right. And guess who's going to run it?" I raised an eyebrow at him. Several beats passed before he sucked in a breath, his eyes wide. My respect for him rose exponentially when he simply nodded his head, accepting the challenge.

It would be his first, real-world press conference and we could all expect it to be a tough one. Too many things had gone from complicated to totally FUBR—F'd Up Beyond Recognition. An assassination attempt on the highest ranking American military officer in Germany, the son of that same officer arrested for drug possession, and a fatal training accident that left one dead and two in the hospital with possible career-ending injuries.

Any one of those things could have caused a major scandal. In my mind, all of them together pointed to something far more sinister.

Jerreau turned back to his computer. "In about twenty minutes, I'd like to brainstorm some of these talking points."

"Of course, sir."

"I'll need all the help I can get."

I smiled. "You'll do fine." I meant it.

I called the Pentagon and told them we'd scheduled a second press conference, warning them the news of the General's son would complicate things. "From what I understand, he is in German custody. I don't know any more details."

The on-call officer yawned and sounded as if I'd woken him up. He apologized for sounding so sleepy. "I'm awake now," he said. "Keep us posted."

Leaning back in my chair, I took a few minutes to think about things, rolling information around in my head. It took a while to muddle through everything that had happened. I wanted to talk to Harry and find out more about the jump accident. And Ramsey still wanted me to talk to Newberg. I'd resisted before, but now I wanted to talk to him. Something was up and he seemed to be in the center of things. I had a long list of questions I couldn't answer without help. The problem was, I wasn't sure if I should enlist the help I wanted, but the questions nagged. No one wanted me to get involved. Hell, I didn't want to get involved, but too many things had happened too quickly to ignore the possibility that they were all linked. And it all felt too close to home. The assassination attempt had happened in my office, the building where I slept, to the man I worked for. How could I ignore it all, sit back and let Ramsey—a man I had little faith in—take control without doing something to help?

I finally sighed, took up my pen and jotted down a list of names. I had no idea if the names I had would lead to anything but at least it was a start.

I tried to look casual as I stopped at Patrovski's desk. "How are you coming with your press release?"

"I'm almost done with a draft. Will you look at it before I show it to the colonel?"

"Of course." I said, wondering how I could ask her for the favor I wanted.

"Is something wrong, Sergeant Harper?"

I shook my head, trying miserably to look innocent but knew I was failing. "Hey, could I talk to you for a minute?"

"Sure," she said as she stood and followed me out of the office. Jerreau looked up and raised an eyebrow at me but I just smiled and kept walking. As soon as we were out the door, I grabbed Patrovski's arm and dragged her to the far side of the room to ensure Owens and Jerreau couldn't hear us. I turned to her and just blurted it out.

"I need you to do something for me. I'll be upfront and tell you that I could catch a bit of flack over it, so if anyone asks you, I want you to tell them Sergeant Harper told you to do it. Is that clear?"

She grinned. "Is this one of your Nancy Drew things?"

I rolled my eyes. McCallen had once accused me of being Nancy Drew-like. I'd taken it as an insult at the time. To be honest, I'd read a couple of the books when I was a kid but couldn't remember them well enough to know if the association should be insulting or not. If it was going to encourage Patrovski to help me, I decided I'd embrace the comparison. "Yes. It's a Nancy Drew thing. No one knows I'm asking you for this and you need to try to keep it that way."

Her eyes practically twinkled. "Okay. What do you want me to do?"

"Do you still have that special friend? The one who works in personnel?"

She blushed so red, I thought she'd explode. Patrovski kept her personal life very private. We didn't ask and she didn't tell, but it was an open secret that she and Major Nadine Swenson from the S-1 shop spent most of their off-time together.

"I'm sorry, Patrovski. I didn't mean to embarrass you."

"Does everyone know?"

"Pretty much and no one has a problem with it. It's not a big deal." It wasn't a big deal for our office, but it was a dangerous thing. If she made any enemies, if anyone wanted revenge, if some boss of hers wanted to be rid of her, they could use her homosexuality as an excuse to expose her, to boot her out of the military. Don't Ask, Don't Tell, or DADT, had ruined plenty of good military careers. Patrovski loved the Army and she loved her job. If I had anything to do with it, I'd never let her sexual preference get in the way of that.

"I need someone to look at this list of names." It was a short list I could count on one hand. There probably should have been a few more, but I had to start somewhere.

"I might have a couple more for you later, but I'd like to start with these. They're people I know are connected to both Newberg and Blunt because most of them are Rangers and most of them have served in the Regiment at one time or another. Most of them are also friends of the family. I need you to go beyond that. Are they friends outside of the unit? Do they belong to any of the same clubs? Did one of them date the other's sister? Are there any resentments, any jealousies. Anything like that. Tell her to start with Beechwood and go from there."

Her face slowly returned to its natural color as she read the list. "She's a big admirer of yours," Patrovski said. "All the shit you've been through. I'm sure she'll want to help."

I smiled. "It would be a huge favor, but you have to tell her what I told you. I'm not officially supposed to be asking these questions."

"Don't you think CID will look into this stuff?"

I pretended to give it some thought. The truth was, I'd never have asked Patrovski to look into the records if I had the slightest hope that Ramsey would venture one inch beyond the attempted murder of General Blunt. It wasn't that I thought the investigator was lazy. He just didn't like things to get messy. Subtleties were easier for him to explain away than to explore and sometimes subtleties were all you had.

"I think CID will want to do one thing. Charge Newberg for doing what a roomful of people saw him do. Beyond that, I don't think they'll care."

Patrovski screwed up her face. "What if you're wrong and it is that simple?"

"That would actually be the best case scenario. Newberg is a self-styled assassin and the case is closed. But I'm not so sure."

"One thing I've always admired about you. You have good instincts," she said.

"Thanks, but I get things wrong a lot more times than I'd like to admit." I still cringed every time I thought about how wrong I'd been about Delray, the soldier I'd lost in Bosnia, but I didn't have time to think about that now.   "Look, I have no idea what consequences there might be for looking into a pile of records that aren't your own. Promise me you'll tell Swenson to only go as far as she is comfortable."

She smiled. "We kind of live on the edge of trouble day-to-day, Nadine and me," she said. "Not much new there."

"What's it—how do you...?"

"Live with keeping most of my life a secret?"

I nodded. She didn't exactly sound bitter, but I could tell it was a question she'd wrestled with many times. She stared at her boots for a second, thought about her response before she answered.

"It's a bit like being a priest I guess. The Army is almost like a calling for me. I can't imagine doing anything else. If it means I have to lie about some things, be celibate, or at least appear that I am, most of the time I can handle that."

"And the rest of the time?"

She scanned the room behind me, looking at Jerreau and Owens. "The other times I worry about making enemies, stepping on someone's toes. The threat is always there, Sergeant Harper. Anyone could ruin my life."

I'd never heard anyone speak ill of my sergeant. She didn't have a lot of close friends, but she also didn't have any enemies as far as I could tell. She seemed to get along with just about everyone and never entered into heated discussions. In fact, as I thought about it, she usually backed down when confronted with conflict. Something I'm sure she learned as a self-preservation tool.

"Trust that we've got your six, Patrovski. You should know that your team is behind you."

She smiled then, and dug out her cell phone. "Wait till I tell Nadine about this conversation. She's gonna freak."

"Thank her for me and keep me posted on what you find out."

She walked past me toward the door, flipping her phone open. She wasn't wasting time and that was a good thing. My experience warned me that, as bad as things seemed now, they could always get worse.

CHAPTER 15

A S PATROVSKI WALKED OUT the front door of our building, McCallen walked in. He saw me, pulled off his cap and stood staring at me, that heated gaze burning a hole in my chest. I tried to pretend I hadn't noticed the desire that sparked from him.

"I'm glad you're back, sir. Let me give you a sitrep." I turned to lead him toward the team, not wanting to be alone with him. He had other ideas.

"We have time for that later. I'd like to see you in my office, please."

I opened my mouth to object then glanced at Jerreau who had heard everything. I flushed in embarrassment. Arguing with Neil wouldn't do any good. He was my boss and he'd made up his mind. The team didn't need to see us in disagreement and we didn't have time for arguments. Getting this little talk over with was the only solution.

"Okay, sir."

I followed him into his office. He tossed his hat on the desk then faced me.

"Close the door," he said.

The simple command set my heart racing. His attentions were too confusing. I didn't understand why he'd suddenly convinced himself that he wanted to be with me. I closed the door thinking maybe it was seeing me with Harry that had ignited the sudden attention. Or maybe it had been the assassination attempt. Standing so close to death may have altered his thinking in some way. Whatever it was, it had to stop.

"I'm just going to get right to the point," he said, inching closer.

"That's probably best."

I stood my ground even though my first instinct was to back away from him. He stopped and looked down at me, his voice softening. "I just wanted to tell you that in a few months, you won't have to call me colonel anymore, Lauren. No more sir-ing me either. I'm retiring."

"What are you talking about?"

"I've taken a job at the Pentagon. A civilian job."

The shock of his decision had me frozen in place. I had so many questions I didn't know where to begin. "Why would you do that? You love the Army. You're not ready to retire."

"Yes, I am," he said, his mouth quirked up into a crooked smile as he stepped closer. "I could stay longer, sure. But I know what I want and I want you."

I took a step back, my hand up to warn him away. "You've made a decision but it doesn't have anything to do with me, Neil. If it did, don't you think you should have asked me first? I would have told you no."

"But I did do it for you, Lauren. Don't you see?"

To say that I was dumbfounded wouldn't have come close to how I felt. "You can't give up your career, Neil. Not for me. That's … that's irrational."

"I love you, Lauren."

"Jesus, Neil," I said, throwing my hands up in frustration. "You don't mean that. You can't make a life changing decision based on that."

"Based on what? The fact that I've loved you for years." He took another step toward me.

"Neil, don't come any closer. I told you I'd listen, but you're not making sense."

He narrowed his eyes at me. "It makes perfect sense and you know it. I was married, had a family. I couldn't leave them, but that didn't change the fact that I loved you, that I still love you."

"Why are you making me listen to this? It won't change anything."

"I know you loved me too, Lauren. You loved me," he said, his voice husky. "I could tell by the way you looked at me. Those times when no one else was around, when you'd stare at me, when we'd see each other, really see each other. We never said it out loud, not in words, but you loved me, Lauren. I know you did. And that kiss. You can't tell me you don't think about that."

I had loved him. No, that wasn't honest. I still loved him, as misguided as the feelings were. He'd crept closer and gazed down at me. The yearning in his blue eyes took my breath away. The pulse in his neck beat rapidly and his breathing hitched.

"I'm a mess, Lauren, can't you see that? When I left Michelle and the kids in the states I felt nothing but relief. I know that sounds horrible, but it's the truth. Then I rushed to Honduras when you were in trouble and I wanted to tell you then how I felt but it never seemed the right time. And in truth, I didn't think you'd ever believe me, believe that this is how I really felt. I decided to show you, to prove it to you. So, I scheduled my retirement."

"Neil, you knew I was meeting, Harry. You knew what my plans were."

"Part of me thought it was just a fling. I mean, how much time have you spent with the guy? The equivalent of a few days? How could that replace all this time, all these years when we knew in our hearts we should be together? And now, now we *can* be. This isn't the right time either, I know that. But when will it be? You've got to…"

A loud knock on the door jolted us. I moved away from him, all the way to the wall, my arms crossed. He stiffened, took a deep breath and shuddered as he let it out. "What?" he said, running a hand through his short hair.

Patrovski stuck her head in the door. She glanced back and forth between us, flushed with embarrassment.

"What is it, Patrovski," he asked.

She opened the door further and stepped in. Over her shoulder I could see Jerreau at his desk. The minute he saw me, he lowered his head as if concentrating on his computer. He must have felt I needed rescuing and sent Patrovski as the cavalry.

"Sir, Chief Ramsey called. He asked Master Sergeant Harper to come to CID headquarters. He said there was someone she needed to talk to?" The inflection at the end communicated confusion, but Patrovski knew exactly why Ramsey wanted to see me.

"Now?"

"Yes, sir."

"Thank you, sergeant."

When she left, she thankfully left the door open. I glanced at Neil, but knew there was nothing I could say. I put my head down and headed toward the door needing more than anything to leave before he said anything else.

"Lauren, I don't know why you're going over there, but don't let them drag you into this. You have a job to do here."

"Yes, sir." I said.

He pressed his lips together, his face flushed. "That doesn't change a damn thing," he said. "We're not done here."

"Yes, sir." I said as I skirted by him, pulling my hat out of my cargo pocket and arranging it on my head. I strode out the door feeling, for the first time since meeting the investigator, grateful for the opportunity to see Chief Ramsey.

❧❦

I PARKED MY GOVERNMENT sedan in the lot and strode into the CID building in a rush, pulling off my soft cap and halting in my tracks as soon as I stepped through the door. The narrow hallways of the single-story, World War II era building were lined with men, their Ranger tabs and shoulder patches giving away their unit affiliation. I squeezed past men huddled in the entryway, some engaged in private conversation, others leaning against the walls reading or comfortable in their own quiet. They were soldiers waiting. An activity one grew accustomed to the longer you wore the uniform.

Considering how many men there were scattered about, they were unusually quiet. The low voices and grim faces appropriate for their vigil as they waited to be debriefed about an accident that may have ended two military careers and sent another man to his grave.

As I made my way down the hall, men were called into various offices. They would be meeting with investigators and safety inspectors to gather assorted versions of the events.

I picked my way through the crowd furtively searching for Harry. I excused myself past a large man blocking my way and saw Captain Pratt leaning with his back against the wall, his arms crossed. He seemed to be staring at the floor. Major Beechwood stood next to him, gazing off into space. While the men standing around us all seemed a bit roughed up, as if they'd just fallen through the sky from several thousand feet, their hair mussed, their faces dirty and their uniforms wrinkled and sweat stained, Beechwood looked fresh and unfazed by it all.

The stillness and intensity of the two officers spoke volumes to their profession. They'd both faced and overcome the military's most rigorous tests. The Army had spent hundreds of thousands of dollars on each of them in skills and leadership training to maximize their ability to execute the nation's most dangerous missions. They were powerful, fit looking military officers. Professional soldiers.

There was something about the pair that left me feeling unsettled.

Beechwood glanced up and met my gaze, his expression grim.

"Master Sergeant Harper," he said.

"Afternoon, Major. I heard about the accident. I'm sorry."

"Terrible," he said, shaking his head. "Garron was a good man."

"Did you know him well?" It seemed like an innocent question when it popped into my head, but when Beechwood's expression turned dark, I became more curious about his answer. His gaze flicked to Pratt for a moment before he crossed his arms and shrugged.

"I knew him, of course. We all know each other," he said, taking in the crowded hallways.

"Of course," I said, feeling uncomfortable. I'd made him angry and I didn't understand why. His prickly response left me speechless. The more I searched for something to say, the more unnerving his gaze became. Somehow, a stare-down contest had begun between us, one I knew I wouldn't win.

"Well. If you'll excuse me, sir," I said, before turning away. My instinct was to glance behind me, but I felt so ill at ease, I forced myself not to. When I turned the corner, I couldn't help myself. I glanced at the two men, and found them conferring with each other while watching me. I stepped around the corner and sighed in relief.

"Damn," I mumbled. "That was awkward." I glanced up, saw Harry and smiled. He leaned with his back against the wall, his fingers working furiously on his phone as he played some kind of game. Eldnik stood next to him, his hands buried in his pockets, staring into space.

"What was awkward?" Harry asked.

I wanted to explain the creepy feeling I'd had but couldn't figure out how. "Nothing, really." I said. "It's good to see you in one piece."

"It's good to be in one piece."

I glanced at Eldnik. "I'm sorry for your loss, Sergeant Major."

He shook his head and wrapped his arms around himself. "I don't understand what is going on around here. Two people in two days? It's just…" He looked down, running out of words.

"What are you doing here, Lauren?" Harry asked.

I explained that we just had our press conference and that Ramsey wanted to see me. "I'm not sure why. I'll tell you about it as soon as I can."

"That would be lovely," he said, his smile filled with meaning.

We grinned at each other while I reached for the door, but he beat me to it, grabbing the knob before I could, our fingers brushing briefly.

"Allow me," he said, a glint in his eye.

"Thank you, Sergeant Major."

"Cheers."

My gaze remained locked with his as I backed into the room, and he closed the door. Santos cleared his throat.

I turned to find him, his reading glasses pushed up onto his forehead, surrounded by stacks of reports and folders.

"Thank you for coming so quickly," he said.

I glanced around the large conference room, crowded with men and women in dark jackets, white shirts and dull-colored ties. Most of the women wore slacks, one or two wore skirts but they were below the knee and shapeless. How could not wearing a uniform look so much like wearing a uniform?

"No problem," I said. "What's going on?"

He motioned me to follow him so he threaded his way around the conference table, excusing ourselves between people who circled the room. Santos pulled out a chair and indicated I should sit, and then leaned in to deliver his message.

"There are early indications this may not have been an accident."

"I'm listening."

"First of all, it appears as if the initial impact didn't kill him. There are indications his death occurred while on the ground."

"Interesting," I said.

The static line jump is the most typical of military jumps, with the paratrooper's ripcord connected via a hook to a line—the static line—which runs the length of the aircraft. The paratrooper steps off, the hook pulls the ripcord and deploys the chute immediately upon leaving. For mere seconds, they fall in a straight line until their chute catches air and balloons out to form a mushroom over their head.

I've stood in the back of military aircraft, bracing myself to steady the shot as I videotaped scores of jumps. In the darkened belly, everyone lines up, their static lines in hand as they shuffle toward the door or the rear of the plane. As soon as the jump master signals, each soldier steps off, one after the other, no hesitation. The land streaks by below in a patchwork quilt of colors, so beautiful and inviting but a dizzyingly long way down.

I'd always thought you needed to be a bit insane to look forward to such a thing, but many people did it and loved it.

I didn't know the statistics for accidents on jumps like these, but since World War II, jumping from an aircraft was almost as common as riding in a tank. I'd heard of plenty of injuries, but those were mostly orthopedic in nature--knees, ankles, backs and feet--hurt in a single impact accident, or from prolonged abuse.

"What happened exactly?"

"We have heard a number of different possibilities...."

"Only one makes the most sense," Ramsey tossed his suit jacket over the back of a chair and loosened his tie before cocking a hip onto the conference table and crossing his arms. "They shouldn't have jumped with the wind conditions they faced. It was just bad judgment."

Ramsey seemed oblivious to the fact that he'd just overruled his partner's assessment. Santos, ever the gentleman, remained unfazed. "Understand that I am not ruling out an accident," Santos said. "I'm merely saying there are several indications that point to the possibility this death was not accidental."

"Ever the conspiracy theorist," Ramsey said, like someone who'd had the argument many times. "I don't know why you always think the worst. Are you so jaded that everything has to have some hidden meaning?"

Ramsey continued on like that for a bit, calling his partner crazy for thinking something nefarious had happened during the jump while I sat there with my thoughts bouncing about in wild directions in my head, like a handball game with no rules.

"Wait, wait a minute," I said. "If there's the slightest chance that the Captain was murdered, a murder that happened so close to the general's assassination attempt, wouldn't it be prudent to make damn certain there wasn't some kind of connection?"

"You see," Santos said to Ramsey, a taunting grin on his face. "If an amateur can see the potential seriousness of this, why can't you?"

I wasn't too pleased with being called an amateur, but that wasn't the point.

CHAPTER 16

B Y FAR, THE MOST annoying thing about Ramsey—and there were a large number of annoying things about him—was his refusal to believe anything other than the simplest explanation. Subtleties seemed beyond him.

"We have been told a sudden gust of turbulence caused the captain to trip or hit the door upon exit," Ramsey said. "How is that not the most logical explanation?"

"The jump master and the pilots indicate turbulence was not an issue during the time the troops exited the aircraft," Santos said. "Nothing other than what one might expect during a jump at two thousand feet."

"So wait," I said. "He exits, he stumbles and then what happened?"

Santos filled me in. "According to the jump master, he somehow hit the door and flipped sideways. When the chute deployed, his body was not in the right position and his legs became entangled in the lines. He collided with two others as he fell out of control. Those two men have serious injuries but will survive. After a struggle, Garron managed to deploy his reserve chute. He may have been knocked unconscious upon hitting the ground. Evidence indicates he was dragged several hundred feet...."

"The jump master said he tripped," Ramsey interrupted. "What about that is so hard to believe?"

"I am not ruling out the possibility of a trip," Santos said. "However, there are other things about this incident which make me want to look closer at the circumstances and you should too."

Ramsey narrowed his eyes at his partner. "What other things?"

"First," Santos said, "There are conflicting stories. The jump master and pilots say there wasn't any turbulence. It is only the two who jumped after Garron who say there were high winds and turbulence at the time of Garron's exit and subsequently, during their exit."

"Which two officers?" I asked.

Santos gave me a steady stare. "Major Mathias Beechwood and Captain Joshua Pratt."

That information hung in the air for a long beat. I looked at Ramsey. He wore his stubborn expression as if it were carved into his face.

"I'm telling you, this could have just been a bad safety call," Ramsey said. "If there wasn't turbulence, a strong gust as he exited could have pushed him into the door."

"I am not discounting this possibility," Santos said. "However, the conflicting stories and the fact that all three of these men had attended the press conference in which the general was shot, lead me to believe there may be something more going on here."

I stared at Ramsey. "You're kidding me, right? That doesn't make your hair stand on end?"

Ramsey closed his eyes, pinching the flesh between them as if to relieve headache pain. He mumbled. "You might as well tell her the rest of it."

I turned to Santos expectantly.

"He was found wrapped in his chute lines," Santos said. "His neck has deep ligature marks. According to my partner, Garron lost control upon exit, was forced to deploy his reserve at the last minute and then, once on the ground, was dragged by the wind. My partner thinks he was strangled by his own lines."

"Makes perfect sense," said Ramsey.

"I, on the other hand, believe someone took advantage of the high grasses where he landed and intentionally strangled him," Santos insisted.

"Say someone did strangle him," Ramsey said. "Don't you think they would have been seen?"

Santos narrowed his eyes at his partner. "The lines were wrapped around his neck multiple times. It hardly sounds accidental. And who knows? Someone may have seen it. We are not done questioning everyone."

"So your theory is that he was murdered," I said.

"Yes," Santos said, a note of finality to the word.

"Why?" I asked. "Why would someone want to kill him?"

Santos smiled and held up his finger. "Ah. Now you ask the right question. Connections, connections. The deceased, Captain Sylvester, graduated from West Point the same year as Newberg and for a time, was Newberg's roommate."

"That's a connection alright."

"And he's served on Blunt's staff a number of times in various junior positions. He's been in his operations office as a trainer, a planner and even applied to be Blunt's aide but wasn't selected."

"Any indication why he wasn't chosen?"

Santos put his hand on top of a stack of folders as if hoping the answer would come to him through osmosis. "Not yet, and it's unlikely we'll ever know. Why someone isn't chosen doesn't usually end up in a file."

"The Army can be really small. We all run into the same people in our career fields. As a Ranger, that's a small, elite group. You're bound to have connections like that, right?"

Santos sat back in his chair with a heavy sigh. "This must be considered, yes."

"It is a small world." Ramsey mumbled under his breath as he drummed his fingers on the desk. "My partner tends to lean toward the improbable. That leaves me to be more practicle in my deductions."

"A role he fully embraces," Santos said.

"Whatever," Ramsey said. "While I'm still not buying the intentional murder scenario, connections do mean something. I've agreed to entertain further investigation until we can debunk some of his ideas." Ramsey stood and lifted an eyebrow at me. "Have you spoken to your boyfriend yet?"

"No. Have you?"

"I was just about to."

"Please don't put a target on his back," I said. "Don't single him out."

He frowned at me. "This isn't my first rodeo," he said, then grabbed a notebook and started weaving his way out of the room. As if as an afterthought, he turned back to Santos and me. "Well, come on if you're coming."

∂∘⋖

WE'D PASSED HARRY AND Eldnik on the way out, but aside from smiling at him, I didn't let on that we were about to call on him. Ramsey ushered us into a small office then sent a young corporal out to bring Harry to us. The investigator took the chair behind the desk and rolled up the sleeves of his white shirt. I settled into a chair while Santos pulled one up to the desk, his pen and notebook ready to take notes.

Moments later, Harry stepped through the door closing it behind him, his gaze sweeping the room and landing on me first. "Sergeant Harper," he said, sounding official. "Gentlemen."

Harry looked windblown, his cheeks still a bit red from the jump, and smudges of dirt darkened his face beneath his eyes, making the green of them appear bright and vivid. He smelled like fresh air and sweat, his uniform rumpled and his boots covered in dirt. He had the look of a soldier having just returned from a mission, a mission that was a bit dangerous. Seeing him in the flesh after thinking, if only for a moment, that he might have been dead or seriously injured, made it difficult to keep myself from flying into his arms. My heart tripped a wild beat in my chest.

"This might take a while," Ramsey said, indicating a seat next to me. "Can you tell us what happened?"

Harry leaned forward, resting his forearms across his thighs, then ran a hand through his hair and blew out a breath.

"That was rotten luck. Truly rotten," he said. "Some of us tried to render first aid to the two blokes that were injured. One of them, Christ that was a nasty break. Compound fracture way up here," he said, pointing to the top of his thigh. "Hard to see him coming back from that." He looked at his hands as if checking to see if there was still blood on them.

"I felt some buffeting as we gained altitude so I knew the jump would be a bit dodgy in that wind, but Eldnik didn't seem concerned so I figured the lads were all experienced enough to handle the conditions. Perhaps I was wrong."

"You think it was just an accident?" asked Santos.

"Don't you?"

Santos raised an eyebrow in response. "That is the nature of our inquiries."

"If you have any fears," Harry said, "you better get someone to have a butchers at the dead man's kit."

"I'm not even going to ask what that means," Ramsey said.

Santos ignored the sarcastic comment. "If we made it available to you, could you tell if someone had tampered with the equipment?"

"Possibly," he said.

"If someone did tamper with his chute," I said. "Wouldn't it have been noticed during safety checks?"

He puffed out his cheeks and thought on it a moment. "We're all responsible for our own kit of course. The riggers pack the chutes and those are checked and double-checked. Frankly, I think equipment failure would be the least likely thing, but you should still check into it."

"Did you see what happened?" I asked.

He ran both hands down his face, a long exhale communicating his frustration. "I jumped near the middle of the string. I had just settled into the fall, looking up at my lines, when I saw him hit two different people. It partially collapsed their chutes and increased the speed of their descent. The bloke who hit them tumbled several times, the collapsed chute behind him, his legs wrapped up, everyone screaming at him to pull his reserve. It was bleeding hard to watch that and not be able to do anything to help."

"So you didn't see him exit the aircraft?" Ramsey asked.

"No. I went out several people before him. I didn't see his exit."

"If I told you he tripped on the way out the door, would you believe that?" Santos asked.

He waggled his head in possibilities. "Sure, anything is possible, but … well, they describe it as a shuffle to the door. There's a reason for that. Tripping would be a rookie move. It's possible but doubtful."

"Would it seem anymore probable if we told you the preliminary investigation indicates that Garron was not killed in the fall," Santos said.

"No, it wouldn't surprise me. He hit far harder then he would have liked. It could have killed him, but then again, it wouldn't surprise me if that's not what finished him."

"Did you see where Garron landed?" Ramsey asked.

"No,"

"Did you see what happened after he was on the ground?"

"No, I was a bit busy. From the air, I'd seen the one bloke with the busted up leg, so I came down near him and helped patch him up."

"And you didn't see Garron after that?"

"If you landed out of the target area, you landed in tall grasses. Once on the ground, it would have been difficult to see unless you stood up."

"Did you see Garron's body?" I asked.

He leaned back in his chair. "Yes, I saw him later, after the ambulance got there and the wounded men were being loaded up. If I had to guess, the speed he hit the ground could have knocked him out, then he got tangled in the lines, the winds picked up his chute and he was dragged a few hundred feet. The lines around his neck. Is that what killed him then? He was throttled. Nasty business."

Santos cleared his throat. "Is it possible someone could have strangled him and then made it look as if it were an accident?"

Ramsey slapped the desk. "And here comes the conspiracy."

"It's a valid question," I said.

"Nothing's ever simple with you people," Ramsey said.

"Except for the dim one in the room," Harry mumbled.

Ramsey shot him an angry glare. "Okay, smart guy. What's your theory on the possibility of strangulation?"

Harry sat back in his chair. "Yeah, it's possible." He paused and shrugged. "I didn't make a close inspection, but that line looked as if it were wrapped around his neck multiple times. That makes it look a bit dodgy, don't you think?"

"What about how he acted before the jump," Ramsey asked. "Was there any indication that he'd had any disagreements with anyone? Any tension in the group?"

"I was going to mention that." Harry leaned forward again, his hands clasped together. "When I first met these men, they were all friendly. Nice blokes. All having an easy way about them, easy going, except for Garron. He seemed preoccupied, separated from the rest of the men, distant." He shrugged. "But I didn't know the man. Maybe he's usually distant. I just don't know."

"Did anyone else mention Garron's preoccupation?" Ramsey asked.

Harry stood and went to the window, his back to the room. "It's just been the one morning, isn't it? Just waiting round, a bit of chat, bit of horsing about. It's not like they would confide in me or anything, but there was something going on."

"Explain," Santos said.

"It's like, when you walk into a room after some big argument has been going on. You can tell there's tension in the air, but no one wants to admit they were fighting. I acted like I didn't notice. It could have been they always got that wound up before a jump. How could I know? But..."

I waited for him to fill in the final thought. He turned and realized we were all staring at him. "I ah, I brought up the general. The shooting and that."

"And what happened?" Ramsey asked.

"It was just a handful of the men you see. Mostly NCOs, Sergeant Major Eldnik and a bunch of the younger blokes. When I brought it up, they just got quiet, like I'd farted or something."

Ramsey leaned back in the squeaky chair, folding his arms across his chest, unimpressed. "That's it?"

"Maybe I'm not describing it right, but it wasn't natural. Not the kind of reaction you'd expect at all. Just silence, until someone completely changed the subject. Later, Eldnik came back and said it was because they all felt responsible for him. He said the general was one of their own and he'd been injured on their watch. 'How can you be responsible?' I asked him. And he says to me, 'We should have seen it coming.'"

"He's talking about Newberg, right?" I said.

"Exactly," Harry said. "I tried to press him on it, but he just said if they'd paid more attention, they would have seen how disturbed he was. Eldnik said at one point Newberg had been a bit depressed, but that he thought the man had gotten help and wasn't having such a hard time anymore. In any case, he never thought he'd hurt anyone."

"He didn't think he'd hurt anyone," Ramsey repeated. "We questioned some of these guys already. I'll have to go over my notes, see if we spoke to Eldnik yet. Did he say anything else?"

"No, just...I could tell Nick wanted to make light of it all, but there was definite tension in the air." He crossed his arms and propped himself on the windowsill. "I know it's not much to work with."

"It's more than we had," Santos said.

Ramsey closed his notebook and stood, pushing up his sleeves. "You've given us some leads here. If you want to keep hanging out with them...well, whatever you decide." He shook Harry's hand and left the room. Santos followed him. Just before

Santos closed the door, Ramsey shoved his way back in. "I still need you to talk to Newberg, Sergeant Harper."

"Roger, Chief," I said.

"Right away," he said.

"I'll be right there."

He glared at us for a minute before closing the door.

I turned to Harry who was still leaning against the window. As soon as our gazes locked, he stretched his arms out to me. "Come here."

CHAPTER 17

RESTING MY CHEEK AGAINST his chest, my arms around his waist, Harry pulled me close, his hand to the back of my head, cradling me so tight I could barely breathe. Blissful was the word that sprang to mind. He smelled of sweat and earth and felt like a solid place to anchor myself. We stood that way for a while, his chin resting on top of my head, the sound of his heart beating a deep thrum in my ear.

He chuckled, a vibration in the hollow of his chest. "It's ridiculous that I've missed you this much in just a few hours."

"Me too. I'm embarrassed to tell you how freaked out I was when I heard about the accident."

He released his grip on me and stepped back to meet my gaze. "I know that feeling, love. I know how unpleasant it can be. To be honest, it's one of the reasons I've never allowed myself to get seriously involved with anyone. It's too much to ask—to have someone care about you only to leave them worrying."

"So, you choose your job over a love life?"

"You know as well as I do, most times it doesn't feel as if the choice is mine to make."

"The job chooses you. You don't choose the job?"

He nodded his acknowledgement. I wasn't sure if I agreed completely. Yes, there was nothing else I could imagine doing as a career, but wearing the uniform, performing my duty, my dedication to the job was one thing. The level of commitment, the demands, both physical and emotional and the intensity of the self-sacrifice involved in Harry's profession were a whole different animal.

"It's too late to back away from me now, Harry. You have someone who cares enough to worry. You'll just have to deal with that."

He grinned then took my hand. "They're doing some urban warfare training tomorrow out in the box. Eldnik says I can come along again if I want. He's a good bloke, and I get the impression he's feeling something isn't right among the men. I think I can get him to open up."

I could have asked him not to go back, but I knew he'd ignore my request. He would throw himself back into a group of men who could have a killer or killers among them as if it were nothing. Despite knowing his fearlessness, I still had a question that had been bubbling up in my head ever since I'd heard McCallen's crazy talk. I wanted to ask, but I wasn't sure if I wanted to know the answer. "Harry, if you weren't a soldier anymore, what would you do?"

His forehead pulled down into a questioning frown. "Why do you...?"

Before he finished I'd already regretted that I'd allowed the words out of my mouth. "Never mind. I'm being stupid." I attempted a chuckle, but it came out shaky and fake sounding even to my own ears.

"Come here, love," he said, pulling me close again, tightening his embrace. When he spoke, his words warmed my cheek. "It will be a few years before I would start considering that possibility, Lauren. Is it this accident? Were you that worried?"

I sighed and, unable to think straight in such close proximity, I paced away from him trying to get my thoughts together. I couldn't tell him Neil had put the thought of being a civilian in my head. I couldn't tell him how much I hated the abject fear and near panic I felt with just the possibility that he'd been one of the injured and reinforce his belief that staying unattached was better for his profession.

"Up until about six months ago, I thought I had a fairly clear picture what the rest of my life would be like," I said, unable to look at him. "Then Bosnia happened...and other stuff, and you, and I'm just...confused I guess."

"I can't predict the future, Lauren, but I like that you think of me in it."

"I'm just being stupid."

"You could never be that, pet."

∘ℂℂ∘

HARRY LET ELDNIK KNOW he was leaving, telling him the investigators had everything they needed from him. They made plans to meet up the next day. "You alright, mate?"

Eldnik glanced around at his men and shrugged. "I just talked to Garron's wife. He had two kids, ya know? I hate this part of the job." He opened his mouth to say more but then pressed his lips together as if to stop himself. Harry clapped him on the shoulder and shook his hand, no further words necessary.

We followed signs posted on walls, directing us to the detention facility. Harry glanced down at me and we shared a smile. Our natural instinct was to hold hands as we walked side by side, but it simply wasn't done when wearing a uniform so we refrained but it wasn't easy. My hand actually itched to be wrapped in his.

When we found them, Ramsey and Santos stood outside a door marked "Detention Visitation." Santos leaned against the wall scribbling notes, his glasses pushed to the top of his head. Ramsey paced. When he saw us approach, he looked at his watch.

"Your little lovers reunion over finally?" Ramsey asked. "I can't sit around diddling myself all day."

"You mean that's not your normal activity?" Harry said, earning an angry look from Ramsey.

"Has Newberg told you anything since last night?" I asked.

"Not a word." Ramsey's eyes were red-rimmed and had dark circles under them. He looked pale as if he didn't have the energy to confront the complications of the case. He may have been wearing a different suit from the day before but it was hard to tell.

He looked just as wrinkled as he had during the press conference. "As you know, I'm a good interrogator. But this guy…"

"You look knackered," Harry said. Ramsey stared at Harry, a look of confusion on his face.

"He's right. You look like crap," I said. "Newberg has obviously worn you down."

Santos cleared his throat. "I have told him several times he needs to get some sleep. It's like talking to a child at bedtime."

Ramsey stuck both hands in his hair, what little there was of it, and pulled. I tried to hide my smile at his obvious frustration with us, with the interrogation, at the whole situation. "Yes, I could use some sleep. That guy is curled up in his cell, right now, sleeping like a baby while General Blunt is fighting for his life." His face flushed bright red with his indignation. "The only thing he has managed to say is to repeat his request to see his Major…."

"Major Beechwood?"

"And the Sergeant Major," Santos said.

"Command Sergeant Major Eldnik," Harry said. "He's a good friend of mine."

"So," I said. "Why aren't Beechwood and Eldnik here?"

"First of all, Newberg is on suicide watch. He started talking about killing himself as soon as we put him in a cell. More importantly, he's not having any visitors until he cooperates," Ramsey said. "And right now, he's not cooperating. Legally, the only person I'm required to let him see is a lawyer and he hasn't asked for that."

"Chief Ramsey is failing to mention that we did ask Beechwood and his sergeant major if they would come talk to him," said Santos.

"They both said they'd only come if I demanded it," Ramsey said. "Maybe they don't want to be closely associated with him or maybe they just don't like the guy. Who knows?" He stopped and took a long swig from an energy drink. He ran a shaky hand over his head.

"I could probably get Nick to talk to him," Harry said.

Ramsey pressed his lips together as if what he was about to say might make him sick to his stomach. "I may ask you to do that," he said. "But let's give Sergeant Harper a crack at him first. Get something, anything out of him. I don't need a confession obviously, but we need to know why he did it. More importantly—just to satisfy my partner's obsession with conspiracy theories—was this part of some bigger plot? Did he know any reason why someone would want to kill Garron? Are others involved? Will someone else come along to try to finish the job, that sort of thing? Just try to find out why he did it."

"Okay, I'll try."

"Before we go in," Santos said. "You may want to look at this."

He handed me a small, hardcover notebook covered in olive green cloth. Newberg had glued one of his embroidered name tapes on the cover along with a Ranger tab. Most officers and senior NCOs carried similar-looking books—a battle book—meant for note taking. Newberg's was fat with rumpled pages, bits and pieces shoved in between the bound cover and held together with a thick rubber band. It felt intrusive to look at someone else's battle book, like reading their diary or searching through their underwear drawer. One glance inside and it was clear why Santos had wanted me to see it.

"Bloody hell," Harry said, looking over my shoulder.

He'd clipped several *Stars and Stripes* and *Army Magazine* articles about me and had them neatly folded and tucked between pages. Several were about Bosnia. There was also a small one about Honduras. A more recent addition was a picture of General Blunt at some major press event that had caught me standing behind him. I was slightly out of focus, but anyone who knew me would have little trouble recognizing me. The disturbing part about the picture was that he'd circled Blunt in red and driven a diagonal line through him.

"That's creepy," I said.

"There is more, but you can clearly see he has some sort of interest in you," Santos said. "Perhaps it only has to do with your proximity to General Blunt…"

"Or not," Harry said.

The fact that he had collected the clippings was disturbing, but I wanted to think it was normal. We had worked together for a short time and I'd been in the paper a few times. "Maybe it's nothing," I said. "It's not that unusual for someone to follow an old acquaintance in the news, is it?"

Ramsey took the book out of my hands and snapped the rubber band around it. "Don't kid yourself. It's not usual for him to have clippings about you saved in something he carries with him all the time. You were right. It's creepy," he said and tucked the offending book under his arm.

CHAPTER 18

SANTOS SIGNALED TO A soldier standing behind glass who activated an electronic lock sending a loud metallic clang echoing down the hallway. Ramsey shoved down hard on the handle then leaned back as he dragged the heavy door open.

The small room contained three cubical spaces facing a wall of scratched and shatter-proof glass. Each space held a chair, a table and a black phone handset attached to the cubical divider. Ramsey motioned me to the center chair. I sat down and waited. I turned to glance at Harry and he gave me a reassuring smile. He crossed his arms and leaned back against the wall. I had to drag my gaze away lest I stare at him and get lost in inappropriate thoughts. Instead, I turned my attention to the metal table in front of me and the empty room on the other side of the glass and settled into my wait mode, a skill I'd honed over years of non-activity. I didn't have to wait long before the door on the other side of the room clanged open.

Newberg, now wearing an orange jumpsuit with the letter P stenciled on the chest pocket, looked rumpled and disoriented as he stood in the doorway. Fresh sleep-induced wrinkles decorated his cheek. He shuffled forward completely fettered, his feet shackled, his wrists wrapped in handcuffs and both restraints connected together by another chain. I'd never seen someone so trussed up before. The weight of the chains had to be uncomfortable.

He seemed anxious, his eyes open wide, a slight smile on his face, until he saw me. As soon as he realized who had come to visit him he deflated in disappointment, halting in his tracks for a moment as he stared at me, a rush of color flooding his face. He shuffled forward, the heavy chains seeming to weigh him down now, making his slow, rattling steps appear to threaten his balance. He settled himself in the chair opposite me. I lifted the receiver and he did the same, reaching awkwardly for the device despite his weighty impediments.

"Hello, Win."

"Harper. It's good to see you and all," he said, not hiding the disappointment in his voice. "But what are you doing here?"

"Chief Ramsey asked me to come talk to you. He found…well, he figured out that we know each other." I wanted to know what all the clippings were about, what it all meant, but it didn't seem like the right time to confront him about it, so I changed the subject. "I'm obviously not who you expected to see."

"No offense. I appreciate you coming." He sat hunched over the desk with slumped shoulders. He needed a shave and his eyes were bloodshot, but he was still an attractive guy. A man who obviously took good care of himself. When he looked up at me, his eyes were shining as if he were fighting back tears.

"Win?"

"It's okay. I mean it. Thanks. I was feeling ..."

He stopped, his gaze drifting down. If he'd been about to say he was feeling lonely, I wanted to tell him to get used to it. It seemed unlikely, from now on, he would feel much else. I tried to change the subject. "You still wasting your money on lottery tickets?"

He attempted a smile, but it appeared pained. "You can't win if you don't buy a ticket." His face fell into his disappointed expression again, like a child who didn't get the birthday gift he wanted.

"I may be a poor substitute for whoever you expected, but you can consider me a friendly face," I said.

He gave the smile another try and it was a bit more believable. He then glanced at Harry, his gaze lingering as he took a full assessment of him from top to bottom. He then switched his focus to Ramsey, his gaze darkening when he stared at the investigator.

"I'm not that surprised really. They're not exactly bending over backwards to make things easy for me."

"Do you blame them?"

He shook his head, the phone pressed hard against his cheek. "Not really, no."

I figured I'd get the obvious question out of the way. "I have to ask, Win. Why did you do it?"

"Would it make you feel better if I told you the voices in my head told me to?"

That made me pause. "Do you hear voices?"

"Don't you?" The question would have been frightening if it wasn't clear that he was being sarcastic.

"How can you joke about it?"

"How can I not joke about it? What logical explanation is there for shooting someone in public?"

"There isn't one, Win. That's why we're a bit confused."

He didn't respond, instead just leaned back in his chair, relaxed and stared at me, still and solid. Whatever reason he'd had, he seemed okay with his circumstances, even a bit cocky.

"You can breathe a little easier, I suppose, since a murder charge is off the table."

His eyebrows went up. "Really? Why?"

"Didn't they tell you? Win, General Blunt is alive."

"What?" He shot up out of his chair and almost toppled over, temporarily forgetting his feet were shackled together. The guard stepped forward and said something I couldn't hear. Newberg gave him an angry glare, then settled himself slowly back into his chair. I wondered why Ramsey hadn't told him, then figured it might have been some kind of interrogation technique. Well, Newberg knew now.

I heard a rattling sound and realized it was his chains. He bounced a heel or his knee or something, making the chains sing. The roundness of his eyes reminded me of a frightened animal. I wondered why he suddenly seemed so tense.

"He's in an induced coma in a German hospital," I said, watching him closely. "But the doctors expect him to survive."

He stared at me for a long moment, as if checking to see if I were telling the truth. Then he looked down, his knuckles white around the handset as his eyes darted around the desk top. "Mother fuck," he mumbled through clenched teeth as the color drained from his face.

I could almost hear his thoughts skittering about as his hands clenched and unclenched, his breath slightly fogged the glass between us. His body vibrated in his chair. I tried to push him a bit farther.

"I'm told Mrs. Blunt is with him now, and Brianna and Melody," I went on. "You know all of them, right? If he's well enough, they'll transfer him to Landstuhl soon."

His gaze flicked to me. "Landstuhl?"

"Yes."

He chewed his lip and tapped a finger on the desk, almost keeping time with his knee bounce. The nervous movements were disturbing to watch, jerky, borderline neurotic. I noticed the nail he used to tick on the table was perfectly clean, perfectly rounded and well-macured hands. Most soldiers I knew had hands that reflected their work—calloused fingers, jagged nails. His soft hands seemed odd, especially for a special operations soldier.

"That's why, damn it. That's why," he said under his breath.

"What's why, Win? What are you talking about?"

"Nothing. Forget it."

"Jeez, if I didn't know better, I'd think you were upset that you failed."

His face tightened as he glared, first at me, then at Ramsey over my shoulder. "Why are you here anyway? He put you up to this, didn't he?'

Ramsey shuffled around behind me, but I ignored him and remained quiet, waiting to see if Newberg would fill the silence but he stayed mute, gazing around the room, at anything to avoid my eyes. I turned my attention to the men standing behind me. "I think you should leave me alone with him."

Harry stared at me for a long moment, his lips pressed together, arms crossed, in that statue-like stillness of his. He came to a decision then he moved toward the door, a strong hand on Ramsey's arm pushing him in the direction of the exit. Ramsey struggled against him a moment, then allowed himself to be ushered out of the room. I knew they'd be able to go somewhere else to listen in, maybe watch through a security feed. The camera high in the corner had to be a closed-circuit video and I assumed they'd be able to listen in through the phone system.

I turned back to Newberg.

"Looks like you've got a lot of pull around here," he said.

"Looks are deceiving." I shifted around in my seat, stalling, considering where to go next.

"Who else is involved in this, Win?"

"I'm the one who pulled the trigger."

"This is true. We all saw you do it. We have pictures and video of it. That doesn't mean you're the only one involved."

"Gee," he said, in a dry tone. "I'll be famous."

"I have to say, for a military planner, you didn't have a very good plan."

"We make the best use of what is handed to us."

"And who handed you this mission?"

He paused for a long moment, his breathing sounded amplified through the phone. "You don't know me, Harper. I get that. Not many people do. If you did, you'd know I did what had to be done."

"I've been told you not only served with Blunt, you were a friend of the family. What went wrong?"

"Blunt was a fellow Ranger and yeah, I know his family but we were never friends. He's not the kind of man who makes friends."

"What does that mean?"

He licked his lips, his mouth obviously dry. I didn't know much about Rangers aside from the quiet respect automatically afforded anyone who wore the tab. Their training was ridiculously rigorous, the dropout rate high in the qualification course. Many tried, few succeeded in earning a spot in the Regiment and the right to wear the tan beret and the shoulder tab. Surprise attacks, infiltration into enemy territory, shock troop kind of hand-to-hand combat and rescue operations, that's the kind of stuff Rangers did. They seemed fearless, heroes waiting to be pointed at the enemy; any enemy. The man in front of me had been trained to be one of those fearless types, but right now, he looked petrified. He couldn't have just realized the significance of his actions. It had to be something else.

"The way you shot him in public, with so many witnesses…did you want everyone to see it? Were you making some kind of statement?"

"Ha. A statement. I guess you could say that. It was fake media. I know that. Still, all those cameras were a bit hard to resist."

"You're talking, but you're not saying anything, Win. Are you just toying with me? Eventually you'll have to explain yourself, won't you? It was like a public execution…"

"Execution attempt, you mean," he said, obviously unhappy with the outcome.

"You'll have to explain it during the court martial."

"I know my fate is sealed," he said, his eyes shining, his fist clenched now. "Or maybe it isn't."

"You could get the death penalty," I said. Did he not understand the consequences? He'd chosen to either die or spend the rest of his life in prison. What the hell had Blunt done to earn such an enemy?

"The military hasn't put anyone to death in decades. Even if I was sentenced to death, I'd die of old age behind bars. Besides, I never intended to wait for the Army to do it. I'm ready to go." He looked down, his shoulders slumped. "I'm just tired. There's nothing left for me here."

"You can't mean that."

He leaned into the glass, fixing me with an intense stare. "We have a unique profession, you and I. We wear a uniform. We swear an oath. Sometimes we get sent on missions we don't fully understand. Whether we understand them or not, we accept that there can be dangerous consequences. We accept that, ultimately, it's not about us. It's about the mission."

I allowed myself to hear what he'd just said. Mission. Orders. Consequences.

"There's one prevailing truth about every mission you get in the Army. Someone else gives it to us. It might be the person who has direct authority over you, or it could be a higher headquarters. We don't usually make them up ourselves."

He continued to stare at me unflinchingly.

"Did this mission come from someone else, Win?"

"What do you think?"

"I think it did."

He continued to stare, his lips pressed into a thin line.

"Who gave you the mission, Win? Why would you do it when you knew the consequences?"

His steady stare unnerved me. I could tell he had no intention of answering me and I understood why Ramsey had felt so frustrated.

"Have they assigned you a lawyer yet?"

He rolled his eyes and shook his head as if he didn't want to be bothered with the question. "They tell me they have, but I don't want to see one."

"Why?"

"What's a lawyer gonna do for me?"

"They might be able to help you explain what it was …"

"There's nothing to explain. Don't you get it? I'm sick of living. Sick of it."

"You're not making this easy."

He huffed in amusement. "Not exactly my goal here, Harper."

"What about those articles about me? Why are you carrying them around?"

He grinned, his eyes narrowed to amused slits. "I remembered you from Thailand. When I heard about Bosnia, I couldn't believe what had happened to you. That was bad enough. Then that other one…"

"Honduras."

"Yeah. I mean, who gets in that kind of trouble?"

"I do, evidently."

He nodded his head, staring at me. "Yes, it seems you do, but you came out of it okay. And well...heck. I kind of admire that about you."

I shook my head at him, my annoyance becoming too acute to keep under control. "You're enjoying this drama, aren't you? Right now, no one understands why you did this. If you were attempting to send some kind of message ..."

"Oh, there's a message alright," he said, with a brief and humorless chuckle.

"Okay," I said, dragging out the word. "If that's the case, then you may need to translate."

He cocked his head to the side, his face flushed and a flash of anger in his eyes. "Well, how about this for a message?" His voice increased in volume as he built up steam. "I failed in a necessary task. I had a chance and I not only screwed it up, I totally screwed myself." By the end, he was shouting and fat tears rolled down his cheeks. He buried his face in his hands, his shoulders shaking.

"Win? Win, please explain it to me. I don't understand."

He looked up, his hands against the glass, his eyes wide in panic. "Please, you have power around here. Please tell them ... I need to see..."

"Your lawyer?"

"No! I need...damn it!"

The loud clank of the electronic door unlocking behind me made me jump. I turned to see Ramsey step in, a scowl on his face. "Tell him the only other visitor he's going to get is a military lawyer. Not his mother, not his girlfriend and certainly not his buddies from his Ranger unit. I'm done with these games."

I covered the receiver with my hand, furious at his timing. "Are you crazy? He was just about to..."

"To do what? String you along again? He's playing games and I'm not tossing him the ball anymore." He crossed his arms with finality.

I glanced back at Newberg. He'd quickly regained control of himself and used his sleeve to wipe his face.

"Ignore him, Win," I said into the phone. "Just tell me what it is you need."

"Nothing," he said glaring at Ramsey. "I don't need a damn thing."

"Damn it!" I said then covered my mouth with my hand, afraid all the scurrilous words I wanted to shout at the investigator would come tumbling out.

"That's it," Ramsey said. "Time's up."

Newberg put his hand on the glass. "Thanks for coming Harper. I appreciate it."

The guards didn't waste any time. Two of them entered Newberg's side of the room and grabbed him under each arm. I put my hand against the glass. "I'll come back if you want to talk again."

The guards yanked him up and he let the phone clatter to the desk. His eyes were pleading as I read his lips, saying "Math Beechwood. Please," as they pulled him out the door. I hung up the phone and turned to Ramsey.

"What is wrong with you? I cannot believe your timing. I almost had him…"

"You mean, *he* almost had *you* wrapped around his finger. You let him get the upper hand."

"I what? You cannot be that dense."

Harry stepped into the room behind Ramsey, pushing his bulk past where the investigator blocked the door. He leaned against the wall, his arms crossed, brow furrowed.

"Oh, he's thick alright," Harry said, the heat of his frustration turning his neck and cheeks red.

Ramsey ignored both of us and began to pace the room, crossing between Harry propped against the wall, and me, seated in my chair. We ignored his frequent passes and gazed at each other. Harry, angry, brooding, looked totally and completely sexy. I tried to imagine him doing something that didn't look sexy, like maybe … well, I couldn't come up with anything. That thought made me smile.

"I fail to see the humor in this situation," Harry said.

He was really pissed. The temperature in the room dropped about fifty degrees. "I'm sorry. I wasn't smiling at… I know it's serious."

"Then don't bloody piss about."

"The guy talks in circles," Ramsey said, ignoring the chill in the room. "I can't decide if he's just stringing us along or …," he let his thoughts trail away.

"I'm not, Harry. Why are you so upset?" I sounded like a whiney kid.

"Because they're playing you, Lauren. Both this chap," he said, indicating Ramsey, "and that other bent bastard." He turned to leave, yanking on the heavy door. "I need a brew," he mumbled as he left.

I jumped out of my chair to follow him, but Ramsey stepped in my way. "Considering your inexperience, you managed to get him to open up quite a bit."

"And how do you manage to make your compliments sound so much like insults?" I shouldered past him and followed Harry.

CHAPTER 19

SEVERAL MINUTES LATER, BACK in the small office we'd used before, Harry and I, with mugs of tea, sat opposite Ramsey and Santos who gripped their coffee mugs as if the caffeine they consumed provided a lifeline. Ramsey took a sip of coffee followed by a sip of his energy drink, his exhaustion etched deeply into his face.

After a long, uncomfortable silence, Harry voiced what had him so upset.

"You should have told this barmy bastard to get stuffed in the first place, Lauren," he said indicating Ramsey, who stared on with a confused look on his face. "He wants you to sort out the porkers. And since Newberg is rabbiting to you, the plunker can act as if he's redundant, leaving it all to you while he takes the piss."

"Why can't you just speak English?" Ramsey's face looked so red it glowed.

"I *am* speaking English, you gobby get."

Ramsey slammed his coffee mug down, splashing the contents on the table. "You may not be an American soldier, Sergeant Major, but you'd be wise to start treating me with the respect my rank requires."

"Oh, yeah. Respect for your rank since everything's going tickety-boo with you at the helm."

"Now see here!"

"Gentlemen, please," Santo said.

"Harry, don't take it out on them," I said.

In response to my plea, Harry took a noisy sip of his tea and looked away.

"Damn it," Ramsey said, attempting fruitlessly to wipe coffee off his tie. "If he's going to insult me, is it too much to ask that he do it in a way I can at least understand?" He crossed his arms over his chest and actually made a pouty face.

Ramsey's little fit tugged a reluctant smile from Harry which he hid behind his cup. To keep the peace, I tried to hide my smile as well.

"Harry's upset because he thinks you're making me do your job for you."

"What's that porker business?" Ramsey asked me, as if Harry weren't sitting right next to me.

I glanced at Harry, who pressed his lips together, refusing to explain. "It's Cockney rhyming slang. Pork pies. Lies...porkers for short..."

The most interesting thing about the exchange was that the Cockney slang had been developed as code to throw off law enforcement in age-old London, a code I'd only started getting the hang of since spending time with Harry. The fact that I understood some of it didn't soften the knowledge that Harry thought I was being used by both Ramsey and Newberg.

Harry leaned in close, lowering his voice. "First they say they don't want you involved, and then they practically order you to get involved. It doesn't make sense. Newberg could have talked to these blokes when they had the chin wag with him. And that's the way it should be, right? A Rupert questioning a Rupert. So, why did he wait? Why is he rabbiting to you?"

I had no idea why British NCOs called their officers Ruperts, but I wasn't going to ask Harry to clarify that point.

"He didn't say anything significant until I told him Blunt wasn't dead. Why hadn't you told him that?" I directed my question to Ramsey.

He shrugged and looked away. "I didn't want him to think he was facing anything other than a murder charge."

"But a murder charge obviously didn't mean anything to him. Failing to complete his mission was a bigger deal apparently. And now he's frightened." I turned to Harry. "He's suddenly petrified, Harry."

"Petrified over something worse than life in prison or even a hanging?"

"We should find out what that something is," I said, sure that it could be the key to understanding the motivation to the murder attempt. Ramsey, as usual, looked skeptical.

"I'm not as interested in what frightened him as I am in who he collaborated with."

"Perhaps it's the same thing," said Santos. "The person, or persons he is working with will not be pleased that their target is not dead. Perhaps there was some form of blackmail involved. A hostage, so to speak."

"He was forced to do it?" Ramsey said, his words thick with sarcasm. "Not likely."

"Is that why he wanted to see Beechwood and Eldnik?" I asked.

Harry didn't like the implication. "No way is Nick involved. You can put that idea right in the bin bag. If he had something to do with it, why would he refuse to see him now?"

"You have a point," I said. "But, the involvement of someone else could explain why a failure would be so devastating. He could be afraid someone will use whatever it is they have hanging over him."

Harry startled me when he suddenly took my hand and wrapped it in both of his. He leaned in close, his gaze intense. "Can you feel it, Lauren? That pull of them dragging you in? You've got sweet Fanny Adams to do with this." He squeezed my hand even tighter. "Lauren, Newberg is special ops. He's supposed to have a brass set of twigs and berries and yet he's petrified. That tells me he's got something real to be frightened of and my gut is telling me this is all going south with you strapped to the boat."

Santos cleared his throat. "Sergeant Major, I understand your reluctance, but Master Sergeant Harper accomplished more in her brief interview than Chief Ramsey managed in twenty-four hours of interrogation."

"Well … I wouldn't go that far …" Ramsey sputtered.

Santos interrupted. "We are grateful for her assistance and unfortunately, we require more of it."

"You're saying she hasn't a choice."

The stony look Santos returned served as answer.

Harry released my hand with a heavy sigh, settling back in his chair. What I didn't say was that if I'd had a choice, I'd still want to help them. If you'd asked me earlier in the day, I would have said I wasn't part of the investigation and I didn't want to be. But now, I had too many questions, there was too much still up in the air for me to simply turn my back on it. And while I understood why Harry was concerned—considering past results—I knew I'd remain preoccupied with finding the truth until it had all been explained.

I could have told them I'd asked Patrovski's friend to look into some things for me, but I didn't know if she'd turn up anything. Not to mention, I didn't want Harry to know that I'd already been nosing around.

So, I kept my motivations and my previous questions to myself since it was clear any involvement from me would only piss Harry off.

"Tell me you understand my concern," Harry said to Santos. "She's put herself in the crosshairs for you blokes before. Tell me you will protect her this time."

Santos and Ramsey exchanged looks. Santos cleared his throat. "We have discussed the possibility of issuing her live ammunition for her weapon. Of course, she's not an official part of this investigation, but it would make me feel better, if she were armed. Would that be agreeable to you, Sergeant Harper?"

Harry glanced down at the weapon strapped to my thigh. I'd worn the nine millimeter pistol for weeks, forgetting it was there most of the time. A few magazines of ammunition seemed the easiest way to ease Harry's concerns.

"You've seen me in a firefight, Harry. You know I'm pretty good with it. Besides, I don't plan on letting you get too far from me."

"Yes, but I hadn't been that far from you before when you got yourself in it."

"We will issue you the ammunition before you leave today," Santos said. "In the meantime, I suggest we concentrate on who else is involved and, if we are considering some form of coercion, exactly what is being used to motivate the Major to murder."

"Ha, nice alliteration, chief," Ramsey said.

"I'm surprised you understand the word," Harry said.

I rolled my eyes at them, and attempted to ignore their childish exchange. "Well, aside from the obvious, is there anything in Newberg's file that someone might have used against him?"

"What do you mean by the obvious?" Santos said.

Harry and I exchanged looks. "It wasn't obvious to you?" I said.

"No!" Ramsey and Santos said together. It seemed a rare occasion that they agreed with one another.

Harry shook his head. "You didn't see the way he looked at me. Made me feel cheap as chips."

"I did notice him do that," I said with a smile. "Who could blame him?"

"Steady on," Harry's arched eyebrow and sly grin made my heart flutter.

"Oh, come on, you two." said Ramsey. "Take it outside."

Santos cleared his throat.

"What?" Ramsey snapped, his exasperation dripping from the one word.

"I'm merely hoping they will clarify what it was that should have been so obvious."

"So, you didn't notice that he's queer?" Harry said.

Ramsey and Santos exchanged looks again. "What are you talking about?" Ramsey said.

"You're takin' the piss, right?" Harry said, giving me a shocked expression. "For fuck sake. Can you believe this … ?"

I interrupted him before he hurled another insult at the investigator. "Harry is right. Major Newberg is gay. I'd suspected it when we were in Thailand but of course, never had confirmation. Today, he seemed to drop any pretense."

"Well," Ramsey said. "That puts a different spin on things." He turned to Harry. "How did you know?"

"Would you like a definition of obvious?" Harry's tone made me to bite my tongue to keep from laughing.

Ramsey, unamused, pressed his lips together and looked ready to launch into another verbal sparring match. Santos interrupted.

"If what Sergeant Major Fogg said is true, shouldn't we consider that his, ahem, proclivities, may have had something to do with his actions...against the General, I mean."

"His proclivities," Ramsey said. "Is that what we're calling it now?"

"If he is gay, he hides it well," Santos said.

"But he'd have to," I said.

"The bloke rather perfected it over the years, I'd say."

"We may not be asking these days, but that doesn't mean being gay won't get you booted out of the Army." I said.

"Sounds like a good enough motive to me," Ramsey said.

"It may be good enough for you, but it's not the right answer," I said, my sarcasm dripping like tar. "Newberg hasn't been under Blunt's command for years. If Blunt were going to get him discharged for conduct unbecoming, why would he wait this long to act on it?"

"Who knows?" Ramsey said. "That doesn't negate the fact that we have a motive now."

"And for you, any motive will do." I glared at the man. I'd seen what he could do with the slightest hint of a motive. He'd taken my stupid infatuation with my commanding officer and turned it into a motive and evidence that could have put me away for life, not to mention, ruin my career and Neil's marriage. If there was one thing about Ramsey I knew for sure. He was a lazy man. If he could find the slightest excuse to close an investigation, he took it, no matter how slim.

I watched Ramsey take out his notebook and in big letters write, "DADT," the acronym that meant Don't Ask, Don't Tell, the Army policy for dealing with homosexuality. Gay service members could serve as long as they kept their sexual preferences a secret, as long as they pretended they were straight, no different from anyone on their left or right. Suspicion of being gay could mean an investigation and eventual discharge.

"Think about it," I said. "If Blunt was trying to get him booted out of the Army, there would be a paper trail. A long one."

"Unless we completely missed it, there is nothing, so far, to suggest such a thing," said Santos.

"But we weren't looking for it before," Ramsey said.

"It still doesn't make sense," I said. "Killing Blunt wouldn't have stopped Newberg from getting chaptered out. And killing him in front of an audience for revealing something he wanted to keep secret? Not to mention, being forced out of the closet is not what frightened him so much. That's a different kind of fear. It just doesn't add up."

Santos pushed his glasses up and grabbed Ramsey's notebook. He added to what Ramsey had written so that it said: "DADT + ? = motive. Ramsey narrowed his eyes at his partner but didn't cross out the equation.

Written that way, it appeared to be a simple calculation, but the possibilities of what could fill in that question mark seemed endless.

ও◈৩

HARRY AND I STEPPED outside and I took a deep breath, sucking in as much fresh air as I could after spending so much time in the stifling office. More than an hour of going over and over what little information we knew had left us no closer to understanding Newberg's motives.

There were far fewer cars in the parking lot, the street lights had come on and we'd just missed the most colorful part of the sunset. The night insects began to pick up their evening song.

I knew it was just my imagination, but I felt every ounce of the additional weight a ten-round magazine of live ammunition added to the Berretta I'd been wearing for almost a month. The two additional magazines I carried in the cargo pocket of my pants slapped against my leg with each step. Ramsey had insisted that I begin to wear body armor along with the lethal ammunition

"Do you have live rounds in your weapon, Chief?" I'd asked.

"Yes, but.."

"Do you generally wear a vest every day?"

"No, but…"

My expression must have communicated my unwillingness to discuss it any further. He'd thrown up his hands and walked away.

It felt a bit strange to be carrying the weapon. Normally, there are only three reasons why a soldier would carry a loaded weapon on a peacetime military base. First, because they are part of a security force and a weapon is part of their profession. Second, because they're at a range about to train with the weapon, or three, they're about to deploy to a war zone or some other dangerous situation. Aside from those times, weapons and the ammunition associated with them are kept secured in an arms room.

In my entire career, there'd been very few times when I'd needed live ammunition. My deployment to Bosnia had been the longest period. Wearing the M16, literally eating and sleeping with it strapped to me, became second nature.

We weren't in Bosnia anymore, and while I understood Harry's concerns, I thought carrying a weapon every day, all day, just because I was helping with the investigation, was a bit paranoid. Still, if it would make him feel better about things, I was willing to drag along the extra weight.

CHAPTER 20

I PROMISED HARRY, AFTER a quick stop back at the office to tie up some loose ends, we could finally call it a day.

"It has felt rather endless," he said.

"I'll try to be quick about it."

I breathed a sigh of relief to see that McCallen's office was empty, the door wide open. I went directly to the opposite side of the building where the rest of the team sat quietly busy. The phones weren't ringing off the hook as they had been that morning but everyone seemed engaged in something.

Harry pulled up a chair next to Owens and watched him edit video. I stopped to admire the whiteboard Jerreau had started. Anyone stepping up to it would get an immediate sitrep, a situational report of the highest priorities, the open media queries and responses to others so they didn't have to duplicate work. He also had a handy list of what could be released and what couldn't, like details of Blunt's medical situation.

Right now, all we could say was that Blunt was still in critical condition. We held back the information that he was in an induced coma, that they suspected brain swelling, that he could wakeup either so brain damaged he could barely function, or he could come out of the coma with most of his faculties. From the medical reports we'd seen so far, odds were good he'd never lead troops again. It was too soon to drop that bomb on the media. So far, all of our statements to the press indicated that we remained hopeful for a full recovery.

Jerreau had started a separate section to track the queries about the jump accident and an additional section to track questions about Trent Blunt's arrest. They'd issued one statement which struck the right note that Trent was innocent until proven guilty and left it unsaid that there was still a dispute about whether he would be tried in German or U.S. courts.

The good news was, it didn't appear as if the press were linking any of the three incidents except for Trent's relationship to the general. That didn't mean we wouldn't get questions about all of them the next day during the press conference.

Jerreau stepped up next to me as I took in the work, quietly nodding my compliment for his organization.

"We're still working a few media queries," he said. "After we released Newberg's name, most of the media switched their attention to his hometown. Since his duty station is Fort Benning, the PAO there has been busy. We also got a call from the PAO at West Point. Evidently they've been busy with stateside queries about Cadet Blunt.

"Have you coordinated anything with the PAO at Landstuhl?"

"Yes. They're referring everything to us until General Blunt gets there. Also, the German doctors here in Nuremburg want to hold a press conference. I've been trying to get them to agree to simply join our conference scheduled for tomorrow."

"Did you inform the Colonel?"

"No. He ah...left shortly after you did. I haven't seen him since." His eyebrow arched up with a silent question. Evidently, Colonel McCallen and I hadn't been very discreet in the current turbulence in our relationship. I felt my face heating up in embarrassment.

"Crap," I mumbled.

"I don't want to stick my nose in..."

"It's nothing to worry about, Captain Jerreau. It's just a misunderstanding. We'll work it out, sir."

I heard the words coming out of my mouth but didn't know if I believed them myself. Working with the Germans was something McCallen should be doing. If we didn't stop them soon, the doctors would be crowing about the great job they were doing treating the American general who'd just had his brain turned into

Swiss cheese—information McCallen would know if he hadn't been absent all afternoon.

"Any chance he's with General Roderick?"

Jerreau shrugged.

"I'm sure he'll be back soon," I said. "In the meantime, have you been able to get Mrs. Blunt on the phone? Might be a good idea to give her the command messages in case she wants to jump in front of the cameras."

We'd had problems with her doing that in the past. She seemed to like media attention and would often call the press on her own without letting us or even her husband know what she was up to. Most of the time, it was about positive things—fund raisers the officers' spouses club was holding, or promotion of some event or effort—but she was a bit unpredictable. The last thing we needed was unpredictable.

"She's been calling us every few hours with updates. I could tell she wants to speak to the press that have gathered but she agreed to leave it be for a while at least. Since the news about Cadet Blunt, we haven't heard a word from her. I think she should be part of the press conference tomorrow though. Don't you?"

I smiled at his thinking. Pauline Blunt knew how to work the press. Sometimes I suspected it was her keen ability to see the politics and understand the underlying traps of military life that cemented her husband's success. She wasn't like some Army wives who flaunted their husband's rank and demanded, usually through intimidation and manipulation, that they be treated like royalty. Instead, she used kindness, a seemingly endless ability to smile and listen, as well as a great sense of humor, to win people over. Pauline was treated like royalty alright, because people wanted to treat her that way. She made us all think it wasn't something we had to do, but we did it anyway. In the end, she seemed to be able to persuade most people to do her bidding and they did it gladly.

"Is Brianna with her?"

"Yes, and Mrs. Roderick."

I glanced toward the door, looking into McCallen's empty office. As much as I didn't want to speak to him about our personal issues, he had work to do. He needed to talk to Mrs. Blunt and the doctors at the German hospital. If we were going to have another presser, he needed to be the one to arrange it with them.

"Let me know when McCallen gets here, will you, sir?"

"Of course," he said, fingering his charm.

"You're not still worried something is going to happen are you?"

Jerreau raised an eyebrow at me and went back to his desk.

I sat down next to Harry and we both watched as Owens scanned through tape, picking out the best shots and dropping them into his timeline. He was quick, his fingers flying over the keyboard. Harry watched his every move.

"It's like he's playing a bloody instrument," Harry said.

Owens seemed embarrassed by the attention. "Hey, Sergeant Harper," Owens said. "What's up?"

"I was wondering if you could show us the video from yesterday."

He made a face. "It's pretty gruesome. I had a medium shot of him when it happened. I've never shot anything like it."

"I'm not really interested in seeing the actual shooting. I'd like to see what you have of the stuff that happened before the press conference—the people in the room, who was there, that sort of thing."

He tried to hide it, but the look of relief on his dark face was hard to miss. I understood his sentiment. Some things were hard enough to see the first time. Since I knew he'd been required to prepare the footage for distribution when the release order came, I knew he'd already seen the gruesome scene over and over again.

"Sure. Captain Jerreau asked me to include Patrovski's still images with my video," he said, as he called up the file. "She had a lot more of the pre-event than I did. I only rolled for a few minutes before the conference started."

"Show me what you have. Did you edit anything out or is this the raw footage?"

"It's all there. Colonel McCallen said he wanted everything."

"Good. Go ahead and roll." The video started with a wide-shot of the back of the room, people milling around, conversing and looking for a spot to stand. The wide shot captured soldiers taking off helmets, greeting each other, a relaxed atmosphere of curious onlookers. Some of the people entering were the media role players who tended to walk in the room and continue forward to find themselves a seat. Their civilian clothes looked clean and crisp, as if they lived with all the comforts of home.

The soldiers appeared much different. Their grime-covered uniforms and dirty faces made them all look tired, as if they were ready for the end of the exercise; end-x we called it. The word, once uttered, spread from person to person like a virus, everyone quick to pass it on to the next person—the exercise is over, we're done, time to relax. Like me at the time, everyone had attended the press conference knowing it was the last major event before end-x was called.

Then Newberg entered. He pushed his way into the room, followed by Beechwood, Pratt, Eldnik and a couple others, one of them a Captain. I wondered if he was Garron, the poor man who had lost his life in the jump accident, but couldn't get a good look at his name. They came in, one after the other and stood in a cluster, talking, observing. Newberg seemed to interact with the others as if nothing unusual was about to happen. He stood closest to Beechwood. Occasionally, their exchange was exclusive, words spoken only between the two of them. Newberg seemed calm, at ease. Not at all a man who was about to commit murder in a public spectacle.

The video wasn't focused on the Rangers. They clustered at the side of the room, only in the shot as Owens slowly swept the entire area for only about thirty seconds. After that, the image swung to the front of the room where Owens zoomed the shot all the way in, focused, then zoomed out and locked down, waiting for the press conference to start. The video then skipped to Major General Blunt stepping up to the podium.

"You can fast forward through this," I said, not wanting to see the bloodshed.

Owens seemed relieved to scan forward, making the video of the shooting blur past.

"Stop it there," I said. Owens returned the video to normal speed. There was shouting, the camera jostled as people ran past where Owens's camera sat on its tripod, but he'd managed to follow most of the action. There was Newberg, sprawled on the ground, three soldiers on top of him, wrestling his arms behind him. I remembered that he'd immediately dropped the weapon, hadn't put up much of a fight. He lay on his stomach, unperturbed as everyone moved frantically around him, the sounds of disbelief intermingled with sobs from some of the media role players brought back all of the anxious moments I'd felt during the event.

"What is he looking at?" I asked.

Newberg's gaze wasn't directed at Blunt, who lay outside the shot. He seemed to be looking behind him, straining his head up, a look of...what? As if he were asking some sort of question? Eyebrows raised, pleading, looking for forgiveness perhaps, maybe even a ghost of a smile on his face as if he were pleased with what he'd done. All I could do was guess, but there was something about his expression that gave me chills.

"The guys he came in with were all standing over there, I think," Owens said.

"His expression is completely creepy."

Owens chuckled. "A perfect way to describe it, Sergeant Harper." He played the tape again and again, allowing me to confirm that he was looking in the direction where the Rangers stood. I wanted to know what he'd been thinking at that moment.

"Did Patrovski get their reaction? Are there any pictures of the Rangers looking back at him?"

Owens blushed, and a bit of sweat broke out on his forehead. "The more I look at my footage, the more embarrassed I am," he said, looking away from me. "Patrovski was really smart."

He showed me the stills she had captured directly after the event. It was as if by instinct, she knew the shooting meant a total picture of the scene was the most important. Owens had kept a medium shot of the men restraining Newberg, their struggle, Newberg's expression, while all of the activity in the room had happened around them.

Patrovski, who had taken some beautiful close up shots of people before and during the press conference, had suddenly gone wide, shooting larger portions of the room. She must have clicked off a hundred shots in rapid fire, like an M16 on full auto. In three-round bursts, she took in as much of the room and the chaos as possible.

I turned to Owens and smiled. "It's experience," I said. "You won't make that same mistake again."

"No, I won't" he said, shaking his head.

He toggled through her images, giving each one about twenty seconds' worth of video before moving on to the next. While the Rangers were not the focus of her shots, because of the wide angle she chose, she managed to capture some of them in the periphery.

One shot that drew my attention showed Sergeant Major Eldnik leaning forward as if he wanted to rush in to help restrain Newberg, but Beechwood and Pratt held him back. Eldnik's face is red with shock, his mouth open as if he were shouting. Pratt, with eyes wide, looked as if he had to strain to hold Eldnik back. Beechwood had his sergeant by the arm, his lips pressed into a line. I kept staring at his image. Did he look shocked? Was there a note of surprise on his face? Or was that revulsion? While everyone around him seemed to be transparent in their reaction, I couldn't tell what Beechwood might be thinking.

The images progressed in Patrovski's rapid-fire way until we landed on one that showed Eldnik, with both hands on top of his head, looking helpless and paralyzed with disbelief. His emotions clearly etched on his face. Beechwood and Pratt are looking at each other, some kind of silent communication going on.

After that, Patrovski's images didn't include them anymore.

It seemed clear the men who had come with Newberg, had no idea what had been about to happen. I asked Owens to scan back to the beginning and, after watching it a few more times, I started to have doubts. Did that expression on Beechwood's face mean anything? Why did Pratt and Beechwood stop Eldnik from rushing forward to help? Isn't that what Rangers do? What did that communicative look between Pratt and Beechwood mean?

I'm not sure how successful I was in hiding the frustration I felt at not having answers to any of my questions. The only thing I knew definitively was that spending more time with the pictures wouldn't clarify anything. My theories were all over the place built on nothing but imagination and suspicion. I finally had to step away from the edit desk as if propinquity to the images caused interference. Despite the distance, the questions continued to roll around in my head, first in one direction, then another, like the silver ball in a maze game, trapped by dead ends at every turn, the slightest tilt changing the game until the elusive center hole seemed further away than ever.

Games can be fun and diverting, but the more I looked into this one, the more I became convinced that I was completely ignorant of the rules.

CHAPTER 21

OWENS HAD SWITCHED SEATS with Harry, showing him how to make easy edits, dropping shots into a timeline, moving audio to fit the images. Harry quickly understood the basic concepts, but scratched his head at most of the technology.

"You make it look easy but it's definitely not that," he said to Owens.

"They sent me to school for months to learn this stuff, but I didn't really know what I was doing until I started working for Sergeant Harper. She's a master at this stuff," he said.

"Thanks, Owens," I said and smiled at the surprised look on his face as he realized I'd been listening in. He flicked a shy smile my way.

"Well, it's true," he said.

"You're a talented broadcaster, Owens. Don't let anyone tell you any different." I would have said more, but heard the front door slam. I excused myself from Harry and Owens, hoping it was McCallen coming back. We had a lot to talk about, but I had plenty of reason to want to avoid him as well. I went to the door of the office and caught him removing his cap, looking toward me with the same level of reluctance I felt. He froze, his lips pressed together.

"Sergeant Harper. A moment please," he said, motioning me follow him to his office. I stepped in and purposely didn't close the door behind me. When he turned back to me from behind his deck, he noticed the door had been left open, but he didn't say anything, just clenched his teeth and sat down, hunching his elbows onto his desk.

I didn't know what he wanted to talk to me about but I knew what subject I wanted to avoid, so I started first.

"Owens has finished his editing and put together this DVD for CID."

"Ramsey called me looking for this," he said, taking the disk and laying it on his desk, before clasping his hands together, his knuckles white.

"Captain Jerreau tells me you may need to have a conversation with the German doctors. It might be a good idea to invite them to join us for our press conference tomorrow so they don't hold one of their own."

"Already done," he said. "It will be the German doctors, Mrs. Blunt with Brianna at her side. General Roderick will not attend and I've decided to take this one. I don't want to send Jerreau in there with everything that's going on. I'm told Trent might be released by then as well."

"The team is prepared, sir. The press kits are already made and Jerreau has good talking points." When he continued to stare at his clenched hands I took the opportunity to make an exit.

"If there's nothing else, sir. I'll see you in the morning," I said, already moving toward the door.

"Sit down, Sergeant Harper."

The impatient note in his voice made me want to object, but I decided what the hell? Playing the avoidance game wasn't working. I sank into the metal chair in front of his desk. He leaned back, staring at me, a cool, professionally detached look. Then his gaze flicked around the room as if he'd come to a decision, one he wasn't comfortable with.

"You know that I served under Blunt for three years when I was a captain, right?"

"Yes," I said, hiding the surprise I felt at the subject he raised.

"He was a Lieutenant Colonel at the time. A hard charger. Promoted ahead of his peers. Everyone knew he was headed for star territory."

I nodded, listening. It felt as if he was working himself up to something and he needed time to get there.

"There were...rumors." He fidgeted. It was that kind of fidget people have when they're about to impart what they consider to be gossip. Things they'd heard, unsubstantiated rumors. I could tell he didn't want to speak ill of the man he admired. He needed a bit of prodding.

"If it has anything to do with what Newberg did, it could be helpful colonel."

"I wanted to tell you this earlier but ..."

He didn't have to finish the sentence. All of our emotional crap had gotten in the way. Like his declaration of love, his announcement of his retirement and divorce and his plea that I give him a chance. Any one of those things had been enough to divert us from the most important subject—why had Newberg tried to kill Major General Blunt?

"Well, you can tell me now, sir."

He sighed, settled himself. "There were these rumors that being around Blunt meant bad luck, especially if you had something he wanted. There was one story from very early in his career, about how Blunt had been on the waiting list to go to airborne school. The first standby. Someone who had a slot broke his leg in a training accident, and Blunt took his place."

"That's why they have standby lists, isn't it? To make sure the class is full."

"Sure, and if that was the only thing, no one would have paid attention. But there were other things."

He looked out the window, still having a hard time meeting my gaze. The outside lights made his eyes luminous, such a bright blue it seemed as if a sunny sky was reflected there instead of a moonless evening. His gaze flicked to me and away and he continued his story. "When I was a captain, Blunt was trying to get into War College. He'd been offered a slot in the distance learning course, but he wanted to go to Carlisle Barracks, to be in the full-time resident course. He talked about it all the time. Even when he was told he'd have the distance learning slot, he said he would end up at the resident course. And he did somehow. I don't know how he worked it, but his orders were changed, and he went to the school. That was the last time I worked for him, before I came to work for him here."

"Are you saying he has pull somewhere? Someone who can make sure he gets the things he wants?"

Neil rubbed his eyes, his shoulders slumped as if he couldn't carry the weight of what he'd just said.

"Part of me doesn't want to believe it, but..."

"Neil, all of this could be important. You know that, right?"

"I overheard him," he said, a quiet mumble I almost didn't understand.

"You heard him?"

"A couple months ago. It was late. I'd gone up to the command group offices to see his aide. I didn't expect Blunt to be there, but he was. He was in his office, but the door wasn't closed all the way. He was on the phone with Trent and he was angry. It stuck with me because he never got angry like that, to the point where he was yelling at the kid."

I nodded in understanding. Blunt wasn't the yelling type. "How did you know it was Trent?"

He gazed up at the ceiling for a moment, took a deep breath then fixed me with an intense stare. "He said...well, he yelled it. He said, 'you have no idea what we went through to get you into that school, boy. Most of it wasn't even legal.'" He shook his head. "It could have just been a figure of speech."

"Right, an exaggeration to make a point or something," I offered.

"Maybe," McCallen said. The angry flush to his cheeks told me he had more to say. "The point is, if he pulled strings to get his kid into the academy. If he made some kind of underhanded move to get his son in..."

"Then Trent took the place of someone more deserving," I said, finishing the thought.

"What I'm saying is Blunt doesn't like it when he doesn't get what he wants. What I heard, plus the other stuff, people suddenly injured. People who withdraw from a course or a job he wanted. His promotions always came ahead of schedule and he's spent more time in the Ranger Regiment than most. Most of it is all just rumor but, after what I heard, I'm not sure. From the outside at least, the man seems to have had a smooth ride toward everything he wanted."

He stood and walked to the window, his hands buried deep in his pockets. "He may never wake up, Lauren. It sucks to have this kind of talk swirling around a man who could end up dead or disabled for the rest of his life."

"But, Neil, what if he had something to do with a guy getting his leg broken or with people bowing out of jobs or classes he wanted? That's all kind of sketchy, isn't it?"

"Sketchy yes," Neil said, turning back to me. "But like I said, they're just rumors. Maybe Blunt is just incredibly lucky. Up until now, that is."

"Have you spoken to Chief Ramsey about this?"

"I gave him a statement right after the shooting, but they haven't made it around to me again, yet. So, no. I haven't said anything to him and I don't plan to. I'm telling you."

"But you have to say something. You don't know if it could be important."

He crossed his arms, a sure sign he was going to be obstinate about it. "I'm not going to put rumors like that into the official record. You know those CID guys. You tell them if you must."

"The information doesn't do any good coming from me."

"Because it's probably not worth repeating. Newberg tried to kill General Blunt, end of story. I don't understand what other questions need to be answered here, but you've been curious about it so I told you. That's it. If I had my way, you wouldn't be involved in this investigation in the first place."

"Bloody well, right," Harry said from behind me. I spun around to find him standing in the doorway. He didn't look at me, only stared past me at McCallen.

My gaze bounced between the two men. As far as I knew, they hadn't spoken to each other since Harry first arrived. The tension in the room was palpable. They locked gazes, both wearing neutral looks on their faces, no sign of friendliness, anger or disdain. Somehow, those blank looks seemed aggressive, both men refusing to look away from the other, refusing to broadcast their next move. They were both skilled warriors. Standing between them as they practically breathed fire on each other was uncomfortable.

I stood and put my hands up, arms outstretched between them as if pushing them away from each other. "I get that you're both of the same opinion, but the last thing I need is the two of you ganging up on me." I said it with a smile in hopes of breaking the tension. It didn't work.

McCallen circled his desk, removing the obstacle between him and Harry. "We may agree about this, Fogg, but only one of us has any authority to have an opinion in the matter."

Harry's gaze darkened. If I thought there had been tension before, now the room crackled with it. He took a step further into the room. "Then why don't you use that authority of yours and keep her out of this, mate?"

"I'm not your mate, pal."

"Okay, let's just step back a minute," I said.

"You shouldn't even be here," McCallen said. "I'm only allowing it out of respect for her."

"Trust that I'd much rather have her away from the likes of you," Harry said.

"Hey, I'm standing right here."

They were inching closer to each other, veins protruding from foreheads, necks straining with tension and testosterone levels pinging off the charts.

"She understands her mission comes first," McCallen said, ignoring my interruption. "Being a man in uniform, I'd think you'd understand that as well. Or do they do things differently in your army?"

"Yeah, there might be some difference, sir," Harry offered the honorific in the most condescending way possible. "In her Majesty's Army, commanding officers don't go round asking their NCOs for a bit of slap and tickle."

"Okay, that's enough," I said, raising my voice to be heard. I waved my arms around so they'd stop focusing on each other and look at me.

Both men looked down as if just realizing I stood there.

"I'm not expecting you two to like each other, but can we at least get rid of the open hostility?"

The overwrought silence stretched, both men still bristling. Finally, Harry took a deep breath and stepped back, exhaling his tension. "I'll be out here," he said, before he left the room.

I turned back to Neil and found him staring at me, his face flushed with color. He ran a hand over his head. "I'm sorry," he said. "That was unnecessary."

"It's okay, sir."

He didn't like that I called him sir, his anger evident in the thin press of his lips. He stepped closer and spoke to me in a lowered voice. "I'm doing the best I can under the circumstances, Lauren. He has no idea what you mean to me—what this is doing to me."

"Then I'll try to stay out of your way, sir," I said, backing toward the door.

He closed his eyes for a moment, his fists clenched at his sides, nostrils flaring. When he opened them again, he seemed more in control. "Please inform Captain Jerreau what we discussed for the press conference. I'll be there in a minute to develop the agenda."

"Yes, sir."

"I don't want to fight, Lauren."

"Neither do I, Neil."

He searched my face and, after a long moment, walked behind his desk and sat down. "Close the door on your way out," he said, shuffling papers around and avoiding my gaze.

The dismissal felt final. Walking out, I felt as if I were making a choice, one I hoped Neil would understand, one that I hoped wouldn't completely ruin our relationship. I pulled his door closed taking care to keep it as quiet as possible.

CHAPTER 22

I SPOKE TO JERREAU, passing on the information about the press conference before going to find Harry. He sat on a folding chair in the main room, his elbows resting on his knees, a look of concentration on his face. His size and posture made me think of Rodin's, *The Thinker*, that bulky, bronze statue of a man who, even though rippling with muscle, seemed bent over with the weight of his pondering.

"I'm not sorry," he said before I'd settled into a chair. "That heart-sick look on his face. His superior attitude. It's plain that he's manipulating you. Bloody twat."

"Give me some credit, Harry. I think I understand him pretty well."

"Do you?" His intense gaze made me question my surety. "You understand that he feels you slipping away and he can't have that."

"There's no slipping, Harry. There was nothing to slip from. Besides, it's this investigation. It's got everyone on edge."

"On edge is it? Maybe he's thinking like I am and knows that nothing good ever comes out of you getting involved in these things. Why did you agree to help them in the first place?"

"It's not like it was planned," I said. "Besides, I feel like it's my…"

"Duty, yes. And I say bullocks!"

I was growing tired of having to explain myself, but I hated to have him angry with me. He sat stiff with tension, his green-eyed gaze penetrating. If there was anything that could knock this blossoming relationship off track, it was his annoying overprotectiveness. I understood his motivations, but I bristled at his doubts.

I had to remind myself that there'd been a time, after Bosnia and Honduras, when I'd needed and welcomed his concern, which drove him to call me almost every night.

I'd been through hell and back. Bosnia—well, I'd lived through a woman's worst nightmare. Honduras had been worse, not in terms of my physical injuries, although they had been bad enough. Men had died. Families had been torn apart, and yet I lived. There were days when I could go about my business—go to work, wash the dishes, pick out the best produce at the commissary. On other days, breathing felt like a difficult chore.

And sleep. Sleep was a luxury for people who were more deserving than me.

Harry seemed to know exactly when to call, different hours, and different times, with some uncanny ability to zero in on when I needed it most. Our conversations focused on the mundane, car washing, what I'd eaten that day, the latest Hollywood news. But before we hung up, he'd always ask the one question that kept me going.

"What ya doin' tomorrow?"

It was as if he knew there was a chance I couldn't face tomorrow, and although I'd never said it to anyone, there were days when I felt like tomorrow was a step too far. Why should I live when others hadn't? What right did I have to take a man's life? That instant between life and death, the decision to halt the breath of someone, repeating itself over in my memory. Memories that sometimes made me double up in pain.

Harry's question, though so simple, had saved me. *What ya doin' tomorrow?* It made me think about tomorrow, and if there's anything universal about tomorrow, it's that there is always, no matter how slim, some kind of chance that it will be better than today.

I stared at Harry, the man who seemed to know me better than I knew myself. He reached out and took my hand, one that I realized was balled into a tight fist. He had to pull and tug to bring my fist closer so that he could kiss my knuckles. He allowed his lips to linger for a long moment before he stopped and rubbed his hand over my clenched fist. Eventually, my fingers relaxed and he stroked them with his long and callused ones.

"I did a piss poor job of it in there."

"It did feel a bit like a showdown."

"Please, come closer." He grabbed the seat of my chair and dragged it toward him. "Look, I know I won't be able to get you to leave until this is settled and it seems we're no closer to it being settled than we were a day ago." He stopped, his clenched jaw jumping in his cheek. He stared at the floor and went on. "I just want to get us the bleedin' hell out of here."

"I had no idea you were so uptight about it."

"You had no idea? I'm going out to the box to do patrols and urban warfare games just to give myself something to do before I become a lunatic."

"I thought you wanted to go with Eldnik."

"You think I want to hang out with a bunch of stinking blokes out in the dirt of the box? I want to be with you in a room that has the sound of the ocean coming through the windows. I want to wake up at our leisure, with a bit of sand in the sheets. You've made it clear that I can't have that until you're done with this. So I have to wait for you, even though I would rather spend time feeding you grapes and having you rub tanning lotion on my back and... other bits. "

"It sounds heavenly. I can hardly wait, Harry."

He consulted his clasped hands where his knuckles were white with tension. "We were so close. So close to getting away like we'd planned."

"Harry, it's not like I had a choice ..." But I stopped talking when I saw his gaze turn dark with anger.

"Blunt is your commander. Noted. And things are looking sketchy and you have so many questions. Yes, it's all true. But this is not your job. You are not an investigator and yet you've allowed them to convince you otherwise."

"I didn't really have to be convinced, Harry." I tore my gaze away from him and thought about the exercise we'd just completed. Just a few days before there'd been thousands of men and women in the box. The exercise had stretched our limits, exhausted us, but in the end, we'd come through it all with a feeling of accomplishment and unity. The mission, the tests, the successes and failures of a major exercise are all designed to lead to one thing—to draw everyone closer, to develop a sense of family, a connection with people you grow to respect for playing their part in the collective machine. The exercise gave us the knowledge that, if called upon, we'd be ready, together, to answer the Nation's call. Blunt had been in charge of it all. He'd always been a demanding but fair leader, a man who didn't tolerate excuses but who stood up for his people and accepted accountability for failure even though it was rarely necessary.

"We're here because of that word that plays such a big role in both of our lives. Duty. Don't pretend you wouldn't feel the same sense of duty to your unit, to your men that I do, Harry," I said, turning back to him.

"We always say it's our duty, Lauren, but that's never the only reason. Duty is the excuse we use when we don't want to admit how much we love the job with all of its demands and degradations. We love being in uniform, you and I. I get that." He stopped and took a deep breath, bracing himself. "I'm just keen to know that it isn't something else keeping you here."

He hesitated, opening his mouth to speak and stopping to rethink his words. "Lauren, is it...? I know you've been through hell and back. Is this too soon? Is it being with me? Do you need more time...?

"Harry, no. I've been looking forward to this for months. I worried at first, of course. Especially after what happened in Bosnia, but being with you has been amazing. And I know this is the most time we've ever spent together. It was frightening to think about, but I'm not worried about that anymore. I want this."

He paused, his stare growing more intense, something like fear sparked in his eyes. "Are you sure? Because if it's the Colonel … are you delaying because you want to be near him?"

I grabbed his face with both hands, forcing him to look at me. "Hear this, Harry Fogg. My staying here has nothing to do with McCallen. Don't let that thought take root in your head. It is not him. Okay?"

He nodded his acceptance, but I didn't see acceptance in his gaze. "Then how can you stay here to work with those men? Especially those men?"

"Ramsey's an ass, but I think I can help them…"

"Oh bullocks!" He practically leaped out of his chair, his fingers balled tightly, his forehead wrinkled in a deep frown. When he could finally speak, his words came out harsh and accusatory. "Ramsey is so daft he's dangerous!"

"Harry…"

"He's a dangerous twat and you should stay out of it. This will only end in you getting yourself hurt. Again!"

I'd never seen him so angry. He vibrated with it, then began to pace, glaring down at me as I sat motionless, paralyzed by the intensity of his words, which exploded out as if he'd had them pent up for some time.

"Their response to putting you in danger is to issue you live ammunition? You're walking around carrying a weapon, Lauren. Does that not indicate that they think you might be in jeopardy?"

"Harry, how would you react if I got this freaked out about you doing your job? The scars on your body prove you've been in danger plenty of times. Are you going to give up that life because I'm worried about you?"

"That's different."

"In what universe?" I asked, my voice now matching his in volume. "Because you're a man?"

"NO! Because, I've patched you up, Lauren. I've had your blood on my hands!" He looked at his own hands, as if the blood was still there. "Have you any idea what that was like? And now you want me to stand by and watch you get yourself in the shit again?"

I stood, reached out to him, but he stepped back, his hands up to stop me.

"I'll bloody well help you, I will. Even if you're too bloody stubborn to admit you need it." He turned away from me for a long moment, consulting the floor, his back stiff with tension. When he turned back to me he was still angry, only more in control of it.

"But I'll not stand by and watch it this time. If you insist on doing this, I'm bloody well going to help you and have a say in how it goes. I'll go out to the box tomorrow and I'll see what I can suss out by talking to those blokes that know Newberg, tap into what my friend, Nick knows, but I want you to bleedin' keep me posted on what you learn. Everything you learn."

"Harry, I..."

"And I mean *everything* that you're up to." This he said with an accusatory finger pointed at me. "Don't leave me to find you tied up somewhere this time. Not again!"

His voice shook with the final warning, his chest heaving and his eyes glassy. I took a tentative stop closer to him and he instantly wrapped me up in a hug so tight I thought he would break me.

"I'm sorry, Harry. I'm so sorry." My words came out muffled, my face buried in his chest.

"I've seen death, Lauren. People I cared about. None of us are immune. In Honduras, there was a moment when I thought you were dead, when I saw you..." He stopped and shuddered, taking a deep breath. I squeezed him tighter. "I thought you were dead, Lauren."

"I'm sorry, Harry." It took several minutes for his breathing to become regular. When he released me, he stepped back, wiping a hand down his face. "Bugger all," he said under his breath.

It was hard to meet his gaze and for him to meet mine, our discomfort almost palpable.

"Just a couple more days, Harry. Then I promise, we'll leave whether this investigation is finished or not."

He nodded as if he didn't trust his voice.

"Just please, can we try to get through the next couple of days without you pulverizing my boss?"

He huffed his amusement and shook his head. "We'll see," he said, his gaze softening. We stared at each other for a long moment, a jumble of thoughts rushing around in my head. I wanted to reach out and touch him but knew it would only fuel the heat I already felt. And then a thought made me smile.

"What has tickled you?"

"I think we just had our first fight."

He grinned. "Oh, that wasn't a fight."

"Was too."

"Was not. Do you want to fight about this, too you bloody stubborn woman?"

"Ha, so you agree it was a fight."

⊱⊰

I'D TAKEN A MOMENT to go into the office with the team, shut the door and apologize to them for the shouting match they must have overheard. Patrovski made light of it. Jerreau rubbed his charm and Owens just looked embarrassed for me. I said my goodnights and left, promising to be ready to help with the press conference the next day.

Harry and I returned to our hotel, exhausted but ready for more pleasant activities. We showered and changed in our respective rooms. When he came to collect me for dinner, he stepped through the door, then closed it with a deliberate push and we fell on each other in frantic need. He pressed me against the door, inched my dress up around my waist and slipped my panties off while he paralyzed me with a crushing kiss.

"Need you. Right bloody now."

I mumbled my approval before he took me. It wasn't just make-up sex, although we garbled apologies between other appreciative words. It felt more like an attempt to cleanse ourselves of the argument we'd had, to erase the sheer terror I'd felt at the prospect that he might have been hurt or worse, and to demonstrate why I simply had to accept his propensity for overprotectiveness.

If we had been anywhere else, we would have ordered room service and spent the rest of the evening naked, but the little bed and breakfast didn't offer it, so we went down to dinner preoccupied with returning to our room as soon as we'd satisfied the other kind of hunger.

Our second evening together felt strangely familiar, not because it was our second evening, but because it felt as if we were both exactly where we should be; with each other discussing the day we'd had and the day to come.

"I could get used to this," Harry said, sitting across from me.

"Me too."

The long seconds we spent grinning at each other over this simple statement should have made me feel silly, perhaps a bit embarrassed but I wasn't and, I could tell by the look in his eye, neither was Harry.

Since we both had a full day scheduled starting very early, we talked about mundane things, like what time we would get up to ensure he wasn't late for his trip out to the box, what time I would pick him up later, the general logistics, everyday conversation that warmed my heart with its ordinariness.

And beneath all that ordinary, I knew I had it bad. The heart pounding, gut-wrenching, mind-numbing, new relationship dizzies, and it was so very frightening—more frightening than any emotion I'd ever felt before. In movies and books, women in love always seem so happy, as if love were this wonderful experience that made you want to dance on air. I didn't feel light or buoyant or jaunty. In fact, the pull of gravity seemed multiplied, as if I were recently returned from space and unfamiliar with how difficult it was to walk after being weightless for months on end.

I looked at him across the table from me and wondered if he had any idea how thoroughly and completely he owned me.

Even though we kept the dinner conversation light, the remainder of my mission lurked like a predator—the kind that liked to toy with its prey before devouring them. I'd somehow, without really agreeing to, allowed myself to be dragged into sorting out the mystery behind Newberg's motives when I should have been focusing on the new man in my life and our first vacation together.

Why would Newberg attempt to kill the commander of American troops in Europe in a room full of witnesses? Was the motive money? Revenge? Jealousy? Or some larger political or military reason? None of them seemed plausible, especially not the political one. If he'd had a reason like that, Newberg would be using the media attention to broadcast it to the world. No, it had to be something else. Something more personal.

Newberg wasn't a crazed killer. He seemed rational, calm and alert. He'd not had any tragedy in his life, no problems with his career. If he was gay, as I suspected, then he'd kept it fairly hidden. Since he'd been a Ranger and served with the same men over and over again, they either knew about his sexuality and didn't care or he'd been masterful at keeping his sex life to himself. I wondered which of those were true.

The lingering questions buzzed in my head like an annoying mosquito, the aggravating noise growing louder, making me think the answer was in reach, only to have it retreat again to a safe distance. I kept swatting at it repeatedly, but kept missing.

As my brain buzzed away with my unanswerable questions, Harry and I stared at each other over the table. We'd practically inhaled our food, each of us ordering an entrée and sharing them in halves. The after-dinner cheese and fruit plate sat before us as Harry poured the last of the wine.

"I really missed you today," he said. "I mean really missed you. I'll be feeling the same thing tomorrow."

I smiled. "Well, we'll have to make sure that your absence is worth it. I was thinking we should come up with some CCIRs."

Harry grinned, brought my fingers to his lips and kissed them. Then he leaned back and took a sip of his wine. "Now you're talking, love."

A Commander's Critical Information Requirements—the information necessary to develop plans for a mission can be collected from a wide range of sources. In our case, we would be using HUMINT—human intelligence—information Harry would try to get from Newberg's Ranger buddies.

"It makes sense to have a plan for what are the most important bits," Harry said.

"No one's going to come right out and say Newberg did it because of A or B."

"Unlikely."

"So, we come up with a list of possible factors—trigger points if you will—that could indicate why he may have done it."

"And we identify other blokes in the unit who may know his reasons."

"Exactly. We know the men who came to the press conference with him, but one of the CCIRs could be what his current relationship is to those men."

"And if they had any notion of what he was about to do," Harry said.

"Another thing I've been wondering is if Newberg is gay, did the men know?"

"Bang on. That's something I'm sure Nick would be able to tell me."

We went back and forth like that, bouncing ideas off each other.

"That fact that Nick and I are mates should help to make some fast friends. Might help me wring some information from the blokes."

"What trust doesn't do, I'm sure your natural charm will make up for."

He smiled and reached across the table again to bring my hand to his lips and kissed it as if we were characters in some Jane Austen story. It felt like a very British thing to do. But the simple gesture surprised me with how many ways I reacted to it. I loved how tiny my hand looked in his, how deeply he stared at me, and how that gentle brush of his lips stirred me.

Could I be anymore pathetically enchanted by this man?

"I appreciate what you're doing, Harry. Going out to the field with these guys, I really do. It just feels as if you're heading into the lion's den."

"Worried about me, are you?"

I felt the heat rush to my face. "No more than you are worried about me."

"As unpleasant as I know the feeling is, I like that you care enough to worry."

His words hung like a magnetic pull between us, drawing us closer to each other. My lips parted in anticipation as I focused on the warm look in his eyes, his desire for me evident in his deep gaze.

And then my phone grumbled.

I squeezed my eyes shut in frustration. When I opened them again, he sat back in his chair unsuccessfully attempting to cover his amusement. "If that's that Ramsey bastard throwing a wobbler again..."

I wanted to ignore the grinding buzz that made my clutch slowly vibrate its way across the table, but, no matter the time, phones are answered in my business. Harry and I exchanged smiles while I picked up the call. "Harper, here," I said with a heavy sigh.

"What's this I hear about your boyfriend going out with the Rangers again?"

"I'm fine, Chief Ramsey. How are you?"

"Don't try to change the subject." He didn't sound angry, more like he knew whatever he said would have little influence on the situation. I could tell by the echo that he had me on speaker phone.

"Who's in the room with you?"

"Hello Master Sergeant Harper," Santos said. "I will start with a proper greeting, if my partner won't."

"Always a gentleman," I said smiling. I motioned that Harry should move closer to me, so he stood and brought his chair next to mine then leaned in so he could hear the conversation. I didn't want to put my phone on speaker in the small restaurant.

"You see? Subject change," Ramsey said, frustration coloring his words. "What about this thing in the box tomorrow?"

"We told you earlier that Sergeant Major Eldnik invited Harry. They're old friends. Do you have a problem with that?'

"Don't matter if he has a problem," Harry said. "I'm going."

"Oh, so he's there too?"

"Cheers," Harry said.

"Well, you need to be careful, that's all. I don't want you to reveal anything we've already learned."

"Oh yeah. And exactly what is it you've learned so far?"

Ramsey paused for a long moment, demonstrating that we knew next to nothing. "That's not the point. We're still interviewing people."

"Speaking of which," I said. "When did you plan to interview Colonel McCallen again?"

"It's low on my priorities," Ramsey said. "We've been…"

"You've been missing the opportunity to learn something interesting," I said, knowing Neil would be pissed that I refused to give up the information myself. "Ask him about Blunt's past. Ask him about training accidents. And ask him…"

"If you know all this stuff, why don't you just tell us?"

I sighed. I could tell them about Blunt and the way he seemed to get everything he wanted, but I was sure Ramsey would brush it all off as rumor and coincidence. If the investigator heard the information coming from a colonel instead of an NCO, he'd give it more credence.

"I only know enough to recognize its significance. McCallen is the one with the personal knowledge. Get him to tell you about it. You may have to be…persuasive."

"Rest assured," Santos said. "I will have him in as soon as he is available. Anything else?"

"Wait a minute. Who's running things here?" Ramsey said, like a spoiled child.

"She seems to be coming up with useful information."

I chuckled. Arguing with Ramsey was always a losing prospect. "Why did you call me, chief?"

"Why did I call...?"

Santos mumbled something in the background.

"Oh yeah. Cadet Trent Blunt is being released from detention in the morning. Mrs. Blunt has asked that the press conference be delayed until thirteen hundred. Your colonel has agreed."

I exchanged looks with Harry, finding it significant that I received the news from Ramsey and not my boss.

"Thanks for the heads up."

"But you aren't telling her why Mrs. Blunt wants the delay," Santos said.

"I'm getting to that." This time it was Ramsey who cleared his throat.

"Wait," I said. "Don't tell me."

"She wants Trent and her daughter standing by her side during the press conference."

"Shit." I rolled my eyes. If Mrs. Blunt wanted her son with her, the focus of the media would shift to him and the charges against him. Maybe McCallen could talk some sense into her.

"Okay," I said. "Thanks for letting me know. I assume you've already told McCallen this."

"Yes, he is aware," Santos said.

Ramsey's voice diminished as he walked away from the phone. "Huh. I thought she'd be more upset," Ramsey said. He sounded disappointed.

"I'll see you tomorrow, Chief," I said.

"Good night Sergeant Harper."

I tucked the phone back in my purse as Harry signaled for the waiter, I assumed to ask for the check. Instead he asked for another bottle of wine and another cheese plate. "Don't open the wine and wrap the plate so we can take it with us."

"Still hungry?" My words sounded breathless to my ears.

"Not at this moment, but I'm thinking I may be a bit later."

∽∽

I SMILED TO MYSELF as the sweat dried on my skin. We'd been more confident in our love making and had felt more comfortable to reveal our needs, any walls that may have been built out of nervousness or unfamiliarity quickly crumbled under the burden of our desire. I lay there listening to his deep breathing, replaying the things he'd said to me, the instructions he'd given and my eagerness to comply.

He'd wanted instruction from me as well and needed to hear my pleasure. He liked to watch me, to gauge my reaction, to see the results of his efforts. His gaze felt electric. I couldn't get enough of it.

We'd both been smiling at the end, Harry almost laughing, a joyful completion so satisfying it felt as if I'd been waiting for this, for him, my whole life.

From the moment I'd met him, Harry's presence had made me feel safe, protected. Even though we'd been through so much danger together, his strength still made me feel invulnerable. Making love to him only intensified those feeling, leading me to believe I could be damaged, hurt, wounded, whatever. It would only take an infusion of his potency to bring me back to life. And alive is what I felt when Harry was inside me.

When I woke sometime later, I smiled at the sound of his quiet snores, more like a rumble deep in his chest. I propped myself up on my elbow and watched the slow rise and fall of each breath. As much as I fought it, my thoughts drifted to the L word.

My mother would have said it was too soon. "Desire is easily confused with love," she would say. "If you feel the need to tell a man you love him and you don't have your clothes on, that's probably a good sign to keep your mouth shut. If you feel love for him after he's done something that pisses you off, you may be onto something."

As most of my mother's advice had been, her logic was undeniable. We had had a big fight and his overprotectiveness was infuriating, but I still felt the same way about him. That word was growing louder in my head. I wanted to call my sister to talk it over with her. She'd probably say the same thing my mother would have said, but somehow the deep feelings I had for Harry wouldn't be real unless and until I discussed it with her.

I settled myself back into his arms, my cheek resting on his chest. As I closed my eyes, trying to settle back into sleep, my last thoughts were that he would connect with the Rangers, find out what he could and I should stop worrying. It was Harry after all. Harry could handle just about anything.

CHAPTER 23

IT WAS STILL DARK when I dropped Harry off at the meeting point. Eldnik and the men stood milling about outside their barracks building. When Harry leaned in the window to kiss me, it was to a chorus of catcalls and whistles.

"Bloody plunkers," Harry said, smiling. He brushed the back of his fingers across my cheek, and looked like he was about to say something before he turned and joined the men.

I drove to the office missing him already.

Along the way, I stopped at the donut shop on post, picked up a dozen fat pills in the varieties I knew people enjoyed, along with five coffees, all sugared and creamed the way they liked and showed up bearing much appreciated gifts.

Everyone was up, bustling about, putting away cots, taking showers and thanking me profusely for breakfast and caffeine.

McCallen picked his usual cream-filled chocolate doughnut and his black coffee with one sugar and avoided my gaze. "Thank you," he said, already turning his back to me.

Twenty minutes later, Jerreau stood at the white board, with McCallen, Owens, Patrovski and me, scattered about the room listening to his plan for the upcoming press conference. Since it was similar to the one we'd already held, we only needed to discuss the choreography—who would speak first and what topics each person would cover. General Roderick would talk about the future of 8th Army. Ramsey would talk investigation details, not that he was willing to say anything new about it, and the German doctors would talk about the general's current condition, which wasn't good.

"The media advisory went out last night. We had to send another this morning changing the time from ten hundred, to thirteen hundred hours per Mrs. Blunt's request," Jerreau said. "We've called everyone who RSVP'd last night and I think we're good to go for thirteen hundred. We also developed this fact sheet that has the timeline, General Blunt's current condition, including what we think will happen next."

I took a peek at the document they'd put together. In bullet points they'd listed the shooting, arrest, Blunt's surgeries and condition status, the media advisories and the press conference we'd already held, all the current pertinent information about the event. My eyebrows went up at the clear and concise way they'd combined all the information.

McCallen didn't see me give Jerreau a thumbs-up while he continued to scrutinize the document.

"Good job," he said. "What else?"

"You have the talking points we developed for the fatal jump accident in case it comes up. Also, the statement which can be read in case questions about Cadet Blunt are raised.

I raised my hand, "Is there a speaking role for the cadet? I understand Mrs. Blunt wants him here.

McCallen turned to me. "I spoke to her this morning. Cadet Blunt will not be here."

At the news, everyone exhaled in relief and broke out in wide grins. Convincing Mrs. Blunt to leave her son out of the event was huge. "Thank you, sir." I said.

"I didn't do it for you."

His response was cold enough to freeze everyone in place. He stared back at me, unflinching and steady, then looked away, his face reddening. "Is there anything else?"

"No, sir," Jerreau said.

McCallen stood, tugging down on his uniform. "Alright, I'll be in my office if you need anything." He turned to leave and I felt everyone staring at me. At that moment, I was sure they all knew what had been going on between McCallen and me. I saw confusion from Owens and pity from both Patrovski and Jerreau. I couldn't look at them. Then McCallen stuck his head back in the door.

"And Captain Jerreau, you'll be taking this press conference. You're ready."

Jerreau stood with his mouth open, staring at the doorway where McCallen had stood.

I patted him on the shoulder. "He's right. You can handle it."

"But I…"

"You're ready, Captain."

He grabbed for the charm he wore around his neck muttering in French, then glanced at his watch. "I better call me mere and tell her I be on the TV again. She'll be so mad if she miss it." He gave me a brief smile then turned away, his fingers clutching his necklace.

"Can I speak to you, Sergeant Harper?" Patrovski said, pulling me aside. "Major Swenson had some information she wanted to pass on."

"Great," I said, motioning to follow me. I led her into the main room and sat down in one of the chairs they set up for the press conference."

When I turned to Patrovski, she had that pitying look on her face again.

"It's okay Patrovski. The colonel and I are having differences of opinion."

"Differences of opinion is it?" her raised eyebrows indicating she wasn't convinced of my description.

I smiled. "That's what I choose to call it anyway. Now, what did Major Swenson learn?'

Patrovski flipped through her notebook. "Quite a lot actually, but I'm not sure if any of it means anything. Major Beechwood and the shooter, Major Newberg, were roommates for several years while they were both captains at Fort Benning. After they finished branch school, they were both reassigned to different units. That was a few years ago. Also, at one point, Captain Pratt served as Newberg's XO during his first command."

It must have been a company command with Newberg in charge and Pratt as the executive officer. Those were usually close relationships, between a commander and his XO.

"So the three men know each other very well."

"It appears so," she said. "There are a few more on the list that are connected to each other, but they don't have the same kind of connection to Major General Blunt. But they're all Rangers, so, it makes sense, right? A three-week exercise, a course they took together, any kind of shared experience and any one of these guys could have become close with each other."

"True. We all have field exercise friendships."

"There was one major connection between Beechwood and the general," Patrovski went on. "Major Swenson says it was just an accident that she found it, but now she's searching through every class list from courses Blunt took. I can't believe she even came up with the idea."

"Okay," I said, smiling. "Major Swenson is brilliant. Now, tell me what she found."

"Well, evidently, Beechwood had an older brother...well, stepbrother, I guess. His mom was widowed with one child, then remarried and had Beechwood some years later. Nadine found it all by tracing next-of-kin notification paperwork and wills Beechwood filled out. Evidently, his mother likes Army men because both of her husbands were officers."

"Did Blunt know Beechwood's mother?"

"It's possible, but that's not what was interesting. Evidently, Blunt did know Beechwood's older brother. They were about the same age and went to a couple of different schools together...Officer basic was first, but then they went to Ranger training together."

"The Ranger course? Then they weren't just connected," I said. "They had to have known each other well." Knowing each other didn't mean they were friends, however. "I wonder if Ramsey and Santos know about that connection."

"It would be easy to miss," Patrovski said. "Beechwood's brother went by a different name. Samuels was his name. Christian

Samuels. When Nadine saw that Samuels' next of kin contact information matched Beechwood's, she made the connection."

Patrovski's broad smile communicated her pride and her love for her girlfriend. There was something about the name that sounded familiar. I rolled it around in my head thinking maybe I'd met him somewhere, taken a class with him, maybe a deployment. They were both relatively common names; Christian and Samuels. There'd been a Samuels in my basic training platoon, but that Samuels had been female.

"Where is Samuels now," I asked.

"Well, that's the thing," Patrovski said, with wide eyes and a whisper that added drama to her information. "He died. In some kind of training accident. When Nadine tried to get details, she was told the file is classified."

"Well, that's something," I said. "An accident could be classified for a lot of reasons. They could have been using tactics they wanted to keep classified, or if there was something classified about the location where the event happened."

"Or," Patrovski added. "Maybe the Army classified it to protect the people involved."

I let that roll around in my head for a minute. "We won't know if we can't get a look at those files," I said. "Did Major Swenson say when he died?"

"No, but I can ask her."

I thought about the training accident McCallen had just told me about earlier. The one that conveniently opened a spot for Blunt to get into airborne school. But it seemed a stretch. Would Blunt be willing to actually kill someone just to get into the class he wanted? And not just someone, but a person he knew well. That kind of cold blooded calculation seemed out of character for the general I knew.

"I'll have to see if Ramsey can get access to those files. He may be mostly useless but he at least has the authority to request information like that."

I was just about to offer to call the investigator when the sound of a slamming door drew my attention.

"Mrs. Blunt," I said, standing to greet her.

She stood ramrod straight, the rims of her eyes matching the bright red of her tailored suit. She pushed a lock of her platinum blonde hair back into its perfectly-coifed state before looking down her nose at me.

"Where's Colonel McCallen?" she demanded, her haughty attitude not hiding the puffiness of her eyes. Two women followed her inside. One of them, Melody Spencer, clutched a tissue with shaky hands. She wore her usual bohemian look, consisting of a peasant-style skirt, loose top and cat-eye glasses. The other woman, General Roderick's wife, Julia, crossed her arms and glared at Pauline Blunt, as if she didn't approve of her actions. Whether Julia Roderick approved or not, Mrs. Blunt was angry and she wanted everyone to know it.

I didn't need to call Neil out of his office. He'd heard the commotion and stepped out immediately to greet her. He stopped for a moment, trying to decide if he should shake her hand or hug her. He bent to offer her a hug but she stepped away from him and went to the door, pushing it open.

"Trent, get in here. Now."

"Oh boy," I mumbled. "This should be interesting."

CHAPTER 24

CADET BLUNT STEPPED THROUGH the door, his cheeks red, his face pale. You'd never guess he'd spent the night in jail. His grey West Point uniform looked perfectly pressed, his hair, when he removed his service cap, lay neatly combed with a stark part on the side. He stood taller than his mother, almost meeting Neil's height.

"Good morning, sir," he said. "I realize my attendance is unexpected and perhaps undesired."

Brianna pushed past him, rolling her eyes. "God, when did you get so stuffy? Mom's right. You need to be here." She turned and noticed McCallen for the first time. Her face flushed before she tucked her hair behind her ear and gave him a flirtatious grin.

"Brianna," her mother said, in reproach. "Go sit down or something."

Trent, ignoring the drama the women in his life presented, continued to direct his attention at McCallen. "I assure you, I won't make any comment, sir, unless you direct me to, but my mother has insisted I be here. I feel I must support her in her wishes. Especially now."

McCallen glanced at me, an eyebrow raised, then turned to the cadet and shook his hand. "We'll make it work," he said.

Mrs. Blunt smiled with pride. Despite her obvious grief, she'd taken the time to don the costume of a general's wife—a red power-suit, a short jacket with a small rounded collar, fabric covered buttons done up neatly over an A-line skirt that looked tailor made for her slender frame. Her sensibly-heeled, red pumps and a short pearl necklace completed the outfit. She wore matching pearl earrings and a massive collection of diamonds on her wedding ring and anniversary band. Her silver-grey hair lay perfectly in place despite the drama. Done up in a short and fashionable flip, her hair and clothing made her look like a woman accustomed to getting what she wanted.

"I still don't understand what that nasty little man was doing here. How could he have been allowed in here with a loaded weapon?"

While we'd all been carrying weapons of one sort or another, we'd only been issued blanks, but the nine millimeter ammunition was fairly easy to get your hands on in any civilian market. I started to explain that to her, but something else she'd said sparked my curiosity.

"Ma'am, I understand the family knows Major Newberg fairly well," I said.

Brianna crossed her arms and chewed on the side of her thumb, glaring daggers at me, but her mother didn't notice.

Mrs. Blunt's gaze flicked to the other women in the room, to the floor, then back at me. "Of course we know him," she said, wringing her hands. "We've known him for years. What I didn't know was that he was a crazy man."

When she met my gaze again she seemed to realize that her comment had drawn more interest than she'd anticipated. She pressed her lips together, pulled down on her jacket and seemed to wrestle for a firmer grip on her emotions.

She took a deep breath and brushed a wisp of hair away from her face, collecting herself. She glanced at Neil and hesitated, a shaky hand on his arm.

"Oh Neil. I'm so sorry I told you Trent wouldn't be coming today. But then I saw him this morning and ... well, just look at him. He must be here. Don't you understand?"

Cadet Blunt looked as if he wanted to find the nearest hole to crawl into, but his back remained straight, his service cap tucked neatly under his arm. He did look impressive in his uniform. As long as he could keep his mouth shut, his presence might not be so bad after all.

"It's okay, Ma'am," Neil said. "We've already prepared for the possibility of questions about his arrest. We can discuss them if you like."

Neil tentatively reached a hand out to her and steered her toward his office. She followed him with Mrs. Roderick and Melody Spencer following behind. Neil turned and asked Trent if he wanted to join them. Trent stepped close to Neil. "Not unless I have to, sir."

"It's okay, son." Neil said. "You can wait out here."

Neil closed the door as Trent and Brianna strolled about the room as if getting to know the place.

Jerreau came up next to me, a look of surprise on his face. "She may be right," he said. "That young man has charisma."

"He does have that. Too bad he's in so much trouble."

Jerreau furiously rubbed the charm around his neck. "Who are those other women?"

"One of them is General Roderick's wife, Julia. The other one is Mrs. Blunt's sister, Melody."

"She'd be pretty if she stopped covering her face with those heavy glasses and stopped wearing baggy sacks," he said. I looked at him, surprised that he'd noticed her good looks. He shrugged and stopped rubbing his charm long enough to shove a sheet of paper in front of me. "Here's the draft of my opening statement. I wanted to get your take on it before I show it to him. We've got less than an hour to get ready for this thing."

"This is good," I said, quickly reading the document. "Really good. I'm glad he's letting you take this. It's time for you to do the real thing. Are you nervous?"

Jerreau stared at me for a long beat, then shrugged, a crooked smile lighting up his face. "Mo bon," he said. "Mais, I got a bit of the faiblesse, me, but I be fine."

I wanted to ask him to explain what he'd just said, but he walked away fanning himself, leaving me to assume it meant he would handle himself well.

As Jerreau walked into the office, Owens and Patrovski came out to get the main room prepared. Owens set up a microphone at the front of the room, checking the sound, while Trent stepped in to help Patrovski straighten the rows of metal chairs.

"You don't have to do that, sir," Patrovski said.

"I'm not going to stand around watching you do it, Sergeant," he said.

I glanced at Brianna who rolled her eyes and folded herself into a chair as if to demonstrate her unwillingness to do anything.

We busied ourselves with all the details; sound, lighting, press kits, finalizing the opening statements and talking points. Neil came out of his office, closing the door behind him. "She's all over the place emotionally. I hope she'll get it together."

We looked toward the closed door as if it had the answers. Jerreau, McCallen and I reviewed the plan, Trent standing off to the side, listening in.

Someone at the gate called to say the German doctor, Herr Drexel, had arrived and that media were arriving and were on their way to our building. I sent Patrovski to get the doctor while Owens picked a spot to set up his camera on a tripod. Shortly after that, General Roderick entered the building, followed by his aide and others from the staff. Neil greeted them and invited them to join us in the office as we went over last-minute details.

I rapped twice on the office door and didn't wait to be invited before I opened it and was surprised to see Mrs. Blunt smiling at the two other women, her makeup and hair flawlessly in place.

She rose to greet General Roderick who gave her a fleeting kiss on the cheek before he moved over to his wife and gave her a big hug. They exchanged words in secret, but to the rest of the room, they simply appeared grateful to see each other.

Mrs. Blunt watched the embrace, her lips pressed together, her hands clenched at her side. I noticed Melody seemed to fade from the room, stepping back until she was pressed against the wall as if to attract the least amount of notice.

I called Trent and Brianna into the office, hoping to keep them sequestered inside until the time for them to step in front of the cameras.

We didn't have time for platitudes so I plunged ahead, providing the rundown of the order of speakers. Mrs. Blunt, at first, seemed surprised that General Roderick would speak. She flicked an annoyed glance at the general and his wife, a distinct note of tension in the air between the two women.

"This press conference is about my husband. I fail to see what General Roderick has to do with it." She turned to Mrs. Roderick and said, "I'm sorry, Julia, but that's how I feel."

Julia simply crossed her arms, her regal bearing evident in the upward tilt of her nose. General Roderick addressed Mrs. Blunt. "Of course this is about Preston, but I have to assure our audience that the 9th Army is still in good hands. If it were up to me, I wouldn't be here, but I have direction from the Secretary's office."

She seemed to pointedly avoid looking at Julia again. She gave General Roderick a slight nod who turned to me for the rest of the choreography. She seemed happy when she heard she would be saved until last.

"Ma'am," I said. "I'm sure you understand the need for us to talk about your husband's condition in very general terms."

She picked up a handheld mirror from the desk, checking her hair. "I'm well aware of how these things go," she said dismissively.

"It would be helpful," I said, forging on, "If you would only talk about the family reaction, your support for his recovery, that sort of thing."

She arched an eyebrow at me as if I were telling her things she already knew. While it may have seemed obvious, I'd been bitten too many times by assuming people understood their role during press conferences.

"Ma'am, while Brianna and Cadet Blunt are here, I'm sure you understand that we shouldn't be discussing any issues other than your husband's condition. If any questions are raised about Cadet Blunt's arrest, please allow Captain Jerreau to handle them."

She put the mirror down and tugged on her jacket, her fingers going to the small flag pin she'd attached to her collar. "Of course."

General Roderick took both of her hands. "I'm so sorry for all of this Pauline. I hope this will be the last press event you'll have to do. Then you can concentrate on Preston's recovery and caring for your family."

She stared at him wide-eyed, her mouth agape as if just realizing that the press conference would serve as a handing over of command. A formal ceremony would take place at some point as per military tradition, but this event, in front of the media and the world, scheduled to take place in just a few minutes, would serve as the last time she would be the commanding general's wife. Her gaze flicked to Melody who stepped out of the shadows, aware the implications. They hugged for several seconds then stared at each other, the tears openly flowing.

"Oh, we'll have to do your make up all over again," Melody said.

The sisters sniffled, attempted to find humor in the fact that they'd both come prepared with tissues and handed one to each other. The mirth was short-lived. They gripped each other's hands, their knuckles white. Melody took in a deep breath and attempted a smile. "We'll get through this, Pauline."

"This could go really badly," I said to Neil barely moving my mouth.

"Have faith, Harper," he whispered, as he stood in the door and scanned the room filling quickly with reporters, everyone shouldering and elbowing each other to find the best spot. "We've got the sympathy card. Even if she says something horrible, we can chalk it up to grief, shock, something like that."

"There are plenty of things we can say to excuse what comes out of her mouth," I said, still whispering to him. "But people will ask why we put her up there in the first place."

"Yes, there's that." He looked down at me, his intense blue eyes softened with a playful glint in his eye. He was so close, his breath brushed against my cheek. "But then, what do I care?" he said. "I'm retiring in a few months."

He turned back to glance at everyone in his office. "Ma'am, General Roderick, are you ready?" Mrs. Blunt responded with a curt nod.

"Let's do this thing," General Roderick said.

CHAPTER 26

I WENT BACK INSIDE, found a couple of stray reporters who'd decided to take their time. One of them tried flirting with Patrovski in a useless attempt to get information. Patrovski glanced at me and smiled as she escorted the man outside.

Jerreau sent another reporter out the door then turned to me. He looked exhausted.

"Glad that's over, me," he said.

"Colonel McCallen couldn't have done it better himself. You did an excellent job."

He flashed a rare smile. "Phew, thank you. My heart felt like it was on full auto the whole time."

"Well, you didn't look nervous at all. You remained in control, you didn't get rattled. You've seriously proven your abilities today."

"Thanks to you and the colonel. And now that it's over, and I can think back on it, it was kind of fun."

"I'm glad you enjoyed it because I'm sure this won't be your last press event. "

McCallen stepped up next to me, and smacked a warm hand of greeting on Jerreau's shoulder as if that was all the praise necessary for the good job he'd done.

"You did so well, the general has decided our job is done. We've been ordered to pack it up," McCallen said. "It's end-x. This time for real."

I opened my mouth to argue the wisdom of the decision, but he didn't let me speak. "I know, I know. It will look as if we're abandoning the Blunts, but I've given what advice I can. Roderick has chosen to return to Heidelberg and we have to go with him. Most of the command staff left this afternoon. The rest of them have been waiting around for us evidently."

Patrovski and Owens had heard the talk of the new plans. "I can be ready to go in an hour," Owens offered, sounding relieved to be heading home.

It never took us long to break camp once end-X was called, but the media calls had to be dealt with in some way. There was no way Mrs. Blunt and her family should be left to handle the brouhaha that was sure to continue to follow them. While I would have loved to grab Harry and get started on our leave, everything felt unfinished. What was all this about? Why had Newberg tried to kill Blunt? Was the jump accident an accident or a murder? As I watched Owens packing up his equipment, I felt torn, but there was really only one thing I could do.

"Sir, I think I should stay," I said.

"I knew you'd say that," he said. He crossed his arms and hunched his shoulders. "I agree."

"You do?"

"With you going on leave, I need Jerreau with me and Patrovski is too junior. Mrs. Blunt would eat her for lunch. No offense, Patrovski."

"None taken, sir," she said, already pulling packing cases out of their hiding places to accommodate our vast array of office supplies. She and Owens allowed the phones to ring and roll over to voicemail while they quickly moved to tear down operations.

"That leaves you," McCallen said. "You can stay up to forty-eight hours, help the Blunts do their media dance, but after that, you're going on leave. If they still need support, I'll send Jerreau back to take over. Does that sit well with you?"

"Yes, sir," I said, wondering why he was being so cooperative.

"By the way, the forty-eight hour deadline is a direct order from General Roderick. Do you understand?"

"Yes, sir."

"I think we satisfied the media mob for a while. You can use your discretion if you think the mission is complete prior to that time. I can't imagine you'd be needed for more than a day or two," he said.

"I'm not sure about that, but I hope you're right."

"Don't get me wrong. I don't like leaving you behind, but I have a feeling if I told you to leave now, you'd ignore me."

He was probably right about that. "You make me sound so..."

"Obstinate, hardheaded and insubordinate? Yeah. All of the above."

"Why not persistent or determined?" I sounded defensive even to my own ears.

"Unwavering," Patrovski offered.

"Resolute," said Jerreau.

Owens threw up his hands. "I got nothin'" he said.

We all laughed, probably harder than the joke warranted. At the end of an exercise, as the tension and pressure eased, it was typical to find things to laugh about. It felt good—to laugh with the team, like a release I hadn't had in a long while. I exchanged a look with Neil and felt a stab of nostalgia as his blue eyes locked with mine.

We all fell to packing up, now and then pausing to answer the phones. In no time, the room looked empty, save for my computer and a few spare office supplies I might need. The afternoon ran into the evening. Owens and Patrovski fueled up the two Humvees they would take back to Heidelberg and ran last minute errands. We'd missed lunch so we busted open a case of MREs and ate the Meals Ready to Eat while we answered phones; packed up our personal gear, cots, footlockers and field gear; and discussed issues we'd left back at the office.

The entire time, Harry poked his way into my thoughts. What was he doing? What had he learned? How had his day in the field gone? I checked my watch and began to worry that I hadn't heard from him. It had started to get dark. How long would he be out there?

I answered calls from several reporters. Most of them left frustrated by what we wouldn't say about the general's condition. One of the calls I took was from Melody Spencer.

"Pauline asked me to get in touch. I told her you couldn't do anything," she said, her frustration evident in her clipped words.

"What is it ma'am?"

"The security men assigned to us here at the hospital have been good, but keeping the media out has still been a challenge," she said. "We thought there were a lot before, but ever since Trent got into trouble, they've been ... well, we feel like prisoners here. There's paparazzi everywhere."

"I'm sorry you've had to deal with that," I said. "Is there any chance the general will be moved to Landstuhl soon?"

At least Landstuhl was on a military base and paparazzi wouldn't be allowed within the gates. There was a long pause as she sniffled and gained control of her emotions. When she did speak, her words came out in a whisper. "He's still in surgery and…well, it's not looking good. Landstuhl is probably not an option, at least for a few days. He's just so…diminished."

She couldn't go on. Despite her attempt to muffle them, I could hear her quiet sobs. I could only imagine her feelings at realizing her brother-in-law, the lifelong warrior, could end up a shell of a man.

"But Preston isn't the only reason I'm calling," Melody said. "I've tried all the numbers we were given but no one is answering. Pauline isn't happy with the lawyer they assigned to Trent's case. She seems far too young and inexperienced to be handling this. We're considering hiring a civilian lawyer, but we wanted to speak to the lawyers there first. Why can't I reach anyone?"

I cringed. I didn't want to be the one to give her the news, but someone had to.

"Ma'am, I'm afraid most of the corps staff are preparing to return to Heidelberg."

There was a long pause. "Oh. Oh yes, I see."

From the tone of her voice, it appeared as if she did see and understand all of the implications. "Does that mean we'll be left here alone?"

"Your security staff will stay with you of course, and the general's driver. I'll be here, at least for a few more days. The remaining headquarters staff are leaving in a convoy in about an hour."

Her heavy sigh communicated a range of emotions. "What am I going to tell Pauline?"

"I can call the hospital staff to see what we can do about the photographers. Maybe German law enforcement can keep them a few meters away from the doors at least, so you can come and go." I gave her my cell phone number for her to use in case of emergency. "And I'll consult with Trent's lawyer on the latest, but we've already given the media as much information as we can at this point. Calls are slowing down here, so I think we've placated them for a while. I'm sorry about the rest of the support staff."

"That's probably why Julia left a while ago," she interrupted, the anger dripping from her words. "Next thing you know, she'll be pushing us to move out of the house."

As cold as it sounded, I was sure she wasn't far from wrong. The Corps commander's residence wasn't just the largest military home in the area. The house came equipped with a resident security team, highly secure communications links as well as a small staff for cooking and cleaning. If I knew Julia Roderick at all, she would see living in the commander's home as a right which came with her new position as the first lady of the Corps. Who could blame her? The gratitude officers paid to their families during promotion ceremonies weren't just platitudes. Military rank was achieved through sacrifices made by everyone in the clan. General Roderick owed much of his success to his wife and family and it was clear from my brief meeting with her, that Julia Roderick felt the perks were her due.

For the Blunts' sake, I hoped she'd wait a while before sending the government movers to pack up the Blunts' belongings.

During my time on the phone, I turned to discover the room was now empty. Jerreau, Patrovski and Owens stood around as if waiting for the final signal to leave. I would be left with the entire building to myself, a phone, a few office supplies and an emptiness I could already feel.

And there wasn't anyone to blame but myself. What did Neil say? Stubborn, pigheaded, whatever. They all applied.

"I'm sure Mrs. Blunt will understand how full General Roderick's calendar is, how many things still need his attention ..."

Melody interrupted me again. "Bottom line is, the lawyers are gone and we're stuck with this young girl and have to trust her to help get these charges dropped."

"Who did they assign to you?"

"Captain Jacoby."

I smiled. They would have taken one look at Captain Laney Jacoby and underestimated her. Everyone did. It's what made her such a formidable trial attorney. Short, raven-haired, with a tiny frame and a soft voice, she looked about twelve. "I know her, ma'am. I think you should give her a chance. She's quite skilled and knows what she's doing, not to mention her German is excellent. If anyone in the Staff Judge Advocate office can win a case in German court, it's Captain Jacoby."

"Well, I suppose we don't have any choice at this point."

"You have my cell number. If you have any problems with the media there, please give me a call."

She thanked me and signed off. I sighed with the expectation that she and Pauline Blunt would call me for any and every problem they had, not just issues dealing with the media. I would end up being their secretary. I wasn't happy with the prospect but felt, under the circumstances, they needed all the help they could get. At least for a while.

When Neil came back to the office, I filled him in on the phone conversation, then, around five in the evening, it was time to say goodbye, which felt a bit awkward. Jerreau, Patrovski and Owens each shook my hand. "This is weird," Jerreau said. "You were supposed to be the one saying bye when you went on leave."

I didn't need the reminder. "You guys drive safe. I'll keep you posted about what's going on here."

Neil waited for the rest of the team to leave and for the door to close behind them before turning back to me. His gaze softened as he stepped close and looked down at me.

"Don't rule me out, Lauren."

"Neil, I..."

"I mean it. Let the idea that we could be together settle in there," he said, touching his finger to my forehead. "Give it some time and remember how many times you wished it were possible. If you do that and still tell me you don't want to make a life with me, I'll wish you all the best. But think about it first. Think about me retired. Think about me as a civilian and all that would mean." He stepped closer and leaned down, capturing my face in his hands. I should have pulled away from him, should have put a stop to it, but those thoughts didn't manifest into action. "No more restrictions, Lauren. No more obstacles to us being together."

"Please, Neil. I don't want to give you false hope."

He smiled. "God, you're so damn stubborn," he said before he pulled me to him and kissed me. It was a hard, but fervent kiss and there was no fighting it. It was as if I had no choice in the matter. I simply had to kiss him back. His arms tightened around me, pulling me up on my toes, my back arched up to him. Without me willing it to be so, my arms went around him, my hand to the back of his head until my fingers laced though his short auburn hair. He trembled against me and moaned his approval. And God help me, it felt so good. My head swam with the intensity of it. Memories flashed through my head of the frustration of loving him from afar, the long hours I'd spent wishing to be exactly where I was—in his arms, kissing him, being kissed, showing him how much I wanted him.

When he finally broke the kiss, we were both breathless, his face just inches from mine, his eyes intensely blue and shining. "God, you are beautiful."

He stepped back out of my arms and, as if in need of giving his hands some other task, settled his soft cap on his head, squaring it, pulling down on the brim to a perfectly rounded shade for his eyes, the silver eagle of his rank flashing in the subdued overhead lighting. I'd always loved the way he looked in that hat.

My thoughts in a jumble, I knew there was something I should say, something to clarify what had just happened, but my words, when I finally uttered them, seemed empty. "Neil, this doesn't change anything."

"Yeah, okay," he said. When I opened my mouth to object again, he smiled and didn't let me finish. "Just, call me later, Sergeant," he said, attempting to sound official. He brushed my cheek with his fingers, tracing lightly across my lips. "And take care of yourself."

He didn't wait for a response before he turned and walked out the door leaving me feeling dazed and ridiculous. I shook myself out of my immobilization and followed him to stand in the doorway as the team started up their two vehicles and drove away, the tires crunching over gravel.

CHAPTER 27

I WENT BACK INTO THE building, looking first to Neil's empty office, then straight ahead to the hollow space of the main room, devoid of everything save for the stacks of grey, folded metal chairs, and took a deep breath. My boot heels echoed back at me in the void of the large area as I crossed over to my office and sat down. The empty desks, the cleaned out corners and the quiet could have made me feel lonely, but I felt lighter, a bit buoyant. Neil's kiss had left me feeling muddled but only for a second. Part of me thought that I would always have some nostalgia for what had never been, but a greater part of me knew it was for the best.

With Neil gone, I could at least force all of that drama out of my head for a month or more. In forty-eight hours or less, whether the questions about Newberg and Blunt had been answered or no, whether the media had found some other story to concentrate on or not, I'd be leaving.

If we had stuck to our original plans, Harry and I would have been wrapping up our tour of Heidelberg and repacking for our trip for a leisurely month of sand and beach. We'd only booked a flight and a hotel in Athens. After that, our intention was to take ferries from island to island as the mood suited us. I called the airline, and used the excuse of military orders as a reason for a change in date.

"I'm still not sure when we will be able to fly," I'd said.

"We can hold the tickets for you. You may have to fly standby, but as long as we have a copy of your orders, you will be able to rebook."

After an exchange of the paperwork, the flight arrangements were made as flexible as we needed them to be.

"Thank you for your service," the ticket agent said.

Almost as soon as I hung up the phone, it rang again, a reporter with a request to speak directly to Mrs. Blunt. "A one-on-one interview," the producer said. "An opportunity for her to share her feelings." I politely but firmly turned the offer down explaining that she wasn't the first or the last to ask for such an interview. My guess was Mrs. Blunt wouldn't be ready to do a one-on-one until she returned to the states.

Not long after that, I received a text message from Brianna Blunt. *Plz dnt tell A. Melody what I told u. Plz!!!!!!!!!!!!*

I wondered why Brianna would suddenly have second thoughts about our talk. Something had caused her to use all those exclamation points. I didn't have to wonder long. The phone rang with Melody Spencer on the line, this time asking for help. "Can you come down here and talk to the press. It's such a distraction. I'm not sure how much longer Pauline can take it."

I assured her I'd be on my way as soon as I could. I hung up and stared at my phone, wondering if I should try to call Harry. I didn't want to seem too clingy but it was getting late. He'd been gone all day on what was supposed to be a few hours of exercises. Why hadn't I heard from him? Before my worried thoughts could get out of hand, my phone vibrated.

"I was starting to get concerned," I said.

He sounded tired. "It's been a longer day than I expected. I would have called sooner but I didn't have a signal until now." He paused, sounding as if he covered the phone with his hand, a teasing note back in his voice. "Were you very worried then?"

"You're creeping around in the box with a bunch of trained killers. I'm just a chair-borne ranger. Of course I worried. How was it?"

"A bit of fun but I wasn't expecting them to take it all so seriously. It was a full day of close-quarter combat, hostage situations—these blokes went all out. Still, I was able to talk to a few of them, and might have some interesting tidbits to share."

"Good. I'll look forward to hearing about it. I've got to go to the hospital for an hour or so. Can you wait that long?"

"Nick has asked me to have a drink with them. I wanted to check with you before I agreed." He chuckled. "Look at me. Asking permission. Bloody hell."

I smiled. "You have my permission. I can't wait to see you."

☙❧

ANYONE TRYING TO GET past a particular point in the seventh floor hospital hallway was politely stopped and told to go in another direction by the MP who stood on duty, his black and white brassard and side arm providing enough authority to enforce the detour. I had to flash my ID card and wait for the okay to be relayed over a radio before he would allow me to pass him and make my way toward the waiting area near the general's room.

Melody Spencer and Brianna sat side by side, looking like mirror images of boredom and impatience in uncomfortable looking chairs. Brianna flipped through a fashion magazine, never staying on a page longer than a second or two while her attention kept returning to the opposite corner of the room. Melody gripped an ebook reader but obviously wasn't paying it the least bit of notice, her gaze riveted to the same spot that had captured Brianna's focus.

Mrs. Blunt sat huddled over a small table with two other people, her harsh whispers, evidently, leaving them no room for input. Trent Blunt looked rumpled and exhausted in his West Point grey cadet uniform but he sat at attention, staring straight at his mother, his expression dark. His government assigned attorney, Captain Laney Jacoby had her hands clasped together on the table, her white knuckles and thinly pressed lips displaying her distaste for whatever it was Mrs. Blunt said.

Melody and Brianna seemed to notice me at the same time. Brianna rolled her eyes and sighed dramatically as if my appearance signaled the end of the world. Melody stood and motioned me to follow her down the hallway.

"I'm so glad you're here," she said, gripping my arm until it almost hurt. "You'd think Pauline would be grateful Captain Jacoby was able to get Trent out of jail, but she's so angry she can hardly see straight."

"What is it you need me to do, Ma'am?" I pulled my arm away from her as politely as possible. Her hand fell to her side clenched in a fist. She looked like a two-year-old about to cause a scene in a grocery store.

"I don't know," she said, attempting to whisper while wanting to scream. "Have you heard what they're saying about Preston in the news? Pauline sat here and listened to complete strangers discussing whether or not he should be taken off life support. It's … well, it's barbaric. Can't you do something about it?" She flapped her hands around as if fixing something in the news involved magical conjuring. "What is it you people say? Change the message or something."

I'd entered a side door of the hospital after seeing a handful of reporters and a couple of live trucks parked near the entrance. Two days after the shooting, Blunt's condition should have faded a bit from the headlines. The new hubbub brewed when all the outlets started quoting "a source inside the hospital." The leak, juxtaposed with sound bites from our press conference with the doctor earlier in the day, had made the story breaking news again and fattened the wallets of a bunch of medical experts ready to speculate that, from what the source had described, chances were Blunt would never recover.

"How true are the reports, Melody? Is he brain dead?"

It was a question I had to ask, but she didn't take it that way. She narrowed her eyes at me, grabbed my arm and yanked me further down the hall. There'd been little chance that anyone could have heard us from where we'd stood. It felt as if she had grabbed me as an alternative to some more violent action she'd wanted to take. I pulled my arm free with a jerk.

"Don't ever put your hands on me like that again."

"I'm sorry," she said, her eyes wide in shock at the furious nature of my words. "I didn't mean..."

"Yes you did. I'm here to help. I want to help, but I won't allow you to push me around as if I have to cater to your bidding."

"That's not what I..."

"Yes it was, and it's exactly what it looks like Mrs. Blunt is doing in there to Captain Jacoby. You and your sister need to come to terms with what is going on here. The general is no longer in command. Do you understand? I am no longer his subordinate and neither is Captain Jacoby. I'm here as a courtesy. Even if I was still under his command, you have no right to get physical or abusive with us."

Fat tears leaked from her eyes but she took a deep breath and squared her shoulders. She pulled off her glasses and wiped her face, then met my gaze in a steady stare.

"I'm sorry," she said. "I'm feeling a bit...helpless."

I deflated, realizing that I'd suddenly gone into Master Sergeant over-drive, my body stiff and my voice hard with indignation. These women needed my sympathy, not my anger.

"I have to ask again. Is the diagnosis they're talking about in the news accurate?"

Her nod was barely perceptible.

"Please explain."

She took in a shaky breath then looked toward where Pauline Blunt continued to harass Captain Jacoby. Jacoby attempted a word or two before being cut off by Mrs. Blunt's tirade again.

Melody's words dragged my attention back to her. "The surgery they performed today didn't go well. They say the only thing keeping him breathing is the ventilators. Dr. Drexel told Pauline that Preston was brain dead. He asked her about organ donation and ..."

She began to hiccup in violent sobs. I dug in my cargo pocket for a tissue, handed it to her and stood by awkwardly as she tried to regain her composure.

I glanced toward Brianna and found her staring at us. I gave her a head tilt to signal her over and she rushed to Melody's side, wrapping her arms around her. The two women stood huddled together sobbing, their matching heights and hair color blending them together until they were one grieving entity.

Eventually, they quieted, but remained in a comforting embrace.

I cleared my throat and they both looked at me. "Listen, I know this is hard."

"No you don't," Melody said, shaking her head, the anger creeping back into her voice. She and Brianna clutched each other for support, their tear-stained faces so similar, if not for age, they could have been sisters. "It's not just that Preston is dead. Believe me, we all know that. It's just…this changes everything, don't you see? With him gone, we're…we're no longer in the Army. How will Pauline ever come to grips with that?"

I crossed my arms and selfishly sighed with relief. I'd been about to tell them the same thing. The inevitable happened to every soldier's family, but they usually had time to prepare for it, to come to terms with a pending retirement or a decision to separate. Suddenly and without warning, Mrs. Blunt's world was about to change in profound ways. She would always be treated with the respect a general's spouse deserved, but it would be a polite respect. She'd be invited to some official events, but would be eliminated from most of the high profile occasions like State Department dinners or senior leader promotion ceremonies. She would no longer have a driver or assistant to help her keep house, she'd lose her catering budget to throw official parties and people would feel far less obligated to attend any event she chose to hold. She'd no longer have the focused attention from other spouses who would defer to her opinion, and since the Rodericks were already planning their move, in short order, she'd no longer have the commanding officer's quarters. She and her family would have to find somewhere else to live.

I felt relief that I wouldn't have to explain the harsh truth the women already understood.

"Believe me, Ms. Spencer. Ms. Brianna. I am aware of how hard this is. I'm no medical expert but I do know one thing.

Keeping the general on a ventilator won't stop any of those changes from happening." I laid my hand over their white-knuckled fists. "General Roderick is already the acting commander. The military cannot wait for you to finish grieving. I am terribly sorry."

Brianna brushed a lock of hair behind her ear and sniffled loudly. "Yeah, try telling that to my mom."

We turned to look at her where she continued to berate Jacoby. If I knew the young captain at all, I knew Laney wouldn't be able to hold her tongue for much longer. Trent wasn't being much help. His extremely short, military haircut left him an oval of dark, curly hair. The sides of his head, left cleanly shaven and pale, made the redness of his ears more prominent. Despite his obvious discomfort, he sat stiffly and allowed the rant to continue.

Suddenly, he'd had enough. "I'm telling you, it wasn't mine!" he shouted, standing and towering over his mother. Jacoby put a restraining hand on his arm. He halted himself, pulled down on his jacket and seemed to stand at attention, his gaze directed over his mother's head.

"I'm going to see my father," he said, before leaving the room, his mother staring after him in shock. He brushed by us in a rush. Brianna held a hand out to him, but he ignored her and marched into his father's room.

Jacoby stood, watching Trent's departure. When she turned toward Mrs. Blunt, her face red, I figured I might be needed if things grew too heated between them. I rushed toward them just as Jacoby let loose with what she'd been holding in.

"Mrs. Blunt, I realize this is a very difficult time for you, but I will only say this one more time. I am *not* your attorney. I am your son's attorney. He is an adult and I am legally obligated to do what is best for him. If you aren't comfortable with that, then I suggest you hire a civilian defense attorney. I can recommend several in the area who understand both UCMJ and German law. Would you like me to…."

"No. No, of course not."

"Then do you understand my position?"

"Of course I do." Pauline's voice sounded as if she were growing hoarse, her words coming out scratchy and strained. She sat stiffly, her jacket still tightly buttoned up, her hair still held perfectly in place without a stray strand. "But I don't understand why he is subject to the German laws. Doesn't SOFA apply here?"

Melody took Brianna's hand and they crossed the room to sit next to Pauline. Jacoby looked down and took a deep breath and paced as she explained.

"The Status of Forces Agreement between the U.S. and Germany includes provisions which gives U.S. military law precedence over German law for military members stationed here, but as I've said, since Cadet Blunt isn't stationed here and the incident happened off post, SOFA does not apply and the Germans have the right to maintain jurisdiction in this case."

Mrs. Blunt shrank in her chair, all the fight gone out of her. Melody took up the questions. "What will happen to him?"

Jacoby glanced at me before addressing the three women. "There is a slim chance that I can convince the German prosecutor to waive their jurisdiction. It was a very small amount of the drug, which is why they allowed his release and why we're not talking about distribution charges. Only possession. But to convince them to do that, I am sure they will want him to admit the drugs were his and Cadet Blunt is refusing to do that. German courts can be relatively lenient for minor drug offenses, especially a first offense, but if he refuses to cooperate, I am not sure what more I can do."

"I don't understand," Brianna said. "He won't say the drugs are his, even if it means he can go free?"

Jacoby held up a hand of caution. "No one said anything about him going free. Even if the Germans waive their jurisdiction, he'll still be subject to UCMJ and the military courts..."

"But surely the UCMJ would be better for him," Melody said.

Jacoby shook her head. "You'd better speak to my client about what I told him and what his options are. Right now, I have to go." She picked up her hat, hefted her fat briefcase and shot me a communicative look as she turned to go. Mrs. Blunt stood with a helpless look on her face.

"I'll be right back ma'am," I said and rushed to catch up with Jacoby. I caught her at the elevator where she punched the down button with more force than necessary.

"Christ, Harper," she said, directing her angry eyes to me. "Why do I always get these fucking cases? I knew this was gonna be a pain in my ass, but holy crap," she said, her voice lowered so only I could hear her. "They actually think he's gonna walk away from this? Possession is possession. Unless a miracle happens, his time at West Point is over. He'll be a private busting rocks at Leavenworth in no time."

"You really think that if he admits his wrongdoing, the Germans will relinquish jurisdiction?"

Her sigh dripped in exasperation. "Jesus." She pinched her nose between her eyes looking exhausted. "I'm saying that if he doesn't admit wrongdoing, there is no chance whatsoever of him getting out of this. He'll spend time in a German jail. Period. Even if he admits guilt, we're facing a steep uphill battle to get the Germans to allow any change of jurisdiction."

The elevator pinged, the doors slid open and she stepped in as if falling into the arms of a savior.

"What if he is innocent?" I said. She'd stepped to the back of the car and several people filed in around me as if I were an annoying obstruction. I ignored them and shuffled back and forth to keep Jacoby in my sights. "What if someone did plant the drugs on him?"

Everyone in the elevator turned to look at Jacoby. She ignored the attention. "You'd have to prove it, Harper," she said as the doors began to close. "Or create enough doubt that a judge could consider …"

"… that the drugs might not be his." I said to my reflection in the elevator doors. "Or that someone had a reason to plant them on him." My disheveled appearance made me question the logic of putting mirrors on elevator doors in hospitals. If there's one place you never look your best…

"Master Sergeant Harper."

I turned to find Trent and Brianna Blunt looking at me. Trent stood erect, stern, with the same dark shadow of a beard his father usually wore late in the afternoon. It made him look older than his years. The general had kept an electric razor in his desk drawer in order to maintain a clean shaven appearance throughout the day. Evidently, his son would have to follow the same practice. Trent's eyes glistened with emotion, the sadness about to spill over.

"My mother refuses to come to grips with the fact that my father...." He stopped and took up his sister's hand. Brianna buried her face in her brother's shoulder and sobbed. He wrapped a strong arm around her but remained focused on me. "We need to make the necessary notifications to the Army staff that our father is dead."

CHAPTER 28

MRS. BLUNT HAD HEARD Trent's pronouncement that his father was dead. I expected her to scream in denial. Instead she stood frozen for a long moment, her mouth open, her protest halted, then she scrunched her eyes closed as if attempting to avoid a bright light and buried her face in her hands. Melody shot Trent a withering look before offering her sister comfort which Pauline Blunt rejected with an impatient shrug of her shoulders.

Trent watched the scene with a blank expression, as if he'd expected it to play out exactly as it had. He turned away from the drama. "There are family and friends we need to notify. Once that's done, I'd like to work with you on a statement for the press."

He glanced toward his mother again. Melody exchanged looks with him but stayed by her sister's side. Brianna clutched her brother's hand while he spoke to me. She stared off into space, her face pale.

"I want to meet with the doctor as soon as possible." He paused for a moment and swallowed. "We need to determine the best time to disconnect life support. We should do everything we can to ensure his organs are able to help as many others as possible."

"We can schedule the press conference for tomorrow around mid-morning," I said, fighting to keep my own emotions in check. Watching his brave confrontation of the situation made me think of how proud General Blunt would have been of him. A nineteen-year old plebe at the point and Trent was already acting with more dignity than his mother. "We can tell the press you won't be taking any questions but will deliver a simple statement."

"Agreed," he said.

"I'll notify General Roderick's PAO, Colonel McCallen, of the plan so they can be prepared with their own statement and plan a press conference. If we time it right, we might be able to switch the narrative to how 9th Army will continue under new leadership and take the focus off your family."

"Excellent." His steady gaze gave me the impression there was more he wanted to say.

"Is there anything else, sir?"

"I appreciate the sentiment, Master Sergeant Harper, but I'm just a cadet. I haven't earned the right to be treated like an officer. Trent will do." He gave me a crooked smile, a deep dimple in one cheek. He turned toward Brianna. "Give us a minute, will you Bree?"

She followed his direction without question, releasing his hand and moving toward her mother. He was only a year older, but it was clear his sister respected him.

He clasped his hands behind his back and strolled down the hallway, away from the waiting area and his family. I fell into stride beside him. He was taller than his father, broader and more fit. He looked impressive in the grey, cadet uniform and the kid had natural charisma.

I'd never had a conversation with him but had seen him around base and at events he attended with his family. I had expected him to be more like his sister, a bit self-absorbed, entitled and aloof. It was apparent that I'd been very wrong about him.

"I know we've never formally met," he said, "but my father told me a little about you. About the things you've done."

I kept my mouth shut and let him talk.

"I tried to tell Captain Jacoby this, but things were crazy at the jail and when we got here … and well, my mother…" He actually smiled then, as if her bullying was more amusing than maddening. He stopped and turned toward me, his gaze penetrating. He looked very much like his father at that moment. Confident, focused, determined and in command.

"Someone set me up, Master Sergeant Harper. Whoever it is has been trying to get me booted from the academy since day one."

"Why do you think that?"

"Little things at first...sabotaging my uniforms and locker before an inspection, that sort of thing. Then more serious stuff. They planted a stolen item in my room then told the commandant, anonymously, where to find it. That's when I knew things had escalated. A month ago, I was accused of cheating on a test. The test was the worst accusation. It was easy for some to believe that I'd done it because my integrity had already been called into question with the theft accusation. The commandant almost had to boot me for that one."

"Why didn't he?"

He arched an eyebrow at me. "I didn't understand it myself until the commandant finally let it slip. The commandant and my father are old friends." The look he gave me made the description loaded. "Evidently, they served together or something, but I got the impression...well, that there had been a good deal of pressure applied."

He blinked rapidly, as if to stop the flow of emotion. "My father...I loved him and respected him, but he never took no for an answer. Never." He took a deep breath and started walking again. "Anyway, the commandant gave me time to prove myself innocent on every occasion. The inspections weren't that big a deal. I was given the usual gigs. I wore out a couple pairs of shoes and missed several weekend passes while I walked the quad for punishment. The theft. Well, I was able to prove that I couldn't have stolen that watch. I was on the other side of post when it happened."

"And the test?"

"That was harder. The commandant allowed me to take the test again. A completely different test and I had to give my answers orally."

"Sounds grueling."

"Military history. It kicked my ass." He chuckled and grinned.

I was amazed by his attitude. He wasn't angry, simply stating fact. Someone, or more than one person, had attempted to smear him. If I'd been in his boots, I would have been freaking out.

"I'm grateful, but I have to wonder what my father had on the commandant to force his actions in that way. And whoever set me up was smart about the infractions, starting with small things to bring my character into question then escalating. The only thing that saved me was the commandant and his support. Whatever it was my father had on him forced General Mason—a man with a hard-core reputation—to basically be his puppet."

"How do you know your father had anything to do with it?"

"General Mason told me. He said he would have expelled anyone else, but that my father actually threatened retaliation in some fashion. He wouldn't go into details."

"So your father saved you, but why would anyone set you up in the first place?"

He shook his head, his ears reddening. As uncomfortable as the conversation was, he seemed loose but intense, like a boxer preparing for a fight, ready to deal out violence if necessary but trying to be smart about it and not lose his reason. "I have no idea," he said. "I'm not the most popular guy there, but I've never had any hostility with anyone. If I have enemies, they've hidden it pretty well. I wish someone was openly hostile. Someone I could point to and say— 'Hey, why are you being such a dick?'"

His smile was disarming. How could you not like this kid?

"Why are you telling me this, sir?"

He stared at me for a long moment. "Do you...could there be some connection? I mean, a man just shot and killed my father. Maybe, whoever it was that did this, came after me too?"

Before he finished the thought, he was already shaking his head. "I know it sounds crazy. I just... What if? What if they planted the drugs because they knew it was the one chance to get at me where the commandant couldn't step in?"

It only took a few seconds of consideration for it to make sense.

"Sergeant Harper, you have to believe me. I've never touched a drug of any kind. I barely drink."

"Sir, I believe you. I really do. I just don't know how you're going to prove it."

He deflated. "I don't either." He turned and began to stroll back to the waiting area. "I never wanted to go to West Point. I thought I'd hate it. But now…"

"Now?"

"Now, I've never wanted anything so much in my life." He gave me that charming smile again, then stopped and gazed at his mother. "It will kill her if I get booted. I don't want to do that to her."

I followed his gaze. She stood at the window, her arms crossed, her back stiff, gazing out at nothing. She'd lost her husband. Her son was about to be booted from the Army Academy. Her position, her power, even her home and her family were all threatened. All of it together might destroy most people. As annoying as she could be, my heart broke for her.

❧❧

"HE'S IMPRESSIVE," I SAID. "And smart. I couldn't have written the statement better myself."

McCallen grunted in approval, his mouth too busy chewing the dinner I could hear him eating. I imagined him with his usual—Indian take out with a tall glass of Dunkelweizen. As if to confirm my vision, he paused and slurped a drink and I pictured the dark foam leaving a thin mustache he would lick off. He'd be in sweats and a t-shirt, leaning over his coffee table, a soccer match playing on his muted TV.

I stood in the waiting room alone after watching Trent, Brianna, Melody and Mrs. Blunt enter the general's room with the doctor. They had a difficult night ahead of them. Exhaustion from too much emotional tension and watching these people in their grief made me want to go back to my hotel, curl up with Harry and never let him go. Not to mention I was starving. There were still too many loose ends to call it a night yet.

"It's a good statement. Just the right sentiment," he said. "I assume he wants to be the one to read it."

"The media will be putty in his hands. I don't care if they bring up his arrest. It won't tarnish this kid. I think people will see him, his strength, his character and question the validity of the charges."

"Do you think he should mention anything about the arrest in the statement?"

"No. I suggested he leave it unsaid. No sense conflating the two issues. Besides, people might think he's using his father's death to take focus off his charges."

The hospital paged a doctor to the emergency room. A nurse walked by pushing a cart, the wheels making an annoying rattle that continued all the way down the hall. I waited for him to say something and wondered if he was still there. "Neil?"

"Sorry. I was just thinking about how good at this stuff you are."

I felt my face flush. "I learned from the best, sir."

"Bullshit. It was always the other way around."

Silence stretched. The sound of his steady breathing felt comforting somehow. I shook my head, forcing the thought away. I forged ahead. "So, I've spoken to the hospital spokesperson. She'll issue a media advisory on hospital letterhead and we'll hold the press conference here at ten hundred tomorrow. She can hand out paper copies of the statement of sympathy you prepared from General Roderick at the end and you can hold your presser at whatever time you decide later that morning."

"Sounds good."

"It ah, it would be nice if, sometime during that period, there was some kind of sympathy statement from the Defense Secretary or the President."

"As soon as we hang up I'll call General Roderick. We'll get that stuff in motion."

I could almost hear the tick tock of the tension-filled time stretch, each of us waiting for the other to say something.

"So, do you believe him?" he asked.

"What? That someone set him up?" I'd thought about nothing else since Trent had told me about his suspicions. Did I want to believe him because of his charm and charisma? Maybe. Or maybe his solidness, his openness and, yes, his charisma made him believable because he was innocent.

"Yes. I believe him. And I think…well, maybe it does have something to do with his father. Trent said he thought the commandant at the academy only stood up for him because his father used some kind of influence to force him. You told me Blunt had a reputation for inexplicably getting what he wanted. Maybe he stepped on too many toes and hurt too many people."

"What you're saying is that Blunt's actions are coming back to hurt his son."

Lots of people used favors and connections to get what they wanted. The question was, did Newberg murder Blunt because of something Blunt had done, or did he kill him because of some information Blunt was using against him. If there was one thing that could have been used against Newberg, one that could have motivated him to commit murder, it was his sexuality and the threat that he could be exposed and chaptered out of the Army because of it.

"I don't see Newberg as someone who could have masterminded it," I said. "It would have to be someone who had some reach. Someone who could solicit the help of others."

"Just…just don't get yourself into trouble again, Lauren. Remember, two people are dead already."

"Two? So you're agreeing that the death yesterday wasn't an accident."

"All you have to do is look at the timing. What are the chances it's not connected?"

Evidently, many people in the Blunts' hemisphere had been injured along the way. I didn't want it to be true, but the idea that

Captain Garron's death had been an accident seemed less likely the more I learned.

"And I shouldn't be telling you this," Neil said.

"Well, now you have to tell me," I said, my curiosity piqued instantly.

"I made a quick stop by headquarters before I came home, just to make sure General Roderick didn't need anything. He and his wife were there with his aide and he just motioned me in to join them. As I'm standing there, the general gave his aide the task of determining how soon they could move into the Commander's residence."

"I figured they'd move fairly quickly to do that," I said, not understanding the significance.

"Sure but, well...then Mrs. Roderick said something that got me thinking. She said, 'why should we wait a second longer? We've waited long enough,' or something like that."

"Waited long enough?"

"Yeah. Sounded weird to me too. So after I left, I was walking out with Captain Jones..."

"The general's aide?"

"Right, Roderick's aide. Anyway, I asked Jones what he thought she meant by that and he told me that Roderick had originally been assigned in the command slot. The position would have given him another star. Evidently something changed and Blunt was given the position."

"Maybe Roderick's promotion was held up in Congress? Or maybe Roderick merely thought he should get the job."

Neil made a noise that communicated disbelief. "Maybe. It wouldn't be the first time Congress held up a promotion, but sending Roderick here to serve as deputy to a position he thought he was originally supposed to get? That seems particularly insulting."

What could have brought about such a major change in assignment? To have your assignment change from the commander to the deputy commander of such a high profile headquarters would have caused a stir. People would have raised questions. Sure, accidents happened and people broke their legs, paperwork could get screwed up and assignments changed. But like the shifting of faults beneath the earth, the changes would toss people about, destroying hopes, throwing careers out of balance. The one constant in the shifts I'd heard about so far, is that once the aftershocks settled, Blunt seemed to always land in a better position than before.

"Considering all the stuff you've been through, maybe I'm just learning to see things from a more shady perspective. Whatever. I just want you to be careful."

"I'll be careful, sir."

He huffed out an angry breath. "Every time you call me sir it's like a reminder of what I've lost."

I listened to the squeaky steps of a nurse's shoes against the tile floor, and the announcement of a hospital code over the intercom, the German words delivered in a calm voice but the underlying urgency still communicated if not fully understood. I pictured General Blunt in his room, machines pushing life into his body, his blood circulating only because his wife hadn't been willing to let him go. Eventually, no matter how horrible, she had to know that he'd left her long ago.

"We're not doing that anymore," I said.

He took a deep drink of his beer. "Okay," he said, in a breathy exhale. "I'm trying."

"Try harder."

He huffed amusement, and balance returned, righting things again.

"What are you going to call me when I'm a civilian?"

"Things I can't call you now without facing court martial."

His chuckle lightened the mood enough to move on to other things. We exchanged a few more details about the plans for the next day, then said our goodbyes. I hung up thinking it would be very strange not to have him to talk to now and then. Very strange if he simply wasn't in my life anymore. We'd been through too much, had known each other too long to suddenly live completely separate lives.

Melody stepped out of the general's room looking exhausted, wisps of her hair forming a fuzzy halo around her head. She glanced my way and headed toward me, her slow gait displaying her fatigue. "The hospital chaplain is with them," she said. "Pauline has dragged me to church for years but it has never been my thing. I'm glad they're going to be with him in the end."

"He'll die with his family around him." It was an empty sentiment and probably not the way a warrior would want to die. If it wasn't any comfort to the general, I'm sure it was a comfort to his family. The subject of family made me think of another question I had.

"Melody, you know Major Beechwood, right?"

She turned her tired eyes to me and shrugged. "Sure. He's been a friend of the family for years."

She cocked her head at me as if to say, so what? I paused, not sure if I should proceed. "Did you know that he had a brother?"

A little wrinkle in her brow appeared as if she were considering the question. "No, I don't think I did. As a matter of fact, I don't think I know much about his family—siblings and such. Isn't that weird?"

She paused, her eyebrows raised as if still waiting to hear the significance.

"I was just wondering," I said, wondering why I'd brought it up.

"Where is this brother of his," she asked. "Is he in the Army too?"

"Evidently he was," I said. The last thing I wanted to do was bring up another death, so I changed the subject thinking it had been a stupid question to ask her in the middle of everything else going on. I shrugged, "Well, we can't know everything about people."

She gave me a blank look in response then sort of shook herself out of her stillness. "Well, I could use a soda," she said. "You want anything?"

I told her no, and watched as she walked down the hallway, toward where the vending machines were. As she passed the elevators, she glanced in the mirrors, tried in vain to smooth her frizzy hair down, then gave up and kept walking, disappearing around the corner.

I paced in the hallway and tried to get Santos on the line, but he didn't answer. I left a brief message then ducked into the restroom to take care of necessities.

When I came out, I tried to call Santos again. With my head down, punching in the password on my phone, I heard Melody's voice. She sounded agitated and angry. It made me curious. I'd just been speaking to her and she'd been calm, fatigued. Her new tension seemed out of character so I stayed tucked into the restroom doorway and listened. I glanced around the corner to watch her as she talked on her cell phone, her shoulders hunched, her finger in the opposite ear as if attempting to shut out the rest of the world.

"Where are you?" She paused. "No, I'm not coming, I told you... I told you to be careful..." Her whispers became more strident. "This is not what we talked about."

She sounded as if she were holding back tears. I wondered who she was talking to and wanted to listen longer, but another woman tried to enter the restroom and didn't like me standing in her way.

"Pardon me," she said, a note of impatience in her voice.

Melody turned toward the sound and saw me. I had no choice but to step into the open. Without missing a beat, she gave me a fake smile of recognition then switched the topic of conversation. "Yes, that's right. Pauline wants to have the memorial service in a couple of days here in Germany," she said, while strolling down the hall away from me. "We'll have a full funeral in the States in a week or so."

I kept watching her. Near the end of the hallway, she glanced back at me once before rounding the corner.

CHAPTER 29

I WAS DISTRACTED WHILE I walked to my car. Who had Melody been talking to? She'd said something had gone too far. What did she mean by that? I ran through several possibilities of who could have been on the other end of the call but none of them made sense.

Just before I put the key in the ignition, my blackberry vibrated with an incoming email. I almost ignored it, but decided to check and saw that it was from Patrovski, the subject line said: *more info!!* The exclamation points accomplished their mission of drawing my attention and I figured the information was probably related to the favor I'd asked of her and her friend. I opened the email and, once I'd read it, felt relieved that I hadn't put it off.

My reply to Patrovski read, *"Wow! Important pieces to puzzle. TKS and the first round for u and ur friend on me."*

I sat still for a moment, letting thoughts weave and dance around in my head as I watched people going in and out of the hospital. Two people in surgical scrubs stepped out the front door, lit up cigarettes and stood on the sidewalk, smoking and talking. I always thought it strange to see people smoking while wearing medical uniforms, as if what they did in their personal lives had nothing to do with their professional ones.

That led me to think about General Blunt. Like any commander, it took a while to get to know him, to understand him to a point where you could anticipate what his intent might be. And while I thought I had eventually grown to know him very well, I had obviously not known him at all.

I suppose the same could be said for anyone you worked with. Who knew what actually took place in people's private lives? It seemed as if, having respect for someone professionally had little to do with the possibility that they lived their personal lives with integrity. The more I thought about it, the darker my thoughts turned. Then my phone rang, altering my state-of-mind one hundred-eighty degrees.

"I'm feeling peckish. Are you free yet?"

I smiled. "Where are you?

"At the pub with Nick and the boys."

"Are Beechwood and Pratt there?"

"No. Not with this lot. We left the officers to their own devices."

I heard laughter in the background, multiple conversations. "I'm just leaving the hospital, but I have to talk to Santos and Ramsey before I can call it a day. Oh, and send a quick email to someone...wait, maybe I should do that first."

"Sounds like you could be a while. Is there anything I can do to help?"

I almost said no, but then thought about it. "Could you pick up something to eat and meet me back at my office?"

"What would you like?"

"Surprise me."

"That, my love, will be my pleasure."

He disconnected the call and I was left wondering about the "my love" part. Was it just a figure of speech? Part of me hoped it was. Another part, perhaps the bigger, more reckless part, hoped it wasn't. It took me a minute to realize I still sat holding the phone to my ear, a smile on my face, staring off into space and not seeing anything.

"Stop being ridiculous," I said out loud while thumbing more numbers into the phone. I finally got through to Santos.

"I wanted to be sure you were informed that the family is taking General Blunt off life support tonight."

"So, this is a murder investigation after all," he said. "Where are you now?"

"At the hospital, on my way back to base." I told him about the plans for the press announcements and went into detail about Trent's claim that he'd been set up.

"As usual," he said. "You have managed to learn things I was unaware of. I know it's been a long day, but I'd like to meet with you briefly, before you leave this evening. Compare notes if you will."

"That's why I called. Can you come to my office? I've still got a ton of paperwork to do."

"He may be reluctant, but I will bring Chief Ramsey as well." Santos said.

"Thanks for the warning," I said with a smile.

⫷⫸

I PULLED INTO THE parking lot and found Harry waiting for me outside my building, his arm weighed down by a paper sack of take out. He opened my car door for me, holding a hand out to assist as if I were alighting from a carriage.

"Me lady," he said.

"I could get used to this."

He kept his grip on my fingers as we walked into the building, his smile bright, his face flushed, his uniform rumpled and disorderly. I let the door close behind us, unable to stop staring at him.

"You look like you might be a little drunk," I said.

He grinned. The tangy smell of Chinese food surrounded us as he wrapped his hand around the back of my neck and pulled me to him for a hard kiss. He tasted like beer. Late evening light filtered through the stained glass windows of the former church bathing the room in warm reds and golds. His cheeks were rough with late-day stubble and it felt as if it had been days instead of hours since I'd last held him, touched him. Already, the way his body fit with mine felt familiar and exactly as it should be.

He stopped kissing me long enough to cradle my face in his hand, taking in my appearance.

"You, on the other hand, look smashing." He moved to kiss me again but stopped, carefully set the bag of food on the floor, cautious not to let it spill, then resumed what he'd started. This time his embrace was more languid, his arms snaking around my back, his hand to the back of my head, drawing a sigh of approval from me as his kiss washed over me. After a time, he wrapped me in his arms, erasing any space between us, his chin resting on top of my head.

"Oh," he said, with a deep exhale. "This is brilliant, isn't it?"

"Yes," I said, my cheek snuggled into his broad chest. "But I've still got so many things to do."

"I know," he said. "Just one minute more."

We allowed the seconds to tick away as we stood there, holding each other, marking the feeling of rightness. A minute later, he kissed the top of my head and mumbled, "No rest for the wicked."

"I'm sorry," I said.

"No need to be. Just know that however knackered I may be, I like the idea of ending my days this way," he said, giving me one final kiss before picking up the bag of take-out and following me into my office.

I cleared off a corner of my desk and watched with amusement as he pulled out several square cardboard containers, opening each one with a flourish. "Spring rolls, shrimp noodles, sesame chicken, pork fried rice and moo shi beef."

"Feeding an army?"

His smile filled my chest with an ache I never wanted to go away. "I will attempt to sate my hunger for food, since I will never sate my hunger for you." He waggled his eyebrows at me, proud of himself.

I took the chop sticks he offered, rolling my eyes. "You're not going to start using words like sate all the time now, are you?"

He devoured half a spring roll in one bite. I took the container of shrimp noodles with me and sat behind my laptop. "I just need five minutes of silence so I can write this email."

"Silence. That could be a tall order, but I will attempt to comply."

He pulled up a folding chair and tucked in. I could feel him staring at me, but I tried to block him out, already drafting the media announcement in my head. I opened my laptop, with every intention of having the work done in minutes, but stopped when I found a necklace lying across the keyboard.

I held up the thin chain and the small medallion.

"What's that?" Harry asked.

"Captain Jerreau's good luck charm. Actually he calls it his protection charm. His grandmother gave it to him..." My voice trailed off. "Why would he leave it for me?"

"Maybe he thought you needed it," Harry said.

I studied the small medallion Jerreau rubbed whenever he got nervous and wondered when he'd left it and why. I'd never seen the circular disk up close before. I'd always imagined it to be like a Saint Christopher medal with some kind of saintly personage, but it wasn't.

The design looked folksy, primitive. A round charm with octagonal edges, the image was made up of eight pitchforks, the long handles all meeting in the center and the business end radiating outward. As a protection charm, I could see how one could imagine himself standing in the middle while having a squad of people armed with potentially deadly weapons standing around you.

I held it up and let the silver disk spin in front of me. It was a tiny thing but I knew it was important to Jerreau. The man never took it off so I knew he'd never have left it if it hadn't been intentional. I imagined he must have reached for it several times, only to remind himself he'd left it for me. Even if I didn't believe the tiny disk could offer any real protection, Jerreau did and I respected him.

I slipped the necklace over my head thinking how sweet it was of him to think of me.

"I wish you'd had such a thing months ago," Harry said. "I hope he's wrong about you needing it now."

I rubbed the disk the way I'd seen Jerreau do it, saying a silent thank you while I waited for my computer to boot up. When I let it go, the disk settled itself between my breasts, the metal surprisingly warm against my skin.

CHAPTER 30

I SENT SEVERAL EMAILS, to the hospital's communications person, to Neil, to the long list of media who had been following the story of the general's assassination. Between typing and sending, I shoved shrimp noodles into my mouth and watched Harry. He'd barely taken his eyes off me since we'd sat down and I didn't mind it at all. It felt so good to have him close by. I didn't want to say anything to get his hopes up, but it felt as if, after the next press conference, we'd be very close to finally starting our leave together. Perhaps we'd still be able to make it to Frankfurt to catch our flight to Athens.

I pushed the thought aside, afraid just thinking about it would jinx the possibility.

I'd just hit send on another email when I heard Santos and Ramsey walk in the door. I had enough time to print off Patrovski's email, as Harry greeted the investigators, offering them both something to eat.

"We've got plenty," he said.

Ramsey declined, holding up an energy drink as if the mega-caffeinated beverage could replace the need for food. Santos rubbed his hands together as if excited about the prospect. "You're going to make yourself sick," Santos said. He turned to me in exasperation. "He's not eating or getting enough rest."

Ramsey tsked and rolled his eyes like a child arguing about much needed bedtime. "Would you stop pestering? Man. You sound like my wife."

His petulant words didn't mask his pale face or the sunken look to his red, glistening eyes. He needed a shave. He'd at least changed out of his suit to Dockers and a polo shirt.

"Enough about me," he said. "I'm curious to know why Santos dragged me here." He stifled a yawn and plopped boneless into a chair.

"Are you sure you're up for it?" I asked. "You look like the walking dead."

"Considerably worse," Santos said. "He refuses to listen to me."

"We can't keep the Rangers here indefinitely," Ramsey said. A couple of generals have already called to demand they be released. We don't have much time if we want more information from them. They may be packing up as early as tomorrow and we're still no closer to learning the motive behind all this. Which is why coming over here was not on my priority list."

Santos said something lengthy in rapid and angry sounding Spanish. Ramsey replied in Spanish which sounded equally insulting. It felt like a familiar routine between them.

During this exchange, the men arranged their chairs in a loose circle in front of my desk. Santos grabbed a plastic fork and the box of fried rice and looked relieved at a chance to put something in his stomach. An overhead florescent light flickered, emitting a buzzing sound like a bee looking for a way out. The lateness of the evening became more evident in the hard-edged shadows that crept toward our circular seating arrangement. The empty office and the fact that we were in an old chapel made the gathering seem like some sort of group therapy meeting.

"Everyone wants us to return the Rangers to duty as soon as possible," Ramsey said. "And yet now, in addition to the attempt on the general's life…check that…in addition to his murder, we have this paratrooper accident and…"

"They're connected," I said.

The look on all of their faces was priceless.

"Are you jumping to conclusions again, Sergeant Harper," Ramsey said, "Or is this based on actual knowledge of something?"

"I'll remind you that my conclusions have landed correctly in the past," I said.

"She's got you there," Harry said, an eyebrow arched.

Ramsey crossed his ankle over his knee, crossed his arms over his chest and took on a "prove it" attitude. I figured he'd be stubborn, as usual, and I knew I only had one shot to convince him. I stood to try to order my thoughts. "Here's what I know. First, General Blunt, while an excellent leader, used any means necessary to further his career."

"Allegedly," Santos said.

I shrugged. "Okay, allegedly. What we know is, some people got hurt during his rise through the ranks."

"We don't have any real evidence to prove those allegations," Ramsey said. "Only rumors and innuendo."

"Until now," I said. "I think what I have to tell you will clarify some of that."

"I'm listening."

"There are two things really. First, there is the mystery of Major Beechwood's stepbrother."

"What stepbrother?" Ramsey said, his impatience an annoying distraction.

"You'll need to let me tell this story, Chief, or we'll be here all day."

"Alright, I'm listening. It's just...I may fall asleep if you go too slow."

I smiled. Ramsey had actually made a joke at his own expense. "You must really be tired," I said.

"Just get on with it."

I reminded them about Beechwood's older stepbrother, Major Christian Samuels, who had been Blunt's roommate at one point and who had died in a training accident.

"Details of the accident were marked classified," I said. "I tried to get you to get your hands on the file but you weren't interested."

"I'm still not interested," Ramsey said.

"Figures. So I asked someone else to try to get their hands on the information. The person I asked was denied access, but she did discover that someone else had recently attempted to look at it. Can you guess who that someone was?"

Ramsey exchanged looks with Santos before he turned his red rimmed eyes back to me with a shrug. "Not a clue."

"Captain Sylvester Garron."

Santos sat forward at the news. "When did he attempt to see the file?"

"In the evening, the day the general was shot," I said.

"Something about that assassination attempt sparked his interest in the file," Santos said.

"Exactly."

Santos began to pace. "So, Captain Garron, perhaps alarmed by the attempt on the general's life, tries to get details about the death of Major Beechwood's brother. The next day, he is killed in a training accident. Yet *another* training accident." He stopped and looked at Ramsey. "Are you interested yet?"

Ramsey buried his face in his hands, his words muffled in them. "Why can't it ever be simple?"

"It would be much easier for you to understand if you'd had some sleep," I said.

Harry huffed in amusement. "Then again, maybe not."

"From what my friend could tell," I said, "Garron was able to look at the file and did learn the details of Samuels' death. Whether or not it meant anything..." I shrugged.

"So, let me get this straight," Ramsey said, a look of concentration on his face. "Major Christian Samuels is an older brother to Major Mathias Beechwood. The same Beechwood who is here now.

"Yes."

"And Major Samuels was killed in a training accident back in the day."

"Exactly."

"The details of said accident are classified."

"Right."

"So, you're inferring that General Blunt had something to do with the accident that killed Samuels and when Garron looked at the file, he was killed."

"Well...yes," I said. "It's possible."

"But if Blunt caused Samuels' death, and Blunt is dead, what is there to keep secret? The only person with a motive to hide the cause of Samuel's death would be Blunt and Blunt is dead."

I suddenly felt a headache coming on. "I don't have all the pieces, but all of these connections can't just be coincidence. There must be a reason behind it."

"So far, you're creating a lot of dots but you don't have the lines that connect them," Ramsey said. "If there is a pattern, you're standing too close to see it."

"It's a tad confused, but you have to admit she's onto something," Harry said. "No matter how wobbly it might be."

"There's more," I said. "Are you ready to hear it?"

"I can hardly wait," Ramsey said with a sigh. "Proceed."

I read a couple of lines from the email Patrovski sent me then paced to order my thoughts.

"We have to go back almost eight years for this one. That's when Major Julius Leonard died in his quarters," I said.

"Who?" Ramsey said.

"I'm getting to that. So Major Leonard died in his quarters," I repeated. "The CID reports never came to any conclusion, but the autopsy said he died from a gunshot wound to the head. There was no evidence of foul play. No evidence of anyone else present at the time of death."

"So, suicide," said Ramsey.

"Why can't you guys ever just say that in your reports?" I asked.

Ramsey and Santos exchanged looks. Santos cleared his throat. "Please proceed, Master Sergeant Harper."

I glanced at Harry for support then forged on. "When Leonard committed suicide, he was attending language school in Monterey, California. He studied Farsi in a year-long course. Major Newberg, a young lieutenant at the time, was in the same class. They had to have known each other."

Ramsey rubbed his face with both hands, his exhaustion broadcast in every movement. "Where in the ever lovin' universe are you getting this shit?"

I ignored the question and plowed on. "Upon graduation, Leonard was to be assigned as Chief of Staff to an airborne unit. A great assignment. A career ladder kind of post."

"Okay. Newberg and Leonard know each other and Leonard has a flourishing career," Ramsey said. He shrugged indicating he wasn't impressed.

"Leonard committed suicide. At the time of his death, he'd had his orders to his new assignment for about six weeks. So why? Why would a man about to go to a great new post, off himself?"

The blank stares were not unexpected. I continued.

"After Leonard's death, guess who ended up taking that assignment that would have been a feather in anyone's cap."

Santos was the first one to make the connection. "Impossible."

"Not impossible," I said. "Blunt was second on the list. Eliminate Leonard and …"

Ramsey stood, his hands up, as if to stop anymore words from invading his brain. "But you said foul play wasn't a factor."

"It wasn't. Blunt was in Europe at the time of Leonard's suicide, so he couldn't have been involved in his death...not in his actual death anyway."

"Okay," Ramsey said, trying to put the pieces together. "So if Leonard committed suicide, how could Blunt have had anything to do with it?"

"By giving Leonard a reason to end his life. Like threatening to end his career by exposing his sexuality," I said.

Ramsey met my gaze and froze, his head tilted to the side, his eyes squinted while he put the pieces together, but I could tell, he needed a bit more grease for his mental wheels.

"Leonard was married. Two kids. I don't have anything to actually prove they had an affair but, Leonard and Newberg co-authored two major assignments while at school together. They also took leave together for every holiday, every chance they could."

"And this is enough to convince you that two men in the army were having an affair?" Ramsey asked.

"No, but listen to this. After Leonard died, Newberg dropped out of the course claiming medical reasons. He took a month of leave. I think he was grieving."

Ramsey plopped back down in his chair. "Where the hell are you getting this information?"

"It helps to ask the right questions," I said. "Look, we know Newberg is gay. We know Blunt hadn't threatened to expose his sexuality. Newberg didn't kill Blunt because of a threat to his career. He killed Blunt for revenge."

Ramsey scratched his head with both hands, the grating sound echoing loudly in the room. It sounded as if he wanted to claw away the fog of his brain so he could understand more clearly.

"Chief, you really need to get some sleep," I said.

"What? Sleep now? When all is about to be revealed?" The sarcastic bite of his words would have hurt if I didn't know how desperate he was to get the same answers I was after. "Tell me, Sergeant Harper. Why did Newberg wait eight years before taking his revenge?"

The question halted me. Why had he waited?

Harry leaned in close. "That's actually a very good question."

"I have them now and then," Ramsey said.

I continued to pace, trying to concentrate. Ramsey, Santos and Harry broke into conversation, I assumed discussing the case, but I blocked them out. Why had Newberg waited eight years? What had changed? What made him decide to act? And what did

Garron's death have to do with it all. Who wanted Garron dead simply because he requested a classified file?

"Chief Santos," I said, and smiled at the surprised look on everyone's face as I interrupted their conversation. "Chief, you said Beechwood was the one who jumped directly after Garron, right?"

"Yes. Major Beechwood," Santos said. "Are you insinuating…"

"Beechwood, again?" I pictured the tall, aristocratic man with the aquiline nose he used to direct his gaze down on the rest of us. His unending confidence slicked off his tongue and came out a thick, southern drawl while telling his colorful stories. What first translated as charm, felt more like disdain on closer inspection. "There's got to be a reason Beechwood would want the details of Samuels' death—his own stepbrother, kept secret"

"You're suggesting Beechwood wanted Garron dead because of something in that file," Santos said.

"And suggesting," Harry piped in, "that Beechwood caused Garron to hit the door somehow. Maybe the man just didn't want anyone to know he had a stepbrother."

"That's what it's looking like to me. Isn't it to you?" When they all gave me blank stares, I knew they needed more convincing.

"I talked to Melody Spencer at the hospital. Beechwood has been a friend of the family for years and yet none of them knew he had a brother. Why do you think that is? Why wouldn't he speak about his family?" When I got more blank stares I tried again.

"How many jumps do you think Garron had under his belt? Would someone with that kind of experience really just trip?"

Harry shrugged. "Beechwood and Garron were near the end of the string. I saw them while we were on the ground. They seemed perfectly friendly with each other, good mates. Beechwood was telling tall tales, entertaining the crowd like a busker in Covent Garden. It's possible the man simply tripped."

"Or maybe," I said, "Beechwood's friendly antics were cover for his plan to hurt Garron."

"Yeah well," Ramsey said. "Whatever he did in the air, didn't kill Garron, right? Cause of death is strangulation."

Giving up on the pacing, I plopped back into my chair. "So, maybe his goal was for Garron to die in the jump, but he resorted to strangulation when that didn't work."

Ramsey drained the last of his energy drink and crushed the can in his fist. "We could sit here guessing all night. Guesses are not facts and facts are what we need."

"She has however, offered us some new avenues of investigation," Santos said.

"Avenues that may just lead to dead ends," Ramsey said. When Santos and I both began to protest, he held up his hand to halt us. "That doesn't mean they aren't worth pursuing." He stood, one knee popping loudly. He put his hands to the small of his back, moving like a man twenty years older. "I gotta get a couple hours of sleep," he mumbled.

Santos threw up his hands. "Finally!"

Harry and I exchanged smiles, until he pulled his vibrating phone out of his pocket.

I ushered Santos and Ramsey out the door, giving them the agenda for the press conferences the next day. They left promising to touch base again after all of the media engagements.

"I'm hoping I'll be able to turn this thing in after tomorrow," I said, my hand resting on the pistol in my thigh holster. "After the media events, I should be done here. I hope so anyway." I glanced at Harry. The thought of finally being able to shuck off my uniform and spend a month with him made my face flush. Santos didn't miss the sentiment and patted my arm knowingly.

"As do I," Santos said. "You deserve it."

"Yeah, yeah. Whatever," Ramsey said. "We'll speak tomorrow. I'm almost dead on my feet here."

Santos said something in Spanish, frustration articulated in his hand gestures. Ramsey responded in clipped words of the same language and they left having an argument I could barely understand.

I turned to find Harry frowning at his phone.

"What's wrong?"

"Well, I didn't tell you because frankly, I wanted to avoid it."

"Avoid what?"

"Nick told me the boys were having a party tonight, in celebration of heading back home. He wanted me to come, but I told him I was knackered. He was kind of insistent. I agreed so he'd stop going on about it."

"A party?" I knew I sounded unenthusiastic. Heading back to the hotel and curling up with Harry was all I had on my mind. "Do you think you might regret not going? Who knows when you'll see him again."

He waggled his head, considering. "You're right about that."

"So, where's the party?"

"Someplace called Mayberry. You know where that is?"

"It's one of the training sites in the box. What is he doing out there?" The box was almost two hundred square miles of training space and, unless you were there for an official exercise, it wasn't smart to be out there at night. Especially if you weren't supposed to be.

"So, what do you say? A party then?"

I thought about my uniform and dusty boots. "Why not? We've got our party clothes on."

CHAPTER 31

IT TOOK ALMOST THIRTY minutes to get to MOUT site Mayberry. We'd taken my government sedan which worked fine for the first ten minutes of the ride on paved roads, but was poorly suited for the dirt roads we'd traveled the rest of the trip. I'd insisted on driving, since I knew the way, but in the wooded darkness, nothing looked familiar. We didn't pass a single other vehicle along the narrow and pitch black tracts that seemed to reach forever deeper into the night. There were no street lights of any kind, no center lines, no shoulders to speak of and we hadn't been gifted with moonlight to alleviate any of the inky dark. The curvy, gravel roads were deeply rutted and took us up and down several steep hills and around curves with sudden drop offs. Harry and I didn't talk as we both strained forward, our eyes open as wide as possible, focused on keeping us on the road. I wished I'd let him drive.

At one turn, we shined a small herd of deer who gracefully bounded to safety. The roads were so bad, we averaged less than twenty miles an hour.

Mayberry, one of the largest of the mock towns in the box, was made up of more than twenty building shells, several streets and alleys and could serve as a small urban setting anywhere in the world. Constructed from bare cement, each building had open windows with no glass, but thick wooden doors that could be kicked in if necessary. Some had narrow, rickety staircases, roof tops perfectly suited for sniper purchases, and hidey holes which offered plenty of opportunity to react to surprise. The empty structures could serve as school houses, homes filled with innocent civilians or terrorist hideouts crawling with bad guys. A structure with a steeple could be a church during one exercise or, with a few modifications, serve as a mosque or temple for the next. The main street, wider than the others, had market stands and several empty vehicles lining either side of the road; built-in obstacles to present added challenges.

During an exercise, the town would be populated with scores of people paid to play the roles of village elders, the local crime boss, a police chief, the busybody school teacher or the kids who begged for candy one minute and tossed hand grenades the next.

I'd been to Mayberry several times during the exercise but I'd never been quite so relieved to finally reach it. The headlights cast an eerie feel on the little town, revealing empty streets, empty buildings as if the place were deserted. I peeled my white knuckles off the steering wheel and shook out my fingers as we rolled slowly into town, wondering where everyone was.

Harry lowered his window, and the heavy thump of a deep, dance beat drifted to us on the night air.

"Nothin' like havin' a knees up in the backside of beyond," Harry said. "At least we know the place isn't deserted."

As we drove slowly down the main street, the tires crunching in gravel, I squinted at something lying in the road. "What is that?" I said.

I put the car in park, left the headlights on and the vehicle running as we both climbed out. As soon as we'd stepped out of the car, the music hit us like a physical presence. The loud Euro-pop cut through the black of the night, sharp and deep. We ignored the clamor and walked around to the front of the car to find someone lying, face up, in the middle of the road. Harry first touched the man's throat, and finding a pulse, shook him roughly. The soldier immediately opened his eyes and sat up.

"Harry!" Eldnik said. "I'm so glad you're here. How did you hear about the party?" He did a cute finger wave at me with a big smile.

"Oye, Nick," Harry said. "You called me, remember?"

Eldnik had a curious look on his face for a minute. He looked around and realized he was sitting in the middle of the street. "What am I ... Oh, yeah. Yeah I did. I called you. Help me up."

"What's going on mate? What are you doing in the middle of the road?"

"Oh, you gotta help me, Harry. I think I'm in trouble."

"Harry, he's hammered," I said.

"No, I'm not," Eldnik said. "You gotta believe me."

I rolled my eyes at Harry, thinking most drunk people thought they were perfectly sober. "I'm gonna go move the car," I said. Harry nodded at me and moved Eldnik out of the road, not that there was any traffic to worry about.

I parked the car beneath a tree at the far edge of the little town and then used the small flashlight I wear on my belt to make my way back to the men. When I rejoined them, Harry had a tight grip on one of Eldnik's arms and had him leaning against a building.

"Seems he approved this little party but not all the extra attractions. He says it's getting out of hand and he's afraid he'll suffer the consequences."

"Thas right, consequenssess," Eldnik said, swaying. "Harry, I didn't drink that mush. Why am I so drunk?"

"How many drinks did you have," I asked him.

"I drove out here," he said, agitated. "I don't drink when I drive, I swear. I had a couple beers with Harry...," he looked at Harry, a big smile on his face then looked at me, throwing his arm around Harry's neck. "I love this guy."

"Yeah, I love you too, Nick," Harry said, then looked at me. "He was drinking that near-beer swill. And he was perfectly sober when I left him." To Nick he said, "So how many beers did you have after that?"

"Juss one. I swear. Juss one." Harry gave me a meaningful look.

"What were you doing lying in the street?" I asked.

He thought about it for a minute. "Oh, I know. I didn't want to fall asleep and make you look for me. I thought...you'd have to run over me to miss me so..."

"That was good thinking, mate. We found you right away." Harry looked at me. "I have to believe him. He's not that much of a drinker."

"Oh Harry," he said, a troubled look on his face. "You should see this party. You should see what they've done. I think I'm in so much trouble."

While it seemed unlikely anyone inside the party would hear us or notice our arrival, it felt as if the darkened doorways and windows hid unknown threats. The tightness in the back of my neck made me think we were being watched. I scanned the buildings. The creepy feeling of being under observation only intensified.

"Some bastard must have slipped him something," Harry said. "They didn't want him to stop the party." The throbbing vein in his forehead communicated his anger at what had been done to his friend.

Eldnik grabbed Harry, yanking on his uniform. "Oh, oh, there was something else I was supposed to tell you. Something really important." Eldnik put a hand to his head and pulled his short cropped hair. "Think, think think...Oh yeah...Oh, this is bad, Harry. You can't tell anybody. Promise?"

"Course, mate. I won't tell a soul. What is it?"

"I think... I think the general's daughter is here," Eldnik said in a panicked, drunken whisper. "If something happens to her, I'm in so mush trouble, Harry. So mush trouble."

"Holy crap," I said. "Brianna is out here?"

"I'm glad you called me, Nicky," Harry said.

"Maybe they drugged him to keep him out of the way of other plans," I said. "What if she is here?"

"We'd better find out. But first, let's put Nick here down for a nap. Would you like that mate?"

"No, no. I want to go with you," he said, swaying with the wind, but his feeble protest couldn't be taken seriously. We walked him back to our car, loaded him into the back seat and watched as he obediently lowered himself to lay sprawled on his side. He was out instantly.

"Right," Harry said. "Let's you and I go have a gander then." He stood then thought better of it. He leaned back in the car and I heard rustling, a couple of grunts from Eldnik. When Harry stood, he had his friend's nine millimeter and holster which he quickly strapped to his thigh.

"That's theft of U.S. government property," I said, my eyebrows raised. "And it's probably not loaded."

"I'll give it back," Harry said with a smile. "And I know where I can get some ammunition." He waggled his eyebrows at me.

I dug in my cargo pocket and handed him one of my spare magazines. "Just don't lose it, or I'll be in so mush trouble." I said, trying for a poor imitation of Eldnik's drunken confessions.

Harry's teeth flashed in the darkness then he looked at his friend, already snoring on the backseat of our car. "Poor bugger," he said as he slipped the magazine into the butt of the weapon and put the weapon on safe, then stuck it into the holster. "Let's hope we don't need these."

"Yeah, let's hope," I said, scanning the darkened windows and doorways of Mayberry. Harry started to leave, but I stopped him and opened my phone to send a quick text.

"Who is that for?" Harry asked.

I showed him the phone, where I'd typed, *MOUT Mayberry. Brianna trouble.* I hit send, but got a message that it failed.

"Shit. No signal," I said. I looked around, thinking I could probably find a signal somewhere but decided finding Brianna trumped finding signal bars.

"Let's just hope we don't need any backup," Harry said.

We followed the thump of the music growing louder as we approached until I could feel the beat of the base in my chest. The door was wide open so we stepped over the threshold onto the dirt floor of the large room they'd converted into a rave party, the kind of underground bash that didn't get announced until the last minute. This rave couldn't have been more exclusive, in the middle of the box, miles from the main post and not a neighbor in sight to complain about the noise. Whoever had planned this had been very creative.

They'd broken chem-lights, the plastic tubes filled with glow-in-the-dark chemicals, and splashed the neon colors across the walls in blinding yellow and green. It was a smart way to embellish the walls since, even after the glowing compounds wore off, no one would care about any evidence their decorative use might leave. Someone had wrapped crinkled foil around a large weather balloon and hung it from the ceiling. The make-shift disco ball bounced the sharp colors around the room in ferocious stabs of blazing shades. I didn't know what was more violent. The battering on my eyes or the attack on my ears with the deafening jerk of the pulsing clamor that passed for music.

The music seemed to be working its magic. A knot of men, most clutching drinks, jumped up and down, their fisted hands raised in the air, pumping their approval, their heads and uniforms sweat-soaked.

Harry leaned down, put his lips to my ear and still had to shout for me to hear him. "That's not Brianna up there, is it?"

I shook my head no. Neither of the two women who gyrated in sexually charged movements could have been Brianna. I would have recognized her blonde and slender frame.

Instead, these women were both dark haired, one with long hair she flung about as she danced. The other wore a short, pixie cut. They danced on a table, raising them up above the mob as if on a stage, a crowd of men their enthusiastic audience. Flashlights dangling directly above each woman ensured their performance remained illuminated. They wore short-shorts, the suspenders worn with tactical equipment belts and nothing else, their pale skin and bare breasts splashed with neon yellow and green. With their arms upstretched, they twirled and teased and I imagined their suggestive moves were normally made more effective with the use of a pole.

"No wonder Eldnik was worried," I shouted.

Despite the bright glow of the neon colors, the spinning disco ball and the makeshift spotlights for the strippers, the room was dark, most of the people appearing as shadowy silhouettes. Still, I was able to spot several other scantily clad women amongst the crowd. I recognized some of the faces of men I'd seen in the CID building when they'd been waiting to be interviewed after the jump accident—a mixture of officers and enlisteds. Not something you'd normally see in a party like this, but it hadn't been a normal exercise for them.

One of the men in their unit had committed murder. Two others had been seriously injured and one killed in a training accident. Surely, the men could feel that things were amiss in their ranks. A tough exercise, fraught with tragedy and shock. Someone had decided they needed to blow off some steam and this wild ruckus was the result.

The music, the neon lights, the booze, the women and even the use of a training site as a party zone didn't bother me. What did bother me was that most of them still carried their weapons.

"I wish they'd locked things up in an arms room before they starting partying," I said.

Harry pulled me out of the way of someone stumbling by us, his M16 slung over his back and a beer in his hand. He stopped in front of me, smiled and leaned in to say something.

"Not a good idea, mate," Harry said. "Move along."

He eyed Harry for a second but was too drunk to care. "No worries," he said and stumbled on his way.

I tried to spot Beechwood but it was impossible, the shoulder-to-shoulder mass of people were all black blobs wearing the same uniform. Then far across from us, I saw someone going up the stairs, his hand outstretched as he pulled a blonde behind him. She seemed to be laughing. When she flung her hair away from her face, I had enough of a glimpse to identify her. I pointed.

"Brianna."

I followed Harry as he attempted to cross the packed space. We'd been standing on the sidelines as we observed. Moving a few feet forward became more difficult as we went. The men were jam packed together, most of them jumping around so wildly, I had to duck several elbows and sweat-soaked bodies. Harry didn't bother trying to be polite about it. He plowed ahead and I followed in his wake, several people throwing us dirty looks as Harry shoved and pushed people aside.

Someone grabbed my arm and spun me around, separating me from Harry for a moment. I screamed his name but he didn't hear me. I found myself surrounded by young men who were drunk, sweaty and completely oblivious to the fact that I didn't want to be there. I tried to push past them, but they'd formed a solid wall.

Harry tuned around and realized I wasn't there. I screamed at him but he scanned the crowd as if he couldn't see me. Then Pratt stepped up behind him and pointed a pistol at his head.

CHAPTER 32

MY PATIENCE FOR THE phalanx of frenzied, partying men disappeared. The man in my direct path to Harry got a severe punch to the gut. He doubled over. Someone else tried to grab me. He got an elbow to the nose, his cry of pain completely drowned out by the cacophony of the music. I kicked and pushed across the dance floor until I reached the bottom of the steps where I'd last seen Harry, but he wasn't there.

I found myself at the bottom of a narrow, wooden staircase and stood in the wash of light that spilled from the floor above. I wanted to go up after him, but hesitated. Everything about that second floor felt wrong, made me want to turn around and leave, but that wasn't an option. Harry and Brianna were up there.

A man, his nose bloody, a furious look on his face, came staggering toward me. I pulled my weapon. He stopped and put his hands up, his look of shock almost comical. Ignoring him, I pressed my back against the wall of the stairs then gazed back at the room full of soldiers, trained heroes, people who were much more capable than me to go after the bad guys, but everyone I saw was completely drunk, oblivious to the drama.

There weren't any other options. I gripped my weapon tighter, kept my shoulder to the wall as I took the steps one by one. At the top of the stairs, I quick-peeked around the corner. A bare wall to the right. A long hallway and several doors on the left. I stepped up and moved to the left, my weapon clutched in both hands, crouched, listening, trying to hear something, anything over the din from below.

And I did hear something, raised voices. A violent scuffle. Someone crying. Brianna. I moved quicker in that direction, toward the door at the end of the hallway. As I got within a few feet, the door flew open. Beechwood had Harry in a choke hold. Pratt stood to the other side with his pistol pointed at Harry's head.

"Wait, wait, wait," I said, frozen in place, my hands up, my weapon dangling from my thumb.

"Put it on the floor," Beechwood instructed.

I moved slowly as I lay the pistol on the floor.

"Kick it here."

I kicked it, but it didn't go far. "Don't you move now," he said to Harry before stepping forward to pick up my weapon. When he stood, he smiled at me. "Come on, now, ya'll," he said, showing too many teeth. "Come join the party."

As soon as I stepped through the door, Pratt switched his aim to my head, knowing a threat to me would keep Harry in check. Pratt wrapped his arm around my neck as if to choke me. All of this while the music continued its furious beat below us and everyone at the party remained in the obliviousness of frenzied dance as if all was right with the world.

Part of me had wanted to think we were being paranoid, overreacting when we first approached the party. A larger part knew something about the party, the timing of it, along with the drugging of Sergeant Major Eldnik, felt hinky, like a setup. Evidently, I'd been right.

The ferocious look on Harry's face made me think, even though he had a gun, Pratt should be the one frightened.

Brianna covered her mouth with her hands, her face streaked in makeup and tears, her body trembling. Beechwood jerked on her arm. "I said, shut up that noise now. Don't make me give you something to cry about."

Pratt slammed the door behind us, cutting off most of the hectic music, but the steady bass beat vibrated under our feet. A camping lantern burned on a table in the corner casting constantly moving shadows around the plain cement walls and bare wood floors. Large, windowless openings offered pitch black views of the evening's surrender to anything good and bright. My stomach cramped in a nervous knot of worry.

"Math, what is going on?" Brianna asked, her voice high-pitched as she sobbed her worry.

"It's alright little one," he said. "We're going to sort some things out now."

Brianna backed away from us, her wide eyes locked onto the weapon in Pratt's hand. "That's my gun, Math? What is he doing with my gun?"

"Good observation," he said, his voice filled with condescension. "That is the gun we've been practicing with. I told you it would come in handy someday."

I pushed away from Pratt, but his grip around my neck only got tighter. "Come on," I said. "I'm obviously not going anywhere. Just let go of me."

Slowly he released me. I shot him a dirty look, then was finally able to turn my head to look at Harry, my gaze drifting to his holster. They'd already taken his pistol. I spotted it lying on a table near the lantern. Harry's very long knife lay next to it. Crap.

"Well," I said, my hands going to my hips. "I'm beginning to think we just did exactly what you wanted us to do."

Beechwood grinned and bowed at me. "You are a sharp one." He wagged a finger at me. "At first I didn't think all that stuff I read about you was true, but maybe I was wrong."

I watched as Harry, out of the corner of my eye, lowered his hands as well, crossing his arms. I knew he'd be surveying the room, making an assessment of what we should do next. Pratt kept the weapon pointed at me, knowing a threat to me would keep Harry from doing anything rash. Harry would never be rash.

"You knew we'd come out here," I said. "You planned on it."

"Exactly," Beechwood said.

"Math, what is going on?" Brianna said, looking as if she were on the verge of losing it completely. "You're not going to hurt them or anything, are you? I don't understand."

"I know darlin'. But there isn't much you do understand, is there?" He patted her on the face then squeezed her cheek until she cried out in pain.

"Owe, Math. That hurts." She sounded more and more like a little girl. He released her and she backed away from him, a look of terror on her face.

"That hurts," he mimicked her, the mask he'd been wearing, gone now, leaving a cruel look for her. It was enough to restart fat tears rolling down her face.

"Where's their car?" He asked Pratt, his tone commanding.

"Under the trees at the East end of town."

I realized the advantage they had over us and glanced at Harry. Beechwood and Pratt had been training in this town for weeks. They knew it inside out and had been watching us since we got here.

"I don't see any problem with leaving it there," Beechwood said. "You?"

Pratt shook his head, his gaze darting between Harry and me.

"People will be looking for us," I said. "People are already looking for Brianna."

"Don't worry. We'll tie up all the loose ends," Beechwood said.

"Is Brianna a loose end?"

The young girl had retreated into a corner, her face awash in tears. She visibly shook, her fear almost palpable.

Beechwood looked at her. "I do feel sorry for her a little. She's just a kid."

"I was told you thought of her like a sister. Was it more than that?"

He turned an angry glare at me. "I had a brother. Once." He walked toward Brianna while she shrank away from him. "He's dead now. My brother is dead. Did you know that?" he asked her as she tried to retreat further from him but the wall blocked her way. "Did you know that my brother died because of you and your family?"

He grabbed a fistful of her hair, forcing her to look at him. "You didn't know. That big, blonde, beautiful empty head of yours didn't know a damn thing, did you?"

I glanced at Harry, wondering what we should do, what we could do. He stood stiff with tension, his hands fisted at his sides. He ignored Beechwood and Brianna, instead focused on Pratt and the weapon he had pointed at my head.

Pratt must have understood what Harry'd been thinking. "I will kill her. Have no doubt about that," Pratt said.

"If you hurt her in any way," Harry said. "I swear to bleedin' Christ I will rip you apart."

"You know what," Beechwood said, in a bright voice. "I believe him. Do you believe him, Pratt?"

"I don't understand you," I said. "What is she doing here? Why are you taking it out on Brianna? She didn't have anything to do with what happened to your brother."

"No," Beechwood said, turning his attention to me. "No, you're right. This little one had nothing to do with what happened to my brother, but her mother did."

"Her mother?" I said, surprised, but only for a moment. In the next instant the clarity hit me, making my arms break out in goose flesh. "Holy crap. General Blunt wasn't your target."

CHAPTER 33

MY MOUTH HUNG OPEN. They'd executed Blunt in a room full of people, not simply because they wanted him dead. They wanted to send a message to someone else.

Beechwood smiled at me. "Of course the general was a target, but it was the second order of effects we were after. Take him out, and Pauline Blunt is no longer a General's wife. Get her son kicked out of school, she's no longer the mother of a West Point officer." He kissed Brianna on the cheek as she stood trembling next to him, her hands clutched in front of her face as if she were begging him to stop.

"This one, though very cute, really doesn't mean much to Pauline in the big scheme of things. Brianna is a pretty, pretty girl, but she'll never be much of anything. She wasn't even really part of the original plan. But, the more I thought about it, the more I figured we couldn't leave her be. After all, she could be an officer's wife someday and we can't have that, can we?"

A fresh wash of tears sluiced down the young girls face. "God, Math. Why are you being so mean?"

"So this is all about revenge on Mrs. Blunt," I said. "An ambitious woman who carved the path for her husband's success."

"At every turn," Beechwood said. "Blackmail, sexual favors, murder, anything she deemed necessary. She didn't care who she hurt. All she wanted was to see her husband become a powerful man. I do believe she wouldn't have rested until he became a member of the Joint Chiefs." His triumphant smile gave me the creeps. "He'll never be that now. Will he, honey?" he said, gently brushing a lock of hair away from Brianna's tear-ravaged face.

"We should get moving," Pratt said.

"What is your stake in this?" I asked Pratt. "Beechwood lost a brother. Newberg lost a lover."

"Oh, I knew she would figure that one out," Beechwood said. "I told you she was smart."

I spun back to Beechwood, taking another step toward him. He seemed to enjoy telling me the story. I wanted him to think listening was my only concern. "How did you convince Newberg to shoot the general in a room full of people? He must have known he would be imprisoned at the very least. He could still face the death penalty."

"To be honest, he was a basket case when I met him. Suicidal. Still pining over his old lover. Really pathetic. He was so lonely, all I had to do was be nice, share a little affection. He thought Julius Leonard was the love of his life. Until he met me." His smile would have been charming if it weren't so disgusting.

I sucked in a breath of surprise. "You became his lover."

"What?" Brianna asked her shock almost greater than it had been earlier.

"Oh relax, Bree. Your mother isn't the only one who will use sex for what she wants. I didn't love him, of course. I mean, I made love to him but…Oh, why all the shocked looks? We're all a little sexually ambiguous nowa days, aren't we?" He smiled, waiting for agreement. When he didn't get any, he shrugged. "Newberg talked about suicide all the time. I made some suggestions for how he could make his death more meaningful, when the time came. I did him a favor, really. I helped him get the payback he wanted and gave him a feeling of self-worth, something to live for, at least for a while anyway. What could be wrong with that?"

Why would Newberg wait eight years to get revenge? We'd asked ourselves that once we found out about the death of his lover. The answer was Newberg didn't wait eight years for revenge. He hadn't thought about revenge until Mathias

Beechwood came along, with his charm and movie star good looks, and captured Newberg's heart. The poor idiot.

"Come on, Math," Pratt said. "We're wasting time."

"Is that why you're helping him?" I asked Pratt. "Because you're in love with him?"

Pratt's look darkened, he raised the pistol he already had pointed at me and walked toward me, threatening.

"You better watch what you say lady," he said.

"No, no. Pratt didn't need that kind of persuasion." Beechwood said. "He's got a brother at West Point. Little Pratt is trying hard, but he's not as smart as his big brother and he's had some trouble passing tests. He's been very helpful though."

"Your brother is the one who set up Trent," I said to Pratt. The flush of color to his face told me I was right. It also told me he wasn't proud of the fact.

"Right again," Beechwood said. "And in return, little Pratt is passing all of his exams with flying colors and a little help from friends of mine. Joshua here has ambitions of his own, don't you Captain? It wouldn't do to have a brother failing at being a warrior."

Pratt withered under my stare, his gaze drifting to the ground. My eyes flicked to Harry. We exchanged a look. Captain Joshua Pratt had been pushed too far. He felt ashamed of his participation.

"God," Brianna said, her voice sounding like a pathetic wail. "I can't believe you. How can you hate me so much?"

"I don't hate you honey, not really. I just hate your mommy." He turned to me. "I hate her so much I don't want to kill Pauline Blunt. I want to watch her as her entire world crumbles."

Pratt didn't like the topic. "Why are you telling her everything? We need to get going."

Beechwood didn't respond, but I knew he was telling me the details of the plan because he loved to tell stories, especially stories where he was the smartest man in the room. Where he was the hero. He couldn't have gone through all of this, seen all of his plans come together, without telling someone about it.

"You bastard," Brianna screamed and lunged at Beechwood. He grabbed her by both arms and shook her, easily taking control. Every instinct told me to help her, but I knew it would do little good. When she didn't stop fighting, he backhanded her and sent her sprawling.

The door slammed open, Melody Spencer stood there, a horrified look on her face. "What are you doing?" she screamed.

"Finally," Beechwood said. "I thought you'd never get here."

Melody ran to Brianna, lifting the young girl to her feet. "Answer me, Math. What is going on here?" I almost didn't recognize her. She wore jeans and black boots, her hair pulled back into a high ponytail. She wore makeup and earrings and had ditched her glasses. Melody Spencer suddenly looked twenty years younger than the woman I'd left at the hospital.

"Just taking some initiative. I thought we could take care ... "

"Brianna was never part of this plan," she said, veins standing out on her face and neck. Her words came out so angry, spittle hit Beechwood in the face.

"That's right," I said. "Melody would never have agreed to this."

His gaze snapped to me. "What do you know about it?"

"I know Melody was in love with your brother, well, your stepbrother really."

From the crazed look on both of their faces, my wild guess had been right. Major Christian Samuels. The stepbrother of Beechwood who had died in a training accident. The same C. S. who had prompted Melody Spencer to have the initials C.S. tattooed on her breast in a blood red heart.

"Wait a minute," I said, more of the story taking shape in my head. "Newberg isn't the only one who would do anything for love."

"What are you talking about?" Beechwood's face looked suddenly drained of color, his self-satisfied smile slowly melting away.

"You're in love with her. It's for Melody that you're doing all of this."

Melody's eyes darted between me and Beechwood. Melody, whose lover was killed in the course of her sister's quest for power. Melody who played the dutiful spinster, following her sister from duty station to duty station, watching the destructive path Pauline Blunt left, biding her time, hiding her beauty, waiting for the perfect opportunity for payback.

"But you can't be doing it for her," I said, arguing with myself. I stared at Melody, at the way she clutched Brianna protectively, her eyes wide. She was frightened.

"I told you not to mess around, Math," Melody said. "I told you she was dangerous."

I shook my head, smiling for the first time since we'd arrived in Mayberry. What an appropriate name for the town. A place where, on the surface, everything seemed so normal, like any-town America. Look behind the doors of the town though, and you'd find empty shells. Some of them dark and lifeless, some lit up in neon colors and others where drama played out in agonizing detail.

"Melody would never approve of what you're doing and you don't even know why. You don't even know her biggest secret."

"What are you talking about?"

"Shut your mouth," Melody said.

"What did you plan to do anyway? Kill me and Harry with Brianna's gun. Make it look like Brianna did it? Maybe she kills herself after?"

"Oh my god," Brianna said through her sobs. "You're such a dick."

Beechwood's eyes darted behind me to Pratt. I turned toward him. Pratt still had the weapon in his hand, but he no longer pointed it at me. His shoulders were slumped, the weapon hanging heavy at his side. I glanced at Harry. He stared intently at Pratt, at the weapon in his hand. I'd have to be ready for when he decided to make a move.

Pratt's look of dejection wasn't lost on Beechwood. "Stick with me, brother. We're almost done."

"It's a good thing she got here to stop you because she never would have forgiven you, would you have, Melody?"

"You don't know what you're talking about." Beechwood sounded less sure of himself.

"Just get them in the car already," Melody said. "We're wasting time."

I shook my head, unable to hide my own smile. "She never would have forgiven you if she found out you killed her daughter."

Brianna stared at me, her mouth open in surprise. She turned to Melody then pushed away from her, a look of disgust on her face. "What? What are you talking about?"

"Come on, Math," I said. "Think about it. Didn't she ever tell you? The woman you love and all. The one you're willing to kill for?"

"You're pathetic," Melody said. "That's ridiculous."

Beechwood stared at her. Then finally took in the two of them, standing together. The blonde hair. The blue eyes. The pointy chins.

I raised my eyebrows. "See the resemblance now? And Melody's plans for revenge never included Brianna, did they? She hurt everyone in that family, except her own daughter. Haven't you ever wondered why Melody followed them everywhere? I mean, her sister was responsible for the death of the only man she ever loved. Why would Melody stay with her?"

"That's impossible. You're not my mom. Are you?" It was hard to tell from Brianna's child-like voice, if she wanted it to be true or not.

"The only reason to stay with them was to be near her daughter," I said. "Surely you see that."

Beechwood's eyes began to dart around the room.

"Did Melody encourage you to befriend Brianna? But I'd bet she told you to keep your hands off her. Didn't you ever wonder why?"

"She's too young," he said, angry now and defensive. "What interest would I have in a girl her age?"

"What interest indeed," I said. "Look at her. Brianna's hot. And she's completely infatuated with you. Wouldn't that have been the perfect revenge? To make her love you, then leave her. But Melody didn't want that. She didn't want to encourage you to have an affair with your niece." I shuddered at the idea. "Yuck."

"My uncle?" Brianna said. "Oh my god!"

"It was all about the image right?" I said, looking at Melody. "Mrs. Blunt, the super successful general's wife, the one who went to State dinners and traveled the world alongside her husband the general. She couldn't have a sister with an out-of-wedlock child. Hell, Brianna and Trent look nothing alike. It's obvious to me. Wasn't it obvious to you, Math?"

"That's enough," Melody said. "If you're not gonna kill this bitch, I will."

She grabbed for the pistol in his hand, surprising him and shoving him off balance. He yanked his hand away, losing his grip on the weapon, sending it flying into the corner. Without the weapon, Melody came at me anyway with her claws out. I hate it when women scratch.

Behind me I heard Harry go at Pratt. I couldn't see what they were doing, but from the violent noises, Harry had his hands full.

It only took one punch to her nose to make Melody crumble, her hands going to her face to stop the rush of blood. Beechwood, not bothering to go after the weapon, came directly at me, broadcasting his punch. I ducked and came up, slamming my fist into his gut, but his abs were rock hard. Pain shot up through my knuckles to my shoulder. This was a man with far more training in hand-to-hand than I would ever have. I never had a chance.

He swept out with a kick, knocking me off my feet. I fell hard, the impact snapping my head back, slamming me to the floor. I was stunned for a moment. During the entire exchange, Brianna screamed, a long, high pitched desperate scream. A scream that mixed with the perpetual thump of the music from the rave that had gone on uninterrupted.

Beechwood cursed and straddled me, punching me in the face, once and again. Brianna continued to scream. The scuffle and the cursing behind me let me know that Harry remained fully engaged as well.

Then Brianna came up behind Beechwood, with the weapon in her hand, she swung at his head, giving him a good clip but not enough to do much damage. He stood, a hand to his head, and backhanded her, sending her sprawling into the corner. I had to give the poor girl props for trying, even if she hadn't done much damage, but she had given me enough time to get to my feet, a bit unsteadily, before he came at me again, fast. I took a couple of steps back, leaned far to the side and using a kick boxing move, snapped my leg out, my foot landing in the middle of his chest, shoving him away. It hadn't felt like I'd hit him hard. I'd felt, at the time, disappointed in the strength of the kick, but it was enough to make him stagger back, his arms pin-wheeling as he attempted to regain his balance. When he hit the windowsill at the back of his thighs, it was as if he slowed down and slowly tumbled backwards out the window, disappearing from view. The riotous music muffled any scream he may have uttered, any sound he may have made when he hit the ground.

I rushed to the window, afraid he'd go running away. We were only on the second floor. I'd assumed he would survive a fall like that. One look out the window, at the impossible angle of his neck, at the total stillness of his body and it was clear he wouldn't be going anywhere.

The noise in the room seemed to disappear as I gazed down at his body, so still, so obviously not alive. Already, the replaying of the moment started. I'd never forget that look of shock on his face, that wide-eyed, helpless expression he'd worn, staring at me, as if I could do something to stop it, as if to ask why, just before he tumbled to his death.

My hand drifted to my chest and landed on something warm beneath my fingers. Jerreau's protection charm. I lifted it, turned it around in my shaking figures and with an icy shudder, realized, I was alive because Beechwood was dead. The body, still and lifeless, his eyes open and unseeing.

A clamor as if from a far distance, reached me. I looked down to see Brianna on the floor, her back against the wall, her legs splayed out in-front of her, her face in her hands as she sobbed. More sound reached me. I looked over at Melody. She stared at me with a panicked question in her gaze, the lower part of her face covered in her own blood. "Math?" she asked. "Math?" A note of panic in her voice.

I shook my head. She scrunched her eyes closed, and slumped into a fetal position.

"You alright, Lauren?" Harry asked.

If felt as if my ears popped, like they would in a plane, suddenly sound coming through the way it should. I realized Harry had been calling to me, his voice becoming more strident.

"Lauren? Lauren, are you alright?"

I turned to face him and took a minute to decide, staring at Melody, whose revenge had been years in the making, but which had gone so horribly wrong, at the protection charm with the question ... if I hadn't been wearing it ... but I couldn't go there. I hadn't meant to kill Beechwood but I had and he'd been so full of himself just a moment before.

"Lauren?"

"Yes," I said, the room spinning a little.

"You sure?"

"Yes. I'm okay, Harry."

He'd used Pratt's belt to bind his hands. Harry's cheek was a bit red and Pratt had some abrasions on his face, but they didn't look like they'd exchanged many blows. Harry must have seen the question in my eyes.

"He didn't have much fight in him," he said.

"There was no honor in this," Pratt said, indicating Brianna. "I just wanted to help my brother. It got out of hand. And that bastard ..." He stopped, shaking his head. "Is he dead?"

Brianna sobbed even harder. I went to her, wrapped her in my arms, knowing how profoundly her world had changed.

☙❧

"OUCH!" I SAID, TRYING to push Harry's hand away, one of which cradled my chin, the other held a cotton swab coated in some kind of stinging antiseptic he continued to dab in the worst possible places, particularly on my eyebrow where I'd earned a rather large gash. The medic said I needed a stitch or two.

"If you can't stitch it up right here, right now, then I don't need any damn stitches," I'd said.

"You have to go to the emergency room, Ma'am. I'm not authorized to do it here."

I turned to Harry. "You heard the man. He's not authorized, Sergeant Major Fogg. You have a choice. You either stitch me up now, or we spend hours and hours in an emergency room..."

He'd put his hands up in a halting motion, politely asked the medic if he could borrow his kit, then did what I'd requested. "Bloody, stubborn woman. Here I am. Patching you up, yet again," he said, attempting to hide a grin. Aside from the gash on my eyebrow, which hurt, my split lip bothered me even more. It felt as if it had ballooned to twice its size and I'd probably have a black eye. Again.

The blue and red lights of a squad car washed over Harry's face, and scores of people milled around us, the hustle and bustle of a crime scene feeling a bit commonplace.

Santos had received the text I'd attempted to send, my phone finding enough bars at some point to deliver it. He'd rallied a team to come out, break up the party and put the bad guys away. Pratt would be just down the hall from Newberg in the detention facility.

I'd told Santos that Harry and I would tell him the story. He could record it and then we were leaving. Ramsey objected. Of course. He said we'd be obstructing the investigation.

"I'm not going to repeat myself over and over again," I said. "We tell it once and then you have to let us go. We've got a plane to catch in the morning. Besides, I'll bet you a hundred dollars Pratt will confess to everything."

Ramsey hadn't wanted to risk his money, so he kept his mouth shut.

"Owe, Harry," I said. The stinging bite of the antiseptic made me want to run away from him.

"Oh my. Does it hurt?" he asked, a wicked look on his face.

"Of course it f'ing hurts, Fogg. Just get it over with."

The pain of Harry's ministrations had distracted me enough that it took me a minute to realize what I was watching, when soldiers wearing white gloves loaded Beechwood's body bag into the back of an ambulance. They closed the doors to reveal Melody Spencer, sitting in the backseat of an MP vehicle. She stared at me for a long moment then looked down. She'd end up in federal court somewhere I was sure. Her outrageous plan had gone terribly wrong. She deserved every bit of the punishment she faced.

I looked at Harry, the deep concentration etched into his brow, and the way he bit his lip made me want to bite it too.

"Please darling, hold still for me."

"Poor Brianna," I said. "I wish she hadn't learned the truth about her mom that way."

"She'll be alright. She's tougher than she looks that one."

I smiled at him, at the fake stern look he wore, at the way his gaze darted about my face.

"At least she's alive." He snipped off a suture. "She has you to thank for that."

"And you," I said, halting the painful smile before I cried out again. I loved watching him as he concentrated, that intense look of his, the complete unawareness that he was so pleasing to look at. His gaze flicked to me, catching me staring at him.

"A Beefeater," he said.

"A what?"

"You asked me what I would do if I wasn't in uniform. It's not like I haven't thought about it before. I've been doing this for twenty years. It's getting a bit hard to tumble out of planes and not feel it the next morning. I'd always thought, if I gave up the SAS, I'd like to be one of the Yeoman Warders."

This time, I did smile, my hand going to my lips to try to staunch the sting. "You mean those lovely men who guard the

Tower of London and give the tours?"

"And guard the royal jewels, and serve in Her Majesty's ceremonies and such. Yes. There are less than forty of them in the whole service. It'd be hard to make it in, but if I did, it would be an honor."

As I stared at him, my feeling of disbelief slowly receded. I could picture him in the colorful uniform, his booming voice keeping gaggles of tourists in line, taking his responsibilities seriously and yet serving with dignity, doing his part. He'd never give up being in the service, in one form or another. He would look fantastic in red.

"You'd be awfully good at it."

He bit his lip as he stuck the needle in again, pulling gently, stitching my flesh together. "I'm not ready to do that yet, you understand," he said, speaking gently, as if he were afraid to disappoint me. "But someday, I'd consider it." He met my gaze, then tied off the suture, snipping it expertly. Then prodded the area as if checking to see if it was secure.

"It really hurts, Harry."

He huffed his amusement. "I know it bloody well hurts. One of these days, you'll know what's good for you and you'll stay out of these messes."

"Can't you just kiss it and make it better?"

"Believe me. If I thought it would do any good, I'd be kissing the bleedin' hell out of you." He shook his head and took my chin in his palm, turning my face side to side. "You realize, everyone who sees us together will think I've beaten you."

I smiled, but that hurt too much. "Owe." I winched at the sting of my torn lip. "Harry?"

"Um?"

"It might be days before I'll be able to kiss you properly."

"Oh, I doubt that love. You're the stubborn one, right?" He leaned in and planted a tiny kiss to the corner of my mouth. "The one who never gives up." His lips found an uninjured spot on the other side of my mouth. "Even when all the odds are stacked against you." He found another spot that would accept his kissing without pain. "I'm sure you'll find a way."

Army Acronyms –

Military jargon is filled with acronyms. It is impossible to list all of them here but I've attempted to include those acronyms used in this story. If you find any I've missed, contact me through my website at www.mldoyleauthor.com.

201 File – Army personnel file containing a soldier's training, awards, promotions and transfers from the date of first entry and throughout the soldier's career.

BDU – Battle Dress Uniform; a woodland pattern camouflage uniform. No longer worn by U.S. Army forces. Replaced with the ACU – Army Combat Uniform.

CID – Criminal Investigation Division; Unit tasked with investigating crimes and other violations of military law by members of the Army.

EOC – Emergency Operations Center; a twenty-four-hour center of support for emergency situations, activated when a situation is serious enough to warrant the input of multiple staff offices.

EOD – Explosive Ordnance Detachment; a detachment charged with identifying unexploded ordnance, deactivating explosives and clearing minefields and a bunch of other stuff you have to be a bit crazy to do.

General Order Number One (GO1) – A military order used to outline prohibited activities which are thought to threaten good order and discipline during major military deployments. Activities can include drinking alcohol, gambling, procuring the services of prostitutes and many others. The list of prohibited activities is adjusted at the discretion of the officer in charge to fit the deployment or mission.

Humvee or HMMWV – High Mobility Multipurpose Wheeled Vehicle; a four-wheel drive vehicle produced by GM which serves as the main vehicle for the US Military. The wide-bodied, fat-tired vehicle can be produced with a turret, be up-armored and have a wide range of other modifications depending on usage.

LZ – Landing zone; a place where a helicopter can safely land. Sometimes a permanent location or one designated hastily to accommodate emergency landings.

M16 – U.S. armed forces military rifle which fires 5.56 NATO rounds at semi-automatic or fully automatic rate.

MOUT – Military Operations in Urban Terrain, a cluster of building shells used for urban warfare training.

MP – Military police.

NATO – North Atlantic Treaty Organization; an alliance of countries from North America and Europe used to seek peaceful solutions to member country conflicts.
or
NATO- Normal Army Tea Order; British slang for tea served white with two sugars.

NCO – Non-commissioned officer; grades of soldiers from corporal through sergeant major, sometimes called the backbone of the Army for their leadership skills, and most responsible for carrying out the day-to-day mission of an operation.

OPORD – Operations Order; a document outlining a plan, the objective, the associated tasks, equipment and staffing necessary to complete a mission.

PAO – Public Affairs Officer; an officer charged with providing advice and guidance to the commander on media and communication matters.

PMCS – Preventive Maintenance Checks and Services; a series of checks and services performed on military equipment before, during and after a mission to ensure the equipment is and stays in working order.

PSD – Personal Security Detachment; like bodyguards, soldiers charged with the safety and security of one individual, usually a high-ranking officer.

QRF – Quick Reaction Force; a standby force used by commanders to respond to emergencies.

Sapper - U.S. Army engineer specialized in digging and building fortifications, constructs combat expedient bridges, roads and air fields and handles the disposal of bombs, mines etc.

SAW – Squad Automatic Weapon or section automatic weapon; a weapon used to provide heavier automatic firepower to squads or sections. The type of weapon varies but is usually fed with an ammunition belt and can be carried or mounted on a vehicle or tripod.

TDY – Temporary Duty; orders authorizing movement of military service members and civilians from one travel location to another for a short tour of duty.

TOC – Tactical Operations Center; the headquarters and center used to provide tactical support to the commander.

UCMJ – Uniform Code of Military Justice; the foundation for military law.

Acknowlegements

My years at the keyboard have taught me that I simply cannot write in a vacuum. I've had two writing groups that have had great influence in where I am now as an author. The first was born from a class I took at The Loft in St. Paul, MN. When the critique class ended some of us branched out to form our own group. When I moved overseas, I lost touch with most of them but more than a decade later, I can still thank Kathy Haley for being the one who shepherded us together and for continuing to read the stories I've cobbled together. Her advice has always been spot on and well appreciated.

The most recent cast of characters, the Novel Experience, is born from members of the Maryland Writer's Association. NE has changed a bit here and there, but at the core are Gale Deitch and Cindy Young-Turner, authors to watch. You should also keep an eye out for Jonathan Allen, Brian Connors, Mark Willen and the originals, Victor Brown, Alma Lopez and C. J. Cooper.

Thanks to all of my beta readers, especially Loreen Doyle-Littles, Larry Doyle, Eileen McIntire, Zander Vyne, Susanne Aspley, Gary McCann, Kristin L. Wilson, Barry D. Guertin, Ian Smith and Colleen Riley.

My biggest thanks go to my family for listening to all of my trials and tribulations and for wishing the best for me. Rebecca, Reuben, Ramsey, Kyle and my niece Lauren. I didn't have to go too far to find a good name for my main character!

Most of all, to my mother, Ruth. Thanks for always having your nose buried in a book. I wish you were here to see this.

About the Author

M. L. Doyle has served in the U.S. Army at home and abroad for more than three decades as both a soldier and civilian. She is the co-author of two memoirs which chronicle the lives of prominent women in uniform. Her award winning fiction also features women who wear combat boots.

A native Minnesotan, Mary currently resides in Baltimore where she is furiously penning more adventures.

Look for Mary's adult romance series, *The Limited Partnerships Series*, which is written under the pen name Louise Kokesh. The series is available as four novellas and as an omnibus.

Mary would love to hear comments from readers. Please like her M.L. Doyle Author page on Facebook. You can also reach her on her website at **www.mldoyleauthor.com**.

Also by
M. L. Doyle

Fiction

Master Sergeant Lauren Harper Mysteries:
The Peacekeeper's Photograph
Canceled Plans (companion short)
The Sapper's Plot
The General's Ambition
The Event (companion short – spring 2015)

Romance

The Limited Partnerships series
Part I - Charlie
Part II - Luke
Part III - Wolf
Part IV – Derek
Limited Partnerships Omnibus

Nonfiction

I'm Still Standing;
From Captured Soldier to free citizen, my journey home
With Shoshana Johnson
(Touchstone, 2010)

A Promise Fulfilled,
My life as a Wife and Mother, Soldier and General Officer
With BG (Ret.) Julia Cleckley

www.ingramcontent.com/pod-product-compliance
Lightning Source LLC
Chambersburg PA
CBHW021340250626
47155CB00002B/719